SHIVERS
FOR CHRISTMAS

SHIVERS
FOR CHRISTMAS

Edited by Richard Dalby

MICHAEL O'MARA BOOKS LIMITED

First published in Great Britain in 1995 by
Michael O'Mara Books Limited
9 Lion Yard, Tremadoc Road, London SW4 7NQ

Shivers for Christmas Copyright © 1995 by
Michael O'Mara Books Limited

A CIP catalogue record for this book is available from
the British Library

ISBN 1-85479-919-3

1 3 5 7 9 10 8 6 4 2

Typeset by CentraCet Ltd, Cambridge
Printed and bound by
Clays Ltd, St Ives plc

CONTENTS

THE DISCOVERY OF THE TREASURE ISLES *

Amelia B. Edwards

Amelia B. Edwards (1831–92) was a celebrated
Victorian traveller, feminist and novelist,
and author of the classic travel book
A Thousand Miles Up the Nile.
The following narrative (which was first published
in Routledge's Christmas Annual in December
1864) is probably the earliest 'Bermuda Triangle'
mystery story, describing a particularly bizarre and
horrifying Christmas Day on a very strange island
situated in a parallel dimension somewhere
between Puerto Rico and Bermuda.

I t was on the 26th of October, 1760, at twenty-seven
minutes past ten o'clock, a.m., that I shook hands for the
last time with those worthy merchants and shipowners,
Messrs Fisher, Clarke, and Fisher, of Bristol. I went at once on
board the *Mary-Jane*, then lying alongside the drawbridge by St
Augustine's parade, in the very heart of the old city. It was my

* From a MS found on a bookstall.

first command, so I stepped on deck with some little pride of heart, and bade the men weigh anchor. My exultation may be pardoned when it is recollected that I was only twenty-six years of age, and naturally thought it a fine thing to be captain of a tight little trading schooner like the *Mary-Jane*, with a valuable cargo on board, and a mate, three sailors, and a boy under my absolute authority.

The flags were flying from every masthead and steeple, and the bells were pealing clamorously, as we worked out of port that morning; for it was the very day of the king's* accession, and all Bristol was wild with loyalty. I remember as well as if it were yesterday, how the sailors cheered from the ships as we went down the Avon; and how my men threw up their hats in reply, and shouted, 'Long live King George!' The Avon, however, was soon left behind, and we entered the Bristol Channel with a favourable wind, all sail set, and a sky brilliant with sunshine above our heads. We were bound, I should observe, for Jamaica, and carried a cargo consisting chiefly of printed goods, hardware, and cutlery, which it was my duty to deliver to the consignee at Kingston. This done, my instructions were to ship a return cargo of cotton, indigo, rum, and other West Indian products. Perhaps it may be as well to add, that the *Mary-Jane* carried about a hundred tons burthen, that my name is William Burton, and my mate's name was Aaron Taylor.

The *Mary-Jane* was not a quick sailer, as I soon discovered; but she was a good, sound, steady little craft, and I consoled myself by remembering that safety was better than speed. It was dusk before we reached Lundy Island, and almost daylight next morning when we passed the Land's-End. This was slow work; but as the wind had shifted a point or two during the night, I made the best of matters, and tried to hope we should do better

---

* The writer alludes, evidently, to King George III, who was proclaimed through-out the kingdom on the 26th October, 1760; King George II having died suddenly, at Kensington, on the 25th.

by-and-by. After tossing about somewhat roughly off the Bay of Biscay, we made Cape Finisterre on the 4th of November; and on the 18th put in at Terceira for water. Having remained here for the best part of two days, we put to sea again on the evening of the 20th. The wind now began to set in more and more against us, and ended by blowing steadily from the South; so that, although we had glorious weather over head, we made almost as little way as if we had had storms to contend against. At length, after a week of ineffectual beating about, just as I was going to turn the ship's head and run back to Terceira, the breeze shifted suddenly to the North. The N.W. would have suited us better; but if we could not get exactly the wind we most wanted, we were thankful, at all events, to tack about, and make such progress as was possible.

Thus we went forward slowly towards the tropics, attended by perpetual sunshine and cloudless skies, and enjoying a climate that grew milder and more delicious every day. The incidents of our voyage, up to this time, had been few and unimportant. A Dutch merchantman seen one morning in the offing—a porpoise caught by one of the crew—a flight of swallows on the wing—a shark following the ship. These, and similar trifles, were all the events that befel us for many a week; events which are nothing when related, and yet afford matter for vivid interest to those on shipboard. At length, on the 15th of December, we entered the tropic of Cancer; and on the 19th sailed into a light sea-fog, which surprised us very much at such a season, and in such a latitude; but which was welcome, nevertheless, for the sun's heat was now becoming intense, and seemed as if it would burn the very deck beneath our feet. All that day the fog hung low upon the sea, the wind fell, and the waters were lulled almost to a calm. My mate predicted a hurricane; but no hurricane came. On the contrary, sea and air stagnated more and more; and the last breath of wind died away as the sun went down. Then the sudden tropical night closed in, and the heat grew more oppressive than before.

[3]

I went to my cabin to write, as was my custom in the evening; but, though I wore only a thin linen suit, and kept every port-hole open, I felt as if the cabin was a coffin, and would suffocate me. Having borne it till I could bear it no longer, I threw the pen aside and went on deck again. There I found Aaron Taylor keeping the first watch; and our youngest seaman, Joshua Dunn, at the helm.

'Close night, mate,' said I.

'Queerest night *I* ever saw, sir, in these latitudes,' replied Aaron.

'What way do we make?'

'None, sir, hardly: scarce one knot an hour.'

'Have the men all turned in?'

'All, sir, except Dunn and me.'

'Then you may turn in too, mate,' said I. 'I'll keep this watch and the next myself.'

The mate touched his hat, and with a glad 'Aye, aye, sir,' disappeared down the companion-ladder. We were so small a crew that I always took my turn at the watch, and to-night, feeling it impossible to stay below, willingly charged myself with the double duty.

It was now about ten o'clock. There was something almost awful in the heavy stillness of the night, and in the thin, white, ghastly fog that folded round us on all sides, like a shroud. Pacing to and fro along the solitary deck, with no other sounds to break the silence than the murmuring of the water along the ship's side, and the creaking of the wheel in the hands of the steersman, I fell into a profound reverie. I thought of my friends far away; of my old home among the Mendip hills; of Bessie Robinson, who had promised to become my wife when I went back after this voyage; of a thousand hopes and projects, far enough removed from the schooner *Mary-Jane*, or any soul on board. From these dreams I was suddenly roused by the voice of Joshua Dunn shouting in a quick, startled tone—'Ship ahoy!'

I was alive in a moment at this cry, for we were at war with both France and Spain at the time, and it would have been no pleasant matter to fall in with an enemy; especially as there had been some fierce fights more than once in these very waters since the war began. So I pulled up in my walk, looked sharply round on all sides, and saw nothing but fog.

'Whereabouts, Josh?' I cried.

'Coming right up, sir, under our weather-bow,' replied the steersman.

I stepped aft, and, staring steadily in the direction indicated, saw, sure enough, the faint glimmer of a couple of lanthorns, coming up through the fog. To dash down into my cabin, seize a brace of pistols and my speaking-trumpet, and spring up again on deck, just as the spectral outline of a large brig loomed up almost within a stone's throw of the ship's side, was the work of a moment. I then stood silent, and waited, ready to answer if hailed, and willing enough to slip along unobserved in the fog, if our formidable neighbour passed us by. I had scarcely waited a moment, however, before a loud voice, made louder by the use of the trumpet, rang through the thick air, crying:—

'Ship ahoy! What name? Where from? Whither bound?'

To which I replied:—

'Trading schooner *Mary-Jane*—from Bristol to Jamaica. What ship? Where from? Whither bound?'

There was a moment's silence. Then the same voice replied:—

'The *Adventure*. Homeward bound.'

The reply was informal.

'Where from?' I repeated. 'What cargo?'

Again there seemed some hesitation on the part of the stranger; and again, after an instant's pause, he answered:—

'From the Treasure Isles, with gold and jewels.'

From the Treasure Isles, with gold and jewels! I could not credit my ears. I had never heard of the Treasure Isles in my life. I had never seen them on any chart. I did not believe that any such islands existed.

'What Isles?' I shouted, the question springing to my lips as the doubt flashed on my mind.

'The Treasure Isles.'

'What bearings?'

'Latitude twenty-two, thirty. Longitude sixty-three, fifteen.'

'Have you any chart?'

'Yes.'

'Will you show it?'

'Aye, aye. Come aboard, and see.'

I bade the steersman lay to. The stranger did the same. Presently her great hull towered up beside us like a huge rock; a rope was thrown; a chain ladder lowered; and I stepped on deck. I looked round for the captain. A tall, gaunt man stood before me, with his belt full of pistols, and a speaking-trumpet under his arm. Beside him stood a sailor with a torch, the light from which flickered redly through the thick air, and showed some twenty men, or more, gathered round the binnacle. All were as silent as ghosts, and, seen through the mist, looked as unsubstantial.

The captain put his hand to his hat, looked at me with eyes that glittered like live coals, and said:—

'You want to see the chart of the islands?'

'I do, sir.'

'Follow me.'

The sailor lighted us down, the captain went first, and I followed. As I passed down the cabin-stairs I eased the pistols in my belt, ready for use if necessary; for there was something strange about the captain and his crew—something strange in the very build and aspect of the ship, that puzzled me, and put me on my guard.

The captain's cabin was large, low, and gloomy, lighted by an oil-lamp swinging from the roof, like a murderer swinging in chains; fitted with old carved furniture that might have been oak, but was as black as ebony; and plentifully garnished about the walls with curious weapons of all kinds of antique shapes and workmanship. On the table lay a parchment chart, elaborately drawn in red ink, and yellow with age. The captain silently laid his finger on the very centre of the parchment, and kept his glittering eyes fixed full upon me. I leaned over the chart, silent as himself, and saw two islands, a greater and a less, lying just in the latitude he had named, with a narrow strait between them. The larger was somewhat crescent shaped; the smaller inclined to a triangular form, and lay up to the N.W. of the other.

Both were very irregular in the outline. The little island seemed hilly throughout, the large one was scooped into a deep bay on the N.E. side, and was piled up into what appeared like a lofty mountain between the inner shore of the bay and the western coast. Not far from the southern side of this mountain, a small river was seen to take its rise, flow in a north-easterly direction, and empty itself into the bay.

'And these,' said I, drawing a long breath, 'are the Treasure Isles?'

The captain nodded grimly.

'Are they under French or Spanish Government?'

'They are under no government,' replied the Captain.

'Unclaimed lands?'

'Wholly unclaimed.'

'Are the natives friendly?'

'There are none.'

'None? Then the islands are uninhabited!'

The captain nodded again. My amazement became more profound every moment.

'Why do you call them the Treasure Isles?' I asked, unable to keep my eyes from the map.

The captain of the *Adventure* stepped back, pulled aside a coarse canvas screen that had till now closed in the farther end of the cabin, and pointed to a symmetrical pile of golden ingots—solid golden ingots—about seven feet high and four deep, built row above row in transverse layers, as a builder might have laid the bricks in a wall.

I rubbed my eyes. I looked from the gold to the captain, from the captain to the map, from the map back to the gold.

The captain drew the screen to its place with a hollow laugh, and said:—

'There are two hundred and fifty-seven tons weight of silver in the hold, and six chests of precious stones.'

I put my hand to my head, and leaned against the table. I was dazzled, bewildered, giddy.

'I must go back to my ship,' said I, still staring covetously at the chart.

The captain took an odd-looking long-necked bottle, and a couple of quaint beakers with twisted stems from a locker close by; filled out a glassful of some kind of rich amber-coloured cordial, and handed it to me with a nod of invitation. Looking closely at the liquid, I saw that it was full of little sparkling fragments of gold ore.

'It is the genuine Golden Water,' said the captain.

His fingers were like ice—the cordial like fire. It blistered my lips and mouth, and ran down my throat like a stream of liquid lava. The glass fell from my hand, and was shattered into a thousand fragments.

'Confound the liquor,' gasped I, 'how hot it is!'

The captain laughed his hollow laugh again, and the cabin echoed to it like a vault.

'Your health,' said he; and emptied his own beaker as if it had been a glass of water.

I ran up the cabin stairs with my throat still on fire. The captain followed at a couple of strides.

'Good night,' said I, with one foot already on the chain-ladder. 'Did you not say latitude twenty-two, thirty?'

'Yes.'

'And longitude sixty-three, fifteen?'

'Yes.'

'Thanks, sir, and good night.'

'Good night,' replied the captain, his eyes glowing in his head like fiery carbuncles. 'Good night, and a pleasant voyage to you.'

With this he burst into a laugh louder and more hollow than ever—a laugh which was instantly taken up, echoed, and re-echoed by all the sailors aboard.

I sprang down upon my own deck in a towering passion, and swore at them pretty roundly, for a set of unmannerly lubbers; but this seemed only to redouble their infernal mirth. Then the *Adventure* hove off, faded again to a mere spectre, and disappeared in the mist just as the last peal of laughter died away, mockingly, in the distance.

The *Mary-Jane* now resumed her course, and I my watch. The same heavy silence brooded over the night. The same fog closed around our path. I alone was changed. My entire being seemed to have undergone a strange and sudden revolution. The whole current of my thoughts, the very hopes, aims, and purposes of my life were turned into a new channel. I thought of nothing but the Treasure Isles, and their untold wealth of gold and jewels. Why should not I seize upon my share of the spoil? Had I not as good a right to enrich myself as any other man that sailed the seas? I had but to turn the ship's course, and possess the wealth of kingdoms. Who was to prevent me? Who should gainsay me? The schooner was not my own vessel, it was true; but would not her owners be more than satisfied if I brought them back double the value of her cargo in solid ingots? I might do this, and still have fabulous treasure for myself. It seemed like madness to delay even for a single hour; and yet I hesitated. I had no right to deviate from the route prescribed by my employers. I was bound to deliver my cargo at Jamaica within a given time, wind and weather permitting; and we had already lost weeks upon the way. Beset by alternate doubts and desires, I went to my berth at the close of the second watch. I might as well have tried to sleep in the powder magazine of a burning ship. If I closed my eyes, the parchment chart lay before them as plainly as when I saw it on the captain's table. If I opened them, the two islands appeared as if traced upon the darkness in lines of fire. At length I felt I could lie there inactive no longer. I rose, dressed, lit my lamp, took out my own book of charts, and set myself to enter the Treasure Isles in their places on the map. Having drawn them in accurately with pencil, and then traced over the pencillings with ink, I felt a little calmer, and turned in again. This time I fell asleep from sheer exhaustion, and woke, dreaming of riches, just at dawn.

My first proceeding was to go on deck and take an observation of our position. The result of this observation was to show me, beyond all doubt, that we were then distant about seventy-two hours' sail from the coast of the larger island; whereupon, I yielded to a temptation stronger than my will or my reason, and changed the ship's course.

That decisive step once taken, I fell into a state of feverish eagerness, which allowed me no rest of body or mind. I could neither sleep, nor eat, nor sit still, nor remain in one spot for three minutes together. I went up to the masthead twenty times a day on the look-out for land; and raged against the fog, as if it were sent from heaven on purpose to torment me. My seamen thought I was mad; and so I was. Mad with the thirst of gain, as many a sane man has been before and since.

At length, on the morning of the third day, Aaron Taylor came to me in my cabin, and ventured on a respectful remonstrance. We had already deviated, he said, two degrees from our course, and were making straight for the Bahama islands, instead of for Jamaica. Had we kept steadily on our way, we should have shortly touched at Porto Rico for provisions and water; but both were running short, and could not possibly hold out for anything like the time it would take us to make land in the present direction. In reply to this statement, I showed my chart with the two islands sketched in according to their bearings.

He looked at them, shook his head, and said very earnestly:—

'I have sailed in these latitudes for the last fifteen years, your honour, and I'll take my Bible oath there are no such islands.'

Whereupon I flew into a violent fit of anger, as if the mate had presumed to doubt my word, and forbade him ever to speak to me on the subject again. My temper, in short, was as much impaired as my peace of mind, or, indeed, as my sense of duty; and gold, accursed gold, was at the bottom of it all!

Thus the third day passed on, and still the fog hung round and seemed to follow us. The seamen did their work sullenly, and whispered together when my back was turned. The mate looked pale and grave, like a man whose mind was full of anxious thoughts. For my part, I was more resolute than ever, and silently vowed to shoot the first sailor who showed a sign of mutiny. To this end I cleaned and primed my pistols, and hid a Spanish dagger between my waistcoat and my belt. Thus the long, monotonous hours went on, and the sun sank, and yet no land, nor indication of land, had appeared on any side.

Sixty-five hours out of the seventy-two had now gone by, and it seemed as if the remaining seven would never expire. To sleep was impossible; so I paced the deck all night, and watched as eagerly for the first gleam of dawn as if my life depended on it. As the morning drew nearer, my excitement became almost more than I could bear. I even felt as if I would gladly have put off the moment which I had been so passionately awaiting.

At length the eastward grey grew visibly lighter, and was followed by a broad crimson flush all across the heavens. I went up aloft, trembling in every limb. As I reached the top-gallant-mast, the sun rose. I closed my eyes, and for a moment dared not look around me.

When I opened them again, I saw the fog lying all over the calm surface of the sea in fleecy tracts of vapour, like half-transparent snow; and straight ahead, distant some ten miles or so in a direct line, a pale blue peak rising above the level of the mist. At the sight of that peak my heart gave a great leap, and my head turned giddy; for I recognized it instantly as the mountain mapped out between the bay and western coast of the larger island.

As soon as I could command my agitation sufficiently, I pulled out a pocket-glass, and surveyed it narrowly. The glass only confirmed the evidence of my eyes. I then came down, intoxicated with success, and triumphantly bade Taylor go aloft and report all that he should see. The mate obeyed, but declared that there was nothing visible but sky and fog.

I was enraged. I would not believe him. I sent the boy up, and then one of the seamen, and both returned with the same story. At last I went up again myself, and found that they were right. The fog had risen with the rising of the sun, and the peak had utterly disappeared. All this, however, made no real difference. The land was there; I had seen it; and we were sailing for it, right before the wind. In the meantime, I caused the ship's boat to be got ready, directed that a bag of biscuits, a keg of brandy, a couple of cutlasses, a couple of muskets, a couple of sacks, and a good store of ammunition should be thrown into it; and provided myself with a pocket-compass, tinder-box, hatchet, and small telescope. I then took a slip of parchment, and having written upon it the name and destination of the *Mary-Jane*, together with the date of the year and month, and my own signature as her captain, enclosed the whole in a stout glass bottle, sealed it down with my own seal, and stowed it away in the boat with the rest of the stores. This bottle, and a small union-jack which I tied round my waist like a sash, were destined to be hoisted on the mountain top as soon as we succeeded in climbing up to it.

My preparations for landing were but just completed, when the mate sung out, 'Breakers ahead!' I ran at once on deck. The fog had grown denser than ever. There was no land in sight, though I knew we must be within a mile of the shore. Not even the breakers were visible, but we could hear the roaring of them quite distinctly. I gave orders to lay to immediately; and, taking Taylor aside, told him that it was my intention to go ashore in the boat without a moment's delay. He flung up his hands and implored me not to venture.

'I swear to you, sir,' said he, emphatically, 'that's there's no land within four hundred miles of us on any side. These are coral reefs; and to take a boat amongst them in this fog is to rush on certain destruction. For Heaven's sake, sir, stay aboard, at least, till the fog clears off!'

But I only laughed, and refused to listen to him.

'There's land, mate,' said I, 'within a mile. I saw it with my own eyes not two hours ago; and it's a land, let me tell you, that will make the fortune of every man on board. As for the breakers, I'll risk them. If the boat is swamped, it will be no great hardship to swim to shore.'

'It will be death, sir,' groaned the mate.

Of this however, I took no notice, but proceeded to give my instructions. I left the command of the *Mary-Jane* in his hands during my absence, and desired him, if the fog cleared, to anchor in the large bay off which I knew we were lying. I then added that I expected to get back to the vessel before nightfall, but ordered that an exploring party should be sent ashore to search for me, if I had not returned by the end of eight-and-forty hours. To all this the honest fellow assented reluctantly enough, and bade me farewell with as sorrowful an air as if he were attending me to the scaffold.

The boat was then lowered; I took Josh Dunn for my rower, laid my own hands to the helm, and gave the word to put off. The men on board uttered a feeble cheer as we parted company, and in less time than it takes to tell, the *Mary-Jane* was hidden from us by the fog.

'Josh,' said I, as the sound of the breakers grew more and more audible, 'if the boat ships water, we shall have to swim for it.'

'Ay, ay, sir,' replied Josh, briskly.

[13]

'Straight ahead,' I continued, 'lies dry land; behind us the *Mary-Jane*. But a small schooner is more easily missed in a fog, Josh, than an island as big as Malta or Madeira.'

'Ay, ay, sir,' replied Josh, as before.

'If you're wise,' said I, 'you'll strike out for the shore, as I shall. In the meanwhile, we had better fill our pockets with biscuit, for fear of accidents.'

I then divided the contents of the biscuit-bag, and we stuffed our pockets as full as they could hold. By this time, the noise had so increased that we could scarcely hear each other's voices, and the white foam was already visible through the mist.

'Steady, Josh,' cried I, 'there are rough seas before us.'

The words were scarcely past my lips when we were tossing in the midst of the surf, drenched with spray, and well-nigh deafened by the roaring of the waters. I saw directly that no boat could live in such a whirlpool—ours did not hold out for five minutes. Flung from billow to billow like a mere cockle-shell, she laboured onwards for something like a hundred yards, filled, heeled over, and disappeared suddenly from beneath our feet!

Prepared for this catastrophe, I rose like a cork, glued my arms to my sides, kept my mouth and eyes shut, and suffered the waves to carry me along. Finding, however, that instead of bearing me towards the shore, they only dashed me hither and thither among the breakers, I presently gave up all hope of floating in, and, being an excellent swimmer, struck out for land. Blinded, buffeted, breathless, now carried to the summit of a mighty wave, now buried in the very heart of a mountain of green sea, now fighting forward again, in spite of wind and spray, I struggled on with a superhuman energy that only the love of life and riches could have inspired. Suddenly, my feet touched land—lost it—touched again. I threw all my strength into one last, desperate effort, precipitated myself through the raging foam that broke like a vast barrier all along the shore, and fell, face downwards, on the pebbly beach beyond.

I lay there for some minutes, just within reach of the spray, and beyond the line of the breakers, so utterly spent and stupefied as to be scarcely conscious of the danger from which I had escaped. Recovering, however, by degrees, I rose, looked around, and found myself on a shelving belt of shingle that reached far away on either side till lost in the fog. Beyond the shingle ran a line of low cliffs, along the summits of which, looking dim and distant in the misty air, rose the feathery tops of a far-stretching forest of cocoa-nut palms. Here, then, was the island, palpable, undeniable, actual! I took up a handful of loose pebbles—stamped on the shingle—ran along the beach. In all this there was no illusion. I was awake, sober, in full possession of my senses. All was as it seemed—all tried, and proved, and real.

Passing instantaneously from a state of wonder, half confused, half incredulous, to a wild, unbounded joy, I ran about for some minutes like a maniac—shouting, leaping, clapping my hands, and giving way to the most extravagant demonstrations of triumph. In the midst of this folly, the thought of Josh Dunn flashed across my mind. I grew sober in a moment. What had become of the poor fellow? I had never seen him from the instant when the boat capsized. Had he swum for the ship, or the shore? Was he saved, or lost? I went backwards and forwards along the beach, dreading to see his corpse washed up by every coming wave, but found no trace of him in any direction. Convinced, at length, that further search was hopeless, I gave it up, and turned my face and footsteps towards the cliffs.

It was now, as nearly as I could calculate, about ten o'clock in the day. The heat was tempered by the fog and the sea-breeze, and I promised myself to reach the mountain-top before sunset. Making straight across the beach to a point where the cliffs looked somewhat lower and more broken than elsewhere, I succeeded in climbing up the face of the rock without much difficulty, and in gaining the skirts of the palm-forest above. Here I flung myself down in the shade, and proceeded to

[15]

examine the contents of my pockets. The rum, ammunition, and other loose stores were lost with the boat; but I found that I was still in possession of all that I had stowed about my person. One by one, I brought out my tinder-box, telescope, pocket-compass, clasp-knife, and other trifles; all of which (except the compass, which was enclosed in a tight tin case) were more or less damaged by the sea-water. As for the biscuit, it was reduced to a nauseous pulp which I flung away in disgust, preferring to trust to the cocoa-nuts for my subsistence. Of these I saw hundreds clustered overhead; and, being by this time quite ready for breakfast, I climbed the tree against which I had been lying, brought down three or four nuts, and made a delicious meal. I then unscrewed and cleaned the glasses of my telescope, consulted my compass and prepared to continue my journey. Finding by the position of the needle that the north lay to the right, following the line of shore below, I concluded that I must have swum to land at some point of the eastern extremity of the bay where I had hoped to anchor. This being the case, I had but to march due west in order to arrive at the foot of the mountain, which I proposed to myself as the object of my first day's exploration. Due west I turned accordingly, and, compass in hand, took my way through the green shade of the forest. Here the coolness, the silence, the solitude, were perfect. I could not hear my own footsteps for the moss that carpeted the ground; and though I saw several birds of brilliant plumage, they uttered no kind of note, but sat like painted creatures on the boughs, and looked at me without any sign of fear. Once or twice, I saw a small long-tailed monkey flitting like a squirrel through the uppermost tree-tops; but it was gone in a moment, and seemed only to make the place more wild and solitary. On every side, like graceful columns supporting the roof of some vast temple, rose hundreds of slender palm-stems, ringed with the natural record of their yearly growth; whilst here and there, through openings in the boughs, came glimpses of blue sky and shafts of golden sunlight.

[16]

When I had walked thus for about a mile and a half, finding the atmosphere growing clearer and brighter at every step, I suddenly emerged upon a grassy plain studded with trees like an English park, and traversed by a small winding river that glittered like moving silver in the open sunshine. Beyond this plain, at the distance of about another mile and a half, lay a second forest, more extensive apparently, than the first; and beyond that again, defined so clearly against the deep blue sky that I could almost have believed I might touch it with my hand, rose a steep and rugged peak, clothed half-way up with trees, and surmounted by some kind of building, with a beacon on the top. The height of this peak I calculated at something less than two hundred feet. I recognized it at once as the same which I had sighted from the masthead of the *Mary-Jane* at sunrise that morning. I also recognized the plain and river, each lying in its proper geographical position, according to the chart.

Finding my every hope becoming corroborated as I went on, I now made no question as to the result of my undertaking, but pushed gaily forward and amused myself by speculating about the treasure. Where should I find it? In what form? Perhaps we should have to mine for it; and in that case I made up my mind to seek all round the island, if necessary, for some safe harbour in which to anchor the *Mary-Jane*. I should then land all my crew, build a few temporary huts, and set the men hard to work at digging and smelting, till our little ship would hold not another ingot. This done, I would sail straight for Jamaica, lodge my treasure in some colonial bank, purchase a large vessel, engage a numerous crew, and return at once for a fresh cargo of riches. What was to prevent me, indeed, from coming again and again, and carrying hence such wealth as no king or kaiser in all the world could boast?

Absorbed in dreams of untold grandeur and power, I felt neither fatigue nor heat, nor was conscious of the miles I traversed. There was now no fog, nor sign of fog, and the atmosphere was magically clear and bright. A soft air blew from the west. The rich grass of the savannah was thick with flowers. Even the mossy glades of the second forest were radiant with purple and scarlet berries which I dared not taste, although they gave out a delicious odour. This forest proved more extensive than the first, and was more closely planted. All at once, just as I began to wonder how much farther it would lead me, I found myself upon the inner verge of the woods, with a strange and startling panorama before my eyes.

The forest terminated abruptly, about half a mile from the foot of the mountain, and lay round it in one vast circular sweep, a zone of living green. Between these woods and the mountain lay the domes, obelisks, and ivymantled walls of a noble city, all deserted and in ruins. In the midst of these ruins rose the great solitary mountain towards which I had been journeying so long. More ruins were clustered about the base of it, and for some way up the lower slopes and buttresses of its sides. Above these came trees and underwood, and, towering higher still against the sky, a lofty peak of rock and rugged precipice. Examining this peak by the aid of my telescope, I saw some kind of small white edifice upon the very summit, surmounted, apparently, by a pyramidal ornament, supporting a glittering beacon. This beacon was the same that I had seen scintillating in the morning light. On reaching the inner verge of the first forest, I observed it long and earnestly. Was it made of glass, or of some reflecting metal? Did it revolve? Or were these brilliant flashes, which seemed almost as if emanating from its very substance, mere refractions of the sunlight? These were questions which I found it impossible to solve without nearer observation. I could only turn my eyes away, dazzled and half blinded, and then press forward, more eagerly than ever, on my way.

A few yards brought me to a huge mound of shattered masonry, which, as far as I could see, ran all round the ruins like a line of fortification, in some places higher, in some lower, and overgrown in every part with trees and creeping plants.

Having scrambled over this first obstacle, I found myself close against the remains of a lofty circular building, with a domed roof. The portals of this building were carved with strange hieroglyphics, and the dome yet showed traces of faded gold and colours. Finding the entrance choked with fallen rubbish, I passed on as quickly as the uneven nature of the ground would permit, and came next upon a small quadrangular edifice, built, as it seemed, of the purest white marble, and engraved all over with arabesques, and mythologic birds and beasts. Being unable to distinguish any kind of entrance, I concluded that it was a tomb. Then came another domed temple, the roof of which was plated with what looked like sheets of solid gold; then a vast number of tombs all together, some of white, some of red, and some of green marble; then a hillocky space of undistinguishable *débris*; then an obelisk inlaid with various kinds of jasper and onyx; and then, partly built up against, and partly excavated in, the rocky base of the central peak, close beneath which I was now standing, a building of grander dimensions than any I had yet seen. The front, defaced as it was, rose to a clear height of at least three hundred feet. The great entrance was supported on either side by a colossal stone image, half man, half eagle, which, though buried in rubbish half way to the knees, yet stood full fifty feet clear in sight. From the middle of the roof rose a kind of low, broad pyramid, fantastically ornamented in gold and colours.

In this temple, I felt sure I should find treasure. My only difficulty would be to force an entrance. The great portals were liberally blocked up by a mass of broken sculpture, that seemed to have fallen from the façade immediately above the entrance. Over and among the rubbish and *débris* had grown a tangled mass of underwood, trailing plants, and huge prickly growths of the cactus tribe. The hand of man could scarcely have barri-caded the approach to the sanctuary of his gods more effectually than time and decay had done.

With only a pocket-knife, I knew that it would be hopeless

[19]

to attempt to cut my way through such a jungle; I therefore left the front, and made a survey of the temple from the sides where it projected from the face of the rock. Even this was no easy matter, for the area all about it was strewn with great mounds of bush-grown rubbish, over which I had to climb as I best could, without heeding how my hands and face were wounded in the effort. All this time I could see no sign of any openings or windows, by which the building could have been lighted, or any other doorway than the great entrance on the other side.

At length it occurred to me that I might find some means of penetrating to the interior of the building by climbing that part of the mountain against which it was reared, and finding some way of dropping down upon the roof. So I went on a little farther, to a point where the ascent looked somewhat less difficult than elsewhere, and succeeded in clambering up to a ledge that commanded the roof of the temple. It lay before me like a vast terrace, with the pyramid in the midst. Comparatively free from the rubble that strewed every foot of the ground below, it was only grass-grown and mossy, with a few young trees and bushes springing up here and there where the dust of ages had deposited sufficient nourishment for their roots. I sprang down upon it, and proceeded to reconnoitre the surface from end to end, taking good care, all the while, lest I should step on some weak spot, and be precipitated into the chasm below. It was well that I did so. Having gone half-way along from the back towards the front, and left the pyramid a few feet behind me, I came suddenly upon what seemed like a great pit, over the edges of which the bushes clung suspended, and linked their tangled boughs together, as if they feared to fall. I drew back startled, for another step would have carried me over. I peered in—all below was dark and unfathomable. I traced the boundaries of the pit, and found that it was an oblong parallelogram, constructed evidently for the purpose of giving light to the interior. Here, then, was an unobstructed opening into the building, but one of which it would be impossible to avail myself without the aid of a ladder. I tore away a bush that grew at the verge of the chasm, and, flinging myself down at full length, shaded my eyes with one hand, and looked into the abyss below. For some minutes I could see nothing—all seemed intensely dark, like the crater of an extinct volcano. At length, one dim outline after another became faintly visible. I distinguished mounds of stones and rubbish, which had probably fallen from the inside of the ceiling, and the lower limbs of another colossal figure, the upper part of which I could only have seen by descending into the building. It was in vain that I leaned over till another inch would have caused me to lose my balance. It was in vain that I tested the strength of every bush and creeper all round the opening. This was all that I had gained, or could hope to gain, in return for my labour in mounting there.

I rose at last, slowly and reluctantly, and paused to think what it was best for me next to do. The city lay at my feet—the mountain rose high above my head. At the level on which I now stood, and for some distance higher up the mountain-side, were scattered several more of those small buildings which I had concluded must be places of sepulture. Should I examine these, in the hope of finding some access to the probable treasures buried with the dust of their inmates? Or should I pursue my first design of ascending the peak, planting the English flag on the summit, and beginning my explorations with a thorough obser- vation of the whole city and surrounding country? I did not waste much time in hesitation. I felt as yet almost unwearied, despite my exertions and my long night's watch; and I decided for the ascent.

It was a difficult task, and needed all the energy and perseverance of which I was master.

The first two hundred yards or so, where the slope was less abrupt, and the terraces were covered with buildings, were comparatively easy; and here I could not resist turning aside for a few minutes, to examine a tomb which seemed to be more dilapidated than any which I had yet encountered. As I drew nearer, I found that it bore every mark of having been broken open at some not very distant time. It was a simple square building of white marble, with a dome-shaped roof. This roof had evidently received several blows from some sharp instrument, and was cracked and chipped in many places. A large portion of the masonry at one end had also been removed, and piled back against the spot where it had been broken open.

An irresistible curiosity impelled me to displace the stones again, and see the inside of the chamber. The blocks were ponderous, and I dragged them out with difficulty. As I did so, one rolled down the slope, and fell crashing through the bushes, a hundred and fifty feet below, whereupon a number of gorgeous birds rose screaming into the air, and flapped heavily away.

'What a fool I am!' I said aloud, as I wiped the perspiration from my brow, and paused to rest; 'what a fool I am to exhaust myself thus, when others have been before me, and have, no doubt, rifled the place of anything that might have been valuable! Well, never mind; those others have, at all events, done the worst of the work, and I may as well see whether it was really a tomb, and whether the rest of them are likely to be worth our trouble hereafter.'

So I went on again with a will, and found to my satisfaction, that when the three or four large marble blocks were fairly rolled away, only small stones and rubble remained. These were rapidly cleared out, and in about another quarter of an hour I had succeeded in making a space large enough to enable me to creep in. Having done so, and found that I could stand upright inside the building, I waited till my eyes had grown accustomed to the darkness. Gradually, as before, one object and then another became visible, and I found that the place was beyond all doubt a sepulchre.

The inner chamber measured about six feet by ten, and was closed in by a ceiling, about three inches above my head. The walls were lined with slabs of the purest alabaster, engraved all over with strange characters. The ceiling was rudely painted with representations of birds, fishes, plants, and beings half human and half brute. Some broken urns of dark blue pottery lay scattered about the floor, and at the farther end of the chamber, on a raised shelf of plain white marble, stood an alabaster coffer, the lid of which, shattered in a dozen fragments, lay close by. It was too dark for me to see to the bottom of this coffer, but I put my hand in, and found it, as I had expected, empty. Just as I was withdrawing my fingers, however, they encountered a small object that felt like a pea. I seized and brought it to light. It was a fine pearl, somewhat discoloured by the damp, but as large as an ordinary holly-berry.

This discovery made my heart leap for joy, and rewarded me for all the trouble I had given myself to break into this tomb. The pearl itself was probably of no great value, but it was an earnest of what I might hope to find in those tombs which as yet had never been disturbed by previous adventurers. I put it inside my tinder-box for safety, and promised myself the pleasure of displaying it to the crew of the *Mary-Jane*, in proof of the booty that awaited us.

'If there is treasure in the tombs,' thought I, exultingly, 'what may we not hope to find in the temples and palaces?'

My head swam with visions of wealth. I pictured to myself temples with costly altars, and sacrificial vessels of gold and silver—palaces with unexplored apartments, containing thrones, and royal furniture, and weapons studded with precious stones—tombs filled with gorgeous ornaments of buried kings. Aladdin's garden of jewels was not more lavish of wonder than became now to me the ruins of this forgotten city. Then came the bewildering thought that all the riches of this vanished race were mine. The island was unclaimed, uninhabited, unpossessed. It was mine to explore, to ransack, to plunder at my pleasure.

I crept out of the tomb and exultingly breathed the fresh air again. I looked up at the great peak, which I could hardly be said to have even begun to ascend. The sun seemed as yet scarcely to have moved in the heavens, and the glorious day was still at its zenith. I sat down for a few moments to rest, and refreshed my parching throat with a few delicious purple berries that grew upon the bushes close beside me. Then I took out my pearl and examined it again in the open daylight. The sight seemed to stimulate me—I rose, replaced it in the box, and resumed my task.

In a few minutes, I had left the last terrace and the last tomb below my feet, and had entered upon that part of the ascent where the rock grew steeper and was overgrown with thorny underwood, through which I had to force a passage as I could. I did force it, however, though my hands and face bled for it, and my clothes were well-nigh torn to pieces on my back. Panting and exhausted, I at length fought through the belt of brushwood and emerged upon the bare rock above.

Hence the barren peak rose, steep and sheer, some twelve hundred feet above my head. At the sight of these awful precipices, my heart sunk within me. There was no visible footing for even a goat, as far as I could see; and scarce a twig, or blade of grass, for the climber to hold by. Thinking that it might possibly be less steep elsewhere, I contrived to work my way round more to the westward, and there, sure enough, found the commencement of what seemed like a gigantic staircase, hewn roughly out from the very substance of the rock. Each step of this ascent was from three to four feet in height. Some were cut in deep shelves, on which three or four persons could have lain down at length; others were so narrow as scarcely to afford space for the foot; and many were quite broken away, which tenfold increased the difficulty of climbing. By the help, however, of perseverance, great natural agility, a cool head, and a resolute will, I sprang, clambered, and swung myself, somehow or another, from shelf to shelf of this perilous staircase, only pausing now and then to rest, and look down at the widening landscape. At length I found my feet on the last step, and the summit, which had hitherto been hidden by the impending precipices, close above my head.

That summit was artificially heightened by a kind of shelving platform, like a pyramid with the apex cut away. On the top of this platform stood a massive square building of white marble, with a large open entrance looking east; and this building served in turn as the pedestal to a gigantic idol, which sat, cross-legged and hideous, with its face to the setting sun. Sitting as it was, the image measured at least twenty feet in height, and wore on its head a large ornament of some strange and dazzling substance, which almost blinded me, at first, by its intolerable splendour. When I had somewhat recovered the command of my sight, I went nearer and examined it. To my amazement, I found this idol to be one incrustation of precious stones, from head to foot. The body was carved in jasper; the legs and arms in red onyx; the hands, feet, and face in the purest alabaster. Round its neck, inlaid upon the surface of the jasper ground, ran a rich collar of turquoises and garnets; round its waist a belt of great emeralds; round its ankles, wrists, arms, and knees, elaborate bands of amethysts and opals. Each eye was represented by a ruby as large as a crown piece. From its ears hung enormous pendants of the purest sapphires, each the size of an ordinary hen's egg, and richly mounted in gold. Across its knees lay a golden scimitar, the hilt of which was carved from a single beryl; while on its head . . . I stared—rubbed my eyes, as if to be sure I was not dreaming—scaled the walls of the building—climbed the shoulders of the idol—examined it from every side—and came at last to the conclusion that this ornament, which I had taken for a beacon far away at sea, was no other thing than one pure, gigantic, inestimable diamond, such as the world had never seen before!

It was almost spherical in shape, though slightly flattened, like the globe, at the two poles; was cut all over in the smallest facets, each of which reflected every colour of the prism; and measured just twenty-two inches and a half in circumference.

When I had in some degree recovered from the state of excitement and wonder into which this great discovery had thrown me, and was cool enough to look down at the scene below, I saw the whole island at my feet, as if drawn out upon a map.

The smaller island lay close by, to the north-west, separated from this one by a strait of about two miles in width; and all around and about, from the verge of the beach below to the farthest limit of the horizon, stretched one rippling, sparkling, brilliant expanse of sapphire sea, unclouded by a breath of vapour, and unbroken by a single sail. I looked for the *Mary-Jane*; but she was hidden by the cliffs that bounded the eastward coast in the direction where I landed. Then I took out my glass, and made a careful observation of both islands. Scattered up and down the hills of the farther one, I saw the remains of various domed and pyramidal buildings, most of which appeared to be plated on the roofs and sides with gold, and glittered to the sun. Beneath my feet, reaching over a much greater extent of ground than I had at first supposed, lay the ruins of a vast number of palaces, temples, tombs, and triumphal arches; many of which, especially to the west side of the island, which I had not before seen, were in a high state of preservation, and richly decorated with gilding, painting, sculpture, and precious metals. In all of them, no doubt, were idols made after the pattern of this on which I was perched so unceremoniously, and treasure of every imaginable description.

However, the present and actual were all that concerned me just then; so I left the investigation of the ruins till such time as I could bring my men to help me, and set to work with my clasp-knife, to secure as much as possible of the spoil within my grasp. My first attack was made of course upon the diamond, which I dislodged with infinite difficulty, it being 'set' into the head of the idol with some kind of very hard cement, that I had to grate to powder as I went on. When, at last, I had quite freed it, I tied it up in the union-jack which had been all this time about my waist, and let myself down upon the east side of the building, where I had seen an opening into the basement. Looking inside this opening, I found the whole interior filled with human skulls; which somewhat startled me. I made room among them, however, for my diamond, and then climbed up again to secure a few more stones. This time I fell upon the idol's eyes and ear-rings, which I soon transferred to my own pockets; and, having knocked out some of the great emeralds from his belt, and one or two of the largest opals from his bangles and bracelets, and taken possession of his golden scimitar for my own use, I made up my mind to rest from my labours for this day, and go back by the way I had come. So I tied the loose stones up with the diamond, secured the bundle to my belt, buckled the scimitar to my side, and prepared to descend the mountain. Loaded as I was now, however, this proved no easy matter; but I got to the bottom at last, after some perilous falls and scrambles; took the same route through the ruins, scaled the outer line of wall as before, and plunged into the forest.

The sun was low in the heavens, and I was thoroughly exhausted by the mental and physical exertions of the day. I doubted whether it would be possible for me to reach the coast before sunset; and I stood in great need of food and rest. The shade and silence of the woods—the springy moss, offering a natural carpet to my feet—the cocoanuts and fragrant berries all around, were temptations not to be resisted; so I decided to spend the night in the forest, and proceeded to choose my lodging. A snug bank at the foot of a clump of banana and cocoa trees was soon found; and here, with a pile of cocoa-nuts by my side, my precious bundle at my feet, and my scimitar lying ready to my hand, I lay down, ate a hearty supper, and settled myself for the night.

The sun went down upon the silence of the forest. Not a bird twittered—not a monkey chattered—not an insect hummed near. Then came darkness and the southern stars; and I fell into a profound sleep.

I awoke next morning with the dawn; breakfasted on a cocoa-nut, drank the milk of two or three others; and set off, compass in hand, towards the coast. As I went along, I remembered all at once, with a sense of shame at having forgotten it till then, that it was the morning of Christmas-day, which, though summer-time out here in this tropical latitude, was a wintry epoch enough far away in England among those who loved me! Christmas-day, when the quiet grey-turreted church in my native village would be garlanded with holly; when many a true heart would ache for my absence; when many a prayer for my safety would be whispered as the Litany was read; and my health be drunk loudly at the Christmas-feast! And I—what had I been doing all this time? Lost in ambitious dreams, had I given a single thought to those who gave so many thoughts to me? Had I longed for wealth, and dared danger and death, to share my riches with them and make them happy? My heart smote me at these questions, and I brushed away two or three remorseful tears. I saw how selfish had been my aims, and soothed my conscience with a number of good resolutions, all of which were to be carried out when I returned to England with a shipload of jewels and gold.

Absorbed in these wholesome reflections, I traversed the mazes of the forest, crossed the flowery savannah, and threaded the majestic glades of the cocoa-woods that lay nearest the shore. Emerging, by-and-by, in sight of the beach and the sea, I saw, to my surprise and satisfaction, the *Mary-Jane* lying close up against the cliffs, in a little rocky cove not half a mile away. The next instant, I had scrambled down the cliff as recklessly as if it had been a mere slope of smooth lawn, and was running towards the ship at my utmost speed, only pausing every now and then to shout and wave my hat, in case any of the crew were on the lookout for me. No answering shout, however, bade me welcome. Not a head appeared above the ship's side. Not even a pennant fluttered from the mast-head. Had the crew deserted the *Mary-Jane*, and gone up the island in search of treasure for themselves?

At this thought I ran on again, breathless, but very angry. As I drew nearer, however, my anger gave place to a kind of terrified bewilderment. I hesitated—ran forward again—stood still—trembled—could not believe the evidence of my eyes; for at every step the aspect of the *Mary-Jane* grew more strange and startling.

She was lying high and dry upon the beach—a wreck! Her shrouds were hanging in shreds; her hull was clustered thick with barnacles; her sails were white with mould; her anchor, broken and covered with rust, lay some yards off, half buried in the sand. Could she be the same little schooner that I had left only yesterday, as trim and stout as when she was turned out of the builder's yard? Was that indeed her name still visible in letters half effaced? Was I mad or dreaming?

I had now come up close under her bulwarks. I walked slowly round and round her, three or four times, quite dumb and stupefied. It was impossible that she could be the same ship. Her build, her size, her name, it is true, seemed precisely those of my little schooner; but common sense, and the testimony of my own reason, forbade me to believe that twenty-four hours could have done the work of twenty-four years. Here was a vessel that had been deserted for perhaps a quarter of a century, and had rotted where it lay. It was a coincidence—a strange, dramatic, incredible coincidence—nothing more.

I looked round for some means of clambering on board this ruin, and succeeded in finding the end of a broken chain. It hung rather short, but I caught it by a leap, and hauled myself up, hand over hand. In another moment I stood upon her deck. The timbers of that deck were all gaping and rotten, and overgrown with rank fungi. A sea-bird had built its nest in the binnacle. Some smaller nests, deserted and gone to wreck like the ship herself, clung to the rotten shrouds. One boat yet hung in its place, by ropes that looked as if a touch would break them to tinder. The other boat—just precisely the small one which would have been missing if this were indeed all that remained of the *Mary-Jane*—was gone from its moorings.

Curiosity, and something deeper than mere curiosity, took me down the crazy stairs, and into the captain's cabin. It was a foot deep in water, and all the furniture was rotting away. The table yet held together, though spotted all over with white mould; the chairs had fallen to pieces, and were lying in the water. The paper was hanging in black rags from the walls, and the presses looked ready to fall on the head of anyone who should venture to approach them.

I looked round, amazed, upon this scene of desolation. Strange! Dilapidated and disfigured as the place was, it yet bore a weird and unaccountable resemblance to my own cabin on board the *Mary-Jane*. My wardrobe stood in that corner of the cabin, just as this did. My berth occupied the recess beside the stove, just as this did. My table stood in the same spot, under the window, just as this did. I could not comprehend it!

I turned to the table and tried the drawers, but the locks were rusty, and the wood had swollen with the damp, and it was only with the utmost difficulty that I broke away the surrounding woodwork, and wrenched them out. They were filled with mildewed parchments, bundles of letters, pens, account-books, and such other trifles. In one corner lay a mouldy looking-glass in a sliding cover. I recognised the little thing at once—recognized it undeniably, positively. It had been given to me by my mother when I was a boy, and I had never parted with it. I snatched it up with a hand that trembled as if I had the ague. I caught sight of my own face reflected upon its scarred surface.

To my terror, I saw that my beard and hair were no longer chestnut brown, but almost white.

The glass fell from my grasp, and was shattered to fragments upon the wet floor. Merciful Heaven! what spell was upon me? What had happened to me? What strange calamity had befallen my ship? Where were my crew? Grey—grey and old in one short day and night? My ship a ruin, my youth a dream, myself the sport of some mysterious destiny, the like of which no man had ever known before!

I gathered the papers together from the table drawers, and staggered up on deck with them like a drunken man. There I sat down, stupefied, not knowing what to think or do. A frightful gulf seemed to lie between me and the past. Yesterday I was young—yesterday I left my ship, with hope in my heart, and brown locks upon my head; to-day, I am a middle-aged man— to-day, I find my ship rotting on a desolate beach, the hair white upon my brow, and the future all a blank! Mechanically I untied one of the packets of letters. The outer ones were so discoloured that no writing remained visible upon them. They were mere folds of damp brown tinder, and fell to shreds as I unfolded them. Only two, which lay protected in the middle of the packet, were yet legible. I opened them. One was from my mother, the other from Bessie Robinson. I remembered so well when I read them last. It was the evening before that misty night when I met the *Adventure* with her cargo of gold and jewels. Fatal night! Accursed ship! Accursed, and thrice accursed wealth, that had tempted me from my duty, and dragged me to destruction!

I read the letters through—at least, all that was legible of them—and my tears fell fast the while. When I had read them a second time, I fell upon my knees and prayed to God to deliver me. After this, I felt somewhat calmer, and having laid the papers carefully aside, began to think what I should do to escape from my captivity.

My first thought was of my crew. The men would seem to have abandoned the *Mary-Jane*. Everything on board, so far as I could perceive, though rotting away, was untouched. There were no signs of plunder; neither had they taken the ship's last boat, in any attempt to put to sea on their own account. I looked down into the hold, and saw the great packing-cases lying half under water apparently undisturbed since the hour when I left the vessel. Surely, then, the men must have landed and gone up the island. In that case, where were they? How long had they been gone? What time had gone by since we parted? Was it possible that they could be all lost—or dead? Was I absolutely and utterly alone in this unknown island: and was it my fate to live and die here, like a dog? Alas! alas! of what use were diamonds and gold to me, if this were the price at which I was to purchase them?

With these bitter reflections pressing on my mind, I roused myself by a great effort, and resolved that my first step should be to institute a thorough search for my men along the coast. In order to do this, it was necessary that I should find myself some place of temporary habitation, either in the wreck or on the shore, to which I could retire at night. Also that I should lay up a store of provisions for my daily use. I likewise determined to set up some kind of signals, here and there, along the cliffs, to guide the men to me, if they were yet wandering about the island. My bundle of jewels, too, needed to be placed in a secure spot, lest any strange ship should find its way into the bay, and other treasure-seekers lay hands upon it. I looked round about me at the rotting timbers and the leaky cabin, and shuddered at the notion of passing a night on board the *Mary-Jane*. The ship looked as if it must be phantom-haunted. It was, at all events, too remarkable an object to be a secure storehouse for my treasures, in case of the arrival of strangers. It was the first place they would ransack. Altogether, I felt it would be safer and pleasanter to stow myself and my jewels in some cavern along the cliffs. I had seen plenty on my way, and I determined to set off at once in search of what I wanted. So I went down again into the cabin to look for some weapon to carry with me, and having found a rusty marling-spike and cutlass still hanging where I had left them behind the door, thrust them into my belt, slung my bundle over my shoulder, let myself down over the ship's side, and started for a walk under the cliffs. I had not gone far before I found just the spot I wanted. It was a deep cavern, about three feet above the level of the beach, the mouth of which was almost hidden by an angle of rock, and was quite invisible from some little distance. The inside of the cave was smooth, and carpeted with soft white sand. The walls were dry, and tapestried here and there with velvety lichens. In short, it was precisely such a retreat as best accorded with my present purposes. I took possession of it at once, by stowing away my bundle of jewels on a sort of natural shelf at the remotest end of the cave. I then traced a great cross in the sand before the entrance, that I might find my lodging again without difficulty, and went out to seek something in the shape of food and firewood.

The first easy path up the face of the cliffs brought me to the outskirts of the palm forests. I climbed the nearest tree, and flung down about twenty nuts. They were by no means such fine nuts as those farther in amid the woods; but I had taken a kind of superstitious horror of the interior of the island, and had no mind now to venture one step farther than was necessary. I then carried my nuts to the edge of the cliff, and rolled them over. By these means, I saved myself the labour of carrying them down, and had only to pick them up from the beach, and store them in the cave, close under the shelf where I had hidden my jewels. By this time, in spite of my troubles, I was very hungry; but the sun was bending westward, and I was anxious to make another excursion to the ship before nightfall; so I promised myself that I would dine and sup together by-and-by, and so proceeded once more in the direction of the *Mary-Jane*.

What I wanted now was, if it were possible to find them, a couple of blankets, a hatchet to break up my cocoa-nuts, a bottle of some kind of spirits, and a piece of tarpauling to hang at night before the entrance to my cavern. I hauled myself up again by the cable-chain, and went down into the cabin. I found my bed a mere shelf-ful of rotten rags. If I hoped to find blankets anywhere, it must be among the ship's stores, in some place more protected from the damp. I forced open the locker in which I used to keep spirits. Here I was fortunate enough to discover two unopened cases of fine French brandy, apparently quite unspoiled. These I at once carried upon deck, and then let myself down into the hold. There I found several pieces of tolerably sound tarpauling, and some packing-cases on the top, which seemed comparatively dry. One of these, which I knew by the marks yet visible on the cover, ought to contain many valuable necessaries, I prized open with my marling-spike, and found filled with blankets, rugs, and other woollen goods. They were damp, and spotted with mildew, but not rotten. I made two great bundles of the best that I could find, and laid them beside the spirit-cases, on the deck. Searching still farther, I came upon a box of carpenter's tools, an old horn-lantern with about an inch of candle left in it, a small chopper, and a bag of rusty nails. There were plenty of barrels of ship's biscuits, pork, gunpowder, and flour in sight; but as they were all more or less immersed in water, I knew it would be mere waste of time to inspect their contents. Besides, the sun was now declining fast, and I was anxious to carry all that I could to my cavern before the sudden tropical night should come.

I then made three loads of my blankets, tarpaulings, spirit-cases, tools, and so forth; lowered them over the ship's side one by one; and in three journeys conveyed them all to my cave before sunset. I had, even then, time to transport thither some large pieces of timber, the fragments probably of former wrecks, which were lying strewn about the beach. With these I made a good fire, which lighted up the inside of my dwelling, and enabled me to make myself quite comfortable for the night. To spread a warm bed of rugs and blankets, to nail up a large tarpauling before my door, and to make an excellent supper of cocoa-nuts, cocoa-milk, and a little brandy, were the occupations of my evening. As my fire began to burn low, I wrapped myself in my blankets, murmured a short prayer for safety and forgiveness, and fell sound asleep.

[34]

I woke next morning with the sunrise, and started directly after breakfast upon my first expedition in search of the crew of the *Mary-Jane*. All that day I travelled along the margin of the bay in a north-west and westerly direction, stopping every now and then to pile up a little cairn of loose stones that might serve as a signal. I returned to my cavern at dusk, having seen no sign of human footsteps or human habitation in any direction, and having walked, first and last, a good twenty miles at the least. This time I brought home some more firewood, and about half a bushel of mussels, which I had found clustered on the low rocks by the sea. I ate the mussels uncooked for my supper, and, having a famous appetite, thought it the most delicious dish I had ever tasted.

The next day, and the next again, and for many days after that, I persevered in my search, trying first north, and then east and south, and finding no trace of my crew. Wherever I went, I raised cairns along the beach and on the edges of the cliffs; and once or twice even laboured to carry up a piece of broken mast and a scrap of ragged canvas to some little headland, and so raised a kind of humble flagstaff where I thought it might be seen conspicuously from either sea or shore. I often stopped in these voluntary tasks, to sit down and shed a torrent of bitter tears. At night I amused myself by shaping my cocoa shells into drinking-cups and basins, and fitting up my cave with shelves and other little conveniences. I contrived, too, to vary my diet with cockles, mussels, and occasionally a young turtle, when I was so fortunate as to find one on the beach. These I ate sometimes boiled and sometimes roasted; and as I grew very weary of so much cocoa-milk, I brought a leathern bucket from the wreck, and used to fetch myself fresh water from a spring about half a mile from home. I likewise searched out a kettle, a couple of hatchets, a pea-jacket but little the worse for damp, two or three pairs of shoes, a chest containing some uninjured stores of sugar and spices, some more cases of wine and spirits, and various other articles, all of which contributed essentially to my comfort. I also found one or two Bibles; but these were so much spoiled that no more than twenty or thirty leaves were legible in each. As these were not, however, the same in each book, I found I had between seventy and eighty readable leaves—in all, about one hundred and fifty-five pages printed in double columns; the perusal and possession of which proved a great blessing to me in my lonely situation, and gave me strength, many and many a time, to bear my trial with fortitude, when I should otherwise have sunk into utter despair.

Thus a long time passed. I took no regular account of the weeks; but perhaps as many as fourteen or fifteen may have gone by in this manner. I devoted at first every day, then about four days, and at last not more than one or two days in each week, to the prosecution of my apparently hopeless search. At last I found that I had explored all that part of the island which lay immediately round about my cavern for a distance of at least twelve miles in all directions. I could now do no more, unless I shifted the centre of my observations, or undertook a regular tour of the coast. After some deliberation I decided upon the latter course, and, having furnished myself with a flask of brandy, a blanket tightly strapped up like a soldier's knapsack, a hatchet, cutlass, compass, telescope, tinder-box, and staff, started one morning upon my journey.

It was now, as nearly as I could judge, about the first week in April, and the weather was enchantingly beautiful. My route, for the first day, lay along the same path that I had already trodden once or twice, up the north side of the great bay. When I wanted food, I gathered some cocoa-nuts from the adjacent woods, and at night I slept in a cavern very much like the one which I now called my 'home.' The next day I pursued the same direction, and provided myself with food and shelter after the same fashion. On the third day, I came to a point where the cliffs receded from the seaboard, and a broad tract of grassland came down almost to the verge of the beach. I was now obliged to have recourse to shell-fish and such berries as I could find, for my daily food. This made me somewhat anxious for the future; for I foresaw that if the palm forests were to fail me for many days together, I should be obliged to give up my design, and return home with my doubts yet unresolved. However, I made up my mind to persevere as long as possible; and, having walked till nearly nightfall, supped on such fare as I could pick up from the beach and the bushes, and slept in the open air, with only the deep grass for my couch and the stars for my canopy.

On the fourth day I pursued the same course, with the savannah still bordering the shore, and on the fifth had the satisfaction of finding the palms, and some other trees, again fringing the beach; sometimes in clumps or plantations; sometimes scattered here and there on rising knolls, like the trees in a well-arranged English park. Among these, to my great joy and refreshment, I found several fine bread-trees and some wild sugar canes; and, towards afternoon, came upon a delicious spring of fresh water, which bubbled up from the midst of a natural reservoir, and flowed away among the deep grasses in a little channel almost hidden by flowers and wild plants. In this charming spot I determined to stay for the remainder of the day; for I was weary, and in need of repose. So I lay down beside the spring; feasted on bread fruit and sugar-cane juice; bathed my face and hands, in the cool spring; and enjoyed some hours of delicious rest. At nightfall I crept into a little nook amid a clump of spreading trees, and slept profoundly.

The next morning I awoke, as usual, with the sunrise. I had been thinking the evening before that this would be the pleasantest spot in which to pitch my tent for the summer, should nothing more hopeful turn up; and I now resolved, before resuming my journey, to reconnoitre the little oasis, and fix upon some site where I might command a good view of the sea, and yet enjoy the benefits of the trees and the grass. A green hill, surmounted by a crown of palms and other trees, and lying about half a mile from the water-line, looked as if it might exactly present the advantages I sought. I went up to it, in the clear, cool air of the early morning, brushing the dew from the grass as I strode along, and feeling quite reinvigorated by my night's rest. As I mounted the little hill, a new prospect began opening before me, and I saw, what I had not suspected while on the level below, that the savannah was surrounded on three sides by the sea, and that by crossing it in a direct line I should save some miles of coasting. A little reflection led me, consequently, to the conclusion that I had now reached the most northerly part of the island, according to the chart, and that from the summit of the hill I should probably come in sight of the smaller island.

Absorbed in these thoughts, I reached the top almost before I was aware of it, and was proceeding to make my way through the trees in search of the view on the other side, when something close by, reared against the stems of three palms which grew near together in a little angle, attracted my attention. I advanced—hesitated—rushed forward. My eyes had not deceived me—it was a hut!

At first, I was so agitated that I had to lean against a tree for support. When I had somewhat recovered my composure, and came to examine the outside of the hut with attention, I saw that it was utterly dilapidated, and bore every mark of having been deserted for a long time. The sides were made of wattled twigs and clay, and the roof, which had partly fallen in, of canes, palm-leaves, and interwoven branches. On the turf outside were the remains of a blackened circle, as if large fires had been kindled there; and in the midst of the circle lay some smooth stones, which might have once served the purposes of an oven. Close by, at the foot of a large bread-tree, about half-way between the hut and the spot where I was standing, rose two grassy mounds of about six feet each in length and two feet in width—just such mounds as may be seen in the corner appropriated to the poor in any English country churchyard. At the sight of these graves—for graves I felt they were—my heart sank within me. I went up to the low arch which served as an entrance to the hut. It was partially closed from the inside by a couple of rotten planks. I removed the planks with a trembling hand, and looked within. All was dark and damp, save where a portion of the roof had fallen in, and hidden the ground beneath. Feverishly, desperately, I began to tear away the wattled walls. I felt that I must penetrate the secret of the place. I knew, as surely as if the hand of God himself had written it on the earth and sky, that my poor sailors had here found their last resting-places.

Oh, heavens! how shall I describe the scene that met my eyes when I had torn the frail fence from its foundations, and lifted away the roof, that had fallen as if on purpose to hide that melancholy scene from the very stars and sun! A bed of dead leaves and mosses—a human skeleton yet clothed in a few blackened rags—three rusty muskets—a few tin cups, and knives, and such poor necessaries, all thickly coated with red dust—some cocoa shells—a couple of hatchets—a bottle corked and tied over at the mouth, as sailors prepare records for committal to the sea—these were the relics that I found, and the sight of them smote me with a terrible, unutterable conviction of misfortune.

I seized the bottle, staggered away to a distance of some yards from the fatal spot, broke it against the bark of the nearest tree, and found, as I had expected, a written paper inside. For some minutes I had not courage to read it. When, at last, my eyes were less dim, and my hand steadier, I deciphered the following words:—

'August 30th 1761.

'I, Aaron Taylor, mate of the schooner *Mary-Jane*, write these words:—Our captain, William Barlow, left the vessel in the small boat, accompanied by Joshua Dunn, seaman, two hours after daybreak on the 24th of December last, A.D. 1760. The weather was foggy, and the ship lay to within hearing of breakers. The captain left me in charge of the vessel, with directions to anchor in the bay off which we then lay, and left orders that we were to send an exploring party ashore in case he did not return by the evening of the fourth day. In the course of the 25th (Christmas Day), the fog cleared off, and we found ourselves lying just off the curve of the bay, as our captain had stated. We then anchored according to instructions. The four days went by, and neither the captain nor Joshua Dunn returned. Neither did we see any signs of the boat along that part of the shore against which we lay at anchor. The two seamen who yet remained on board were then despatched by me in the long-boat, to search along the east coast of the island; but they returned at the end of three days without having seen any traces of the captain, the sailor, or the small boat. One of these men, named James Grey, and myself, started again at the end of a few more days of waiting. I left John Cartwright in charge of the vessel, with orders to keep a strict look-out along shore for the captain or Dunn. We landed, hauled our boat up high and dry, and made for the interior of the country, which consisted apparently of nothing but dense forest, in which we wandered for five days without success. Returning in a south-east direction from the northward part of the forest-land, James Grey fell ill with fever, and was unable to get back so far as the boat. I left him on a high spot of ground sheltered by trees, made him a bed of leaves and moss, and went back to the ship for help. When I reached the *Mary-Jane*, I found John Cartwright also sick with fever, though less ill than Grey. He was able to help in bringing along blankets and other necessaries, and he and I built up this hut together, and laid our dying messmate in it. On the second day from this, Cartwright, who had over-exerted himself while he was already ailing of the same disease, became so much worse that he, too, was unable to get back to the ship, or to do anything but lie down in the hut beside Grey. I did all I could for them, and tried to do my duty by the ship as well as by the men. I went down to the shore every evening to look after the schooner, and went on board every morning; and I nursed the poor fellows as well as I could, by keeping up fires just outside the hut, and supplying them with warm food, warm drinks, and well aired blankets. It was not for me to save them, however. They both died before a fortnight was gone by—James Grey first, and Cartwright a few hours after. I buried them both close against the hut, and returned to the ship, not knowing what better to do, but having very little hope left of ever seeing Captain Barlow or Joshua Dunn in this world again. I was now quite alone, and, as I believed, the last survivor of all the crew. I felt it my duty to remain by the ship, and at anchor in the same spot, till every chance of the captain's return should have gone by. I made up my mind, in short, to stay till the 25th of March, namely, three months from the time when Captain Barlow left the vessel; and then to navigate her into the nearest port. Long before that, however, I began to feel myself ailing. I doctored myself from the captain's medicine-chest; but the drugs only seemed to make me worse instead of better. I was not taken, however, exactly as Grey and Cartwright were. They fell ill and broke down suddenly—I ailed, and lingered, got better and worse, and dragged on a weary, sickly life from week to week, and from month to month, till not only the three months had gone, but three more to the back of them; and yet I had no strength or power to stir from the spot. I was so weak that I could not have weighed anchor to save my life; and so thin that I could count every bone under my skin. At length, on the night of the 18th of June, there came a tremendous hurricane, which tore the schooner from her moorings, and drove her upon the shore, high and dry—about a hundred yards above the usual high-water mark. I thought she would have been dashed to pieces, and was almost glad to think I should now be rid of my miserable life, and die in the sea at last. But it was God's will that I should not end so. The ship was stranded, and I with her. I now saw my fate before me. I was doomed, anyhow, to live or die on the island. If I recovered, I could never get the *Mary-Jane* to sea again, but must spend all my years alone on the cursed island. This was my bitterest grief. I think it has broken my heart. Since I have been cast ashore, I have grown more and more sickly, and now that I feel I have not many more days to live, I write this narrative of all that has happened since Captain Barlow left the ship, in the hope that it may some day fall into the hands of some Christian seaman who will communicate its contents to my mother and sisters at Bristol. I have been living up at the hut of late, since the heat set in; and have written this in sight of my messmates' graves. When I have sealed it in a bottle, I shall try to carry it down to the shore, and either leave it on board the *Mary-Jane*, or trust it to the waves. I should like my mother to have my gold watch, and I give my dog Peter, whom I left at home, to my cousin Ellen. If any kind Christian finds this paper, I pray him to bury my bones. God forgive me all my sins. Amen.

'AARON TAYLOR.
'August 30th, 1761.'

I will not try to describe what I felt on reading this simple and straightforward narrative; or with what bitter remorse and helpless wonder I looked back upon the evil my obstinacy had wrought. But for me, and my insatiate thirst for wealth, these men would now have been living and happy. I felt as if I had been their murderer, and raved and wept miserably as I dug a third trench, and laid in it the remains of my brave and honest mate.

Besides all this, there was a heavy mystery hanging upon me, which I tried to fathom, and could not comprehend. Taylor's narrative was dated just eight months after I left the ship, and to me it seemed that scarcely three had gone by. Nor was that all. His body had had time to decay to a mere skeleton—the ship had had time to become a mere wreck—my own head had had time to grow grey! What had happened to me? I asked myself that weary question again, and again, and again, till my head and my heart ached, and I could only kneel down and pray to God that my wits were not taken from me.

I found the watch with difficulty, and, taking it and the paper with me, went back, sadly and wearily, to my cavern by the sea. I had now no hope or object left but to escape from the island if I could, and this thought haunted me all the way home, and possessed me day and night. For more than a week I deliberated as to what means were best for my purpose, and hesitated whether to build me a raft of the ship's timbers, or try to fit the long-boat for sea. I decided at last upon the latter. I spent many weeks in piecing, caulking and trimming her to the best of my ability, and thought myself quite a skilful ship's carpenter when I had fitted her with a mast, and a sail, and a new rudder, and got her ready for the voyage. This done, I hauled her down, with infinite labour and difficulty, as far as the tide mark on the beach; ballasted her with provisions and fresh water, shoved her off at high tide, and put to sea. So eager was I to escape, that I had all but forgotten my bundle of jewels, and had to run for them at the last moment, at the risk of seeing my boat floated off before I could get back. As to venturing once again to the city of treasures, it had never crossed my mind for an instant since the morning when I came down through the palm forests and found the *Mary-Jane* a ruin on the beach. Nothing would now have induced me to return there. I believed the place to be accursed, and could not think of it without a shudder. As for the captain of the *Adventure*, I believed him to be the Evil One in person, and his store of gold an infernal bait to lure men to destruction! I believed it then, and I believe it now, solemnly.

The rest of my story may be told very briefly. After running before the wind for eleven days and nights, in a northeasterly direction, I was picked up by a Plymouth merchantman, about forty-five miles west of Marignana. The captain and crew treated me with kindness, but evidently looked upon me as a harmless madman. No one believed my story. When I described the islands, they laughed; when I opened my store of jewels, they shook their heads, and gravely assured me that they were only lumps of spar and sandstone; when I described the condition of my ship, and related the misfortunes of my crew, they told me the schooner *Mary-Jane* had been lost at sea twenty years ago, with every hand on board. Unfortunately, I found that I had left my mate's narrative behind me in the cavern, or perhaps my story would have found more credit. When I swore that to me it seemed less than six months since I had put off in the small boat with Joshua Dunn, and was capsized among the breakers, they brought the ship's log to prove that instead of its being the 25th of December A.D. 1760, when I came back to the beach, and saw the *Mary-Jane* lying high and dry between the rocks, it must have been nearer the 25th of December, 1780, the twentieth Christmas, namely, of the glorious and happy reign of our most gracious sovereign, King George the Third.

Was this true? I know not. Everyone says so but I cannot bring myself to believe that twenty years could have passed over my head like one long summer day. Yet the world is strangely changed, and I with it, and the mystery is still unexplained as ever to my bewildered brain.

I went back to England with the merchantman, and to my native place among the Mendip Hills. My mother had been dead twelve years. Bessie Robinson was married, and the mother of four children. My youngest brother was gone to America; and my old friends had all forgotten me. I came among them like a ghost, and for a long time they could hardly believe that I was indeed the same William Barlow who had sailed away in the *Mary-Jane*, young and full of hope twenty years before.

Since my return home, I have tried to sell my jewels again and again; but in vain. No merchant will buy them. I have sent charts of the Treasure Isles over and over again to the Board of Admiralty, but receive no replies to my letters. My dream of wealth has faded year by year, with my strength and my hopes. I am poor, and I am declining into old age. Everyone is kind to me, but their kindness is mixed with pity; and I feel strange and bewildered at times, not knowing what to think of the past, and seeing nothing to live for in the future. Kind people who read this true statement, pray for me.

(Signed)   WILLIAM BARLOW

Discoverer of the Treasure Isles, and formerly
Captain of the Schooner *Mary-Jane*.

ASHER'S LAST HOUR

George Manville Fenn

George Manville Fenn (1831–1909) was one of
the most prolific authors of the Victorian era,
with over 200 books to his credit, half of these
being stirring adventure novels for boys (equally as
popular as those by his friend George A. Henty).
He began his career as a contributor to *All the Year
Round*, helped by the invaluable advice and
encouragement of the magazine's editor Charles
Dickens. 'Asher's Last Hour' is one of the best,
and more unusual and imaginative, stories
inspired by *A Christmas Carol*, and was published
alongside several other seasonal fantasy tales in
Fenn's collection *Christmas Penny Readings* (1867).

'Now, once for all,' said Asher Skurge, 'if I don't get
my bit o' rent by tomorrow at four o'clock, out you
goes, bag and baggage, Christmas-eve or no Christmas-
eve. If you can't afford to pay rent, you'd best go in the house,
and let them pay as will.' And Asher girded up his loins, and
left Widow Bond and her children in their bare cottage, to
moan over their bitter fate.

And then came Christmas-eve and four o'clock, and no money;
and, what was better, no Asher Skurge to turn out Widow

Bond, 'bag and baggage,' not a very difficult task, for there was not much of it. The cottage was well furnished before Frank Bond's ship was lost at sea, and the widow had to live by needle-work, which, in her case, meant starving, although she found two or three friends in the village who were very sorry for her, or at all events said they were, which answered the same purpose.

However, four o'clock grew near—came—passed—and no Asher. It was not very dark, for there was snow—bright, glittering snow upon the ground; but it gradually grew darker and darker, and with the deepening gloom Mrs Bond's spirits rose, for she felt that, leaving heart out of the question, old Skurge, the parish clerk, dare not turn her out that night on account of his own character. Five o'clock came, and then six, and still no Asher; and Widow Bond reasonably thought that something must be keeping him.

Mrs Bond was right—something was keeping the clerk, and that something was the prettiest, yellow-haired, violet-eyed maiden that ever turned out not to be a dreadful heroine given to breaking up, and then pounding, the whole of the ten commandments in a way that would have staggered Moses himself. No; Amy Frith, the rector's daughter, was not a wicked heroine, and now that she was busy giving the finishing touches to the altar-screen, and pricking her little fingers with holly till they bled, she would not let the old man go because young Harry Thornton, her father's pupil, was there. And Amy knew that so sure as old Skurge took himself off, the young man would begin making love, which, though it may be crowned in a church, ought not to be made in the same place.

The young man fumed and fretted; and the old man coughed and groaned and told of his rheumatics; but it was of no use; the maiden pitied them both, and would have set them at liberty on her own terms, but remained inexorable in other respects till the clock chimed half-past six, when the candles were extinguished, the dim old church left to its repose, and the late

[46]

occupants took their departure to the rectory, and the long low cottage fifty yards from the church gates.

'No; it couldn't be done at any price—turn the woman out on such a night; the whole place would be up in arms; but he would go and see if there was any money for him'; and so Asher Skurge partook of his frugal tea by his very frugal fire, a fire which seemed to make him colder, for it was so small that the wintry winds, which came pelting in at keyhole and cranny, all hooted, and teazed, and laughed at it, and rushed, and danced, and flitted round, so that they made a terrible commotion all about Asher's chair, and gave him far more cause to complain of rheumatics than he had before.

So Asher buttoned himself up, body and soul too; he buttoned his soul up so tight that there was not space for the smallest, tiniest shade of a glance or a ray of good feeling to peep out; and then he sallied forth out into the night wind, with his nose as sharp and blue as if it had been made of steel; and, as he hurried along, it split the frosty wind right up, like the prow of a boat does water, and the sharp wind was thus split into two sharper winds, which went screeching behind him, to cut up the last remains of anything left growing.

He was a keen man was Asher; as keen a man as ever said 'Amen' after a prayer and didn't mean it. Ill-natured folks said he only seemed in his element on Commination-day, when, after all the Curseds, he rolled out the Amens with the greatest of gusto, and as if he really did mean it, while the rector would quite shiver—but then the wind generally is easterly at commination time, in the cold spring. He used to boast that he had neither chick nor child, did Asher; and here again people would say it was a blessing, for one Skurge was enough in a village; and that it was a further blessing that his was a slow race. He was a cold-blooded old rascal; but for all that he was warm, inasmuch as he had well feathered his nest, and might by this time have been churchwarden; but he preferred being clerk, to the very great disgust of Parson Frith, who would gladly have been rid of him long enough before.

It did seem too bad to go worrying a poor widow for rent on a Christmas-eve; but nothing was too bad for Asher, who soon made the poor woman's heart leap, and then sink with despair.

Old Skurge was soon back in his own room, and the wind at last blew so very cold that he indulged in the extravagance of an extra shovel of coals, and a small chump of wood, and then he drew his pipe from the corner and began to smoke, filling the bowl out of a small white gallipot containing a mixture, half tobacco, half herbs, which he found most economical; for it did not merely spin out the tobacco, but no dropper-in ever cared about having a pipe of 'Skurge's particular,' as it was named in the village.

Then, after smoking a bit, Asher seemed moved to proceed to further extravagance, in consequence of its being Christmas-eve; so he laid down his pipe, rubbed his ear, and then plunged his hand into his pocket and brought out a small key. The small key opened a small cupboard, wherein hung upon nails some half-dozen larger keys, one of which was taken down and used to open a larger cupboard, from which Asher Skurge brought forth a well-corked and tied-down bottle.

A cunning, inhospitable old rascal, bringing out his hidden treasures to bib on a winter's night alone. What was it in the old black bottle? Curaçoa, maraschino, cherry brandy, genuine hollands, potent rum, cognac? Hush! was it smuggled-up remains, or an odd bottle of sacramental wine? No, it was none of these; but it poured forth clear, bright, and amber-hued, with a creaming foam on the top; and—'blob'; what was that? a swollen raisin, and the grains that slipped to the bottom were rice.

Then what could the liquid be? The old man sipped it and tried to look gratified, and sipped again, and took a long breath, and said 'ha!' as he set down the glass, and proceeded to fish out the raisin and bits of rice, which he threw on the fire, and disgusted it to that extent that it spat and sputtered; after which he let the glass stand again for a long time before he attempted another taste, for the liquid was very small, very sour beer, six months in bottle. Another year, perhaps, might have improved its quality; but one thing was certain, and that was, that it could be no worse.

But Asher Skurge was not going to show that he did not appreciate the sour beverage, for he considered himself quite bacchanalian; and, after one loud gust of wind, he poked his fire so recklessly that the poor thing turned faint, and nearly became extinct, but was at length tickled and coaxed into burning.

'Nine of 'em,' said Asher, as the old Dutch clock in the corner gave warning of its intention to strike shortly; a chirping, jarring sound, as much as to say 'stand clear or you'll be hit'; and just then the clerk stopped short, put down his pipe again, and rubbed the side of his nose uneasily; got up and looked closer at the clock; went to the window and moved the blind to get a peep out, and then came back to the fire and sat rubbing his hands.

'Never knew such a thing before in my life,' said Asher. 'Never once forgot it before. And just at a time, too, when I'm comfortable. All that confounded woman's fault for not paying her rent. Running after her when I'd my own business to attend to.' In fact, the old clerk had been so put out of his regular course that night, what with church decorations and hunting up Widow Bond, that he had quite forgotten to wind up the clock, the old church time-keeper that he had never let run down once for twenty years.

It was a rough job though upon such a night, just as he was so comfortable, and enjoying his beer and tobacco in so jovial a manner. He looked in his almanac to make sure this was the right evening, and that he had not worked his ideas into a knot; but, no; his ideas were all straight and in good order, and this was the night for winding up.

Couldn't he leave it till the morning?

Couldn't he forget all about it?

Couldn't he wait half an hour?

Couldn't he—couldn't he?—No; he couldn't; for habits that

[49]

have been grown into, can't be cast off in a moment. They may be shabby, and they may be bad habits; they may hang in rags about the wearer, but for all that it takes some time to get rid of them; and if Asher Skurge had not wound up the clock upon this particular night, he would have been unable to sleep in his bed, he would have had the weights upon his chest, the lines hanging round his neck, and the pendulum vibrating within an inch of his nose, while the hands pointed at him, and called attention to his neglect.

No; once a week had Asher Skurge wound up that clock; and, 'will he, nill he,' it seemed he must go this night and perform his old duty. But he did wait more than half an hour, and then how he did snap, and snarl, and worry the air—the cold air of the room. He might have been taken for a wiry terrier showing his teeth with impotent rage while worried by the attacks of a flea legion; but there was nothing for it, and he got up and tied his comforter three times round his neck; brought the horn lantern out of the cupboard, and then tried to illumine the scrap of candle at the bottom. But there was no illumination in that candle. To begin with, it was only a fag-end—one where the cotton did not reach the end of the grease, and to make matters worse, it had been extinguished in that popular manner—snuffing out with wet fingers. Consequently the candle end spit, spat, and sputtered; sent off little fatty scintillations, and then went out. Lit again, it went through the same process, and upon repeating this twice, Asher grew wroth, seized the offending morsel, and dashed it into the fire, where it flared up and seemed to rejoice in the warmth, whilst its indignant owner wiped his fingers in his scant hair, and then lit a fresh piece, closed the lantern, and opened the door for a start.

Talk about Will-o'-the-Wisps and hobgoblins, why Asher looked quite the equal of any ugly monstrosity of the imagination, as he went crunching and grumbling along the snowy path on his way to the belfry-door. The wind was colder than ever, while in spite of the howling din, it was bright and clear overhead, and the stars seemed not merely to twinkle, but quiver and dance.

Asher's journey was but a short one, and mostly along the narrow side path which led amongst the tombstones and wooden tablets; but he cared no more for tombstones, and night walks in churchyards, than he did for walks in the meadows; so on he went, 'crunch, crunch,' on the frozen snow, never pausing to admire the beautiful old church in its Christmas mantle, but growling and grumbling, and if it had been any other man we might have said swearing, till he reached the door in the tower and fumbled in the big key.

'Scraun-n-n-n-tch' went the old wards as the rusty key turned in the rusty lock; and 'Crea-ee-ee-ak' went the great door upon its old hinges; and then setting down his lantern, Asher tried to shut the door again to keep out the bitter wind. But the door would not shut, but seemed as if something was pushing it back against him; and it was not until after two or three vigorous thrusts, that the old man stopped to scratch his head, and took up his lantern and examined the hinges; when, sure enough, there was something which prevented the door closing, for there was a great bone stuck in the crack, and it was so squeezed and jammed in that it took a great deal of getting out. But when it was got out, Asher threw it savagely away, for he minded not a bone or two when there was quite a heap in the corner behind him; so he threw it savagely away, and gave the door a bang which made the old tower jar, and the light in his lantern quiver, while just then there was a rattling noise, and something round came rolling up to him and stopped up against his feet so that the old man gave quite a start.

'Bah!' exclaimed Asher directly after, for he made no more account of a skull than the grave-digger in Hamlet. 'Bah!' he exclaimed; and he gave the skull a fierce kick to send it back to the heap from whence it had rolled. But just then Asher gave a leap—a most nimble one, too, for so old a man; for the skull seemed to have seized him by the foot, and stuck tightly to his heavy boot, which he had driven through the thin bone, and half buried in the internal cavity.

'Why, what the—?' What Asher would have said remains unknown, for he stopped short just as a mighty rush of wind smote the door, howled through the bottom of the tower, and nearly extinguished the horn-protected candle. The old man did not say any more, but kicked and kicked at the skull till it was loosened, when it flew off, and up against the stone wall with a sharp crack, and then down upon the floor; while Asher seized his lantern, and, troubled with an unusual feeling of trepidation, began to ascend the ricketty old oak ladder which led up to the floor where the bell-ringers had been that night pulling a few changes out of the five bells.

Asher Skurge crossed the floor, threading his way amongst the ropes, and then began to mount the next ladder; for there was no spiral staircase here. Up the ricketty, loose rounds, and then rising like a stage ghost through a trap-door, the clerk stood at length in the second floor amongst the ropes, which passed through to the bells above; and here, shut up in a gigantic cupboard, was the great clock whose announcements of the flight of time floated over vale and lea.

As the clerk drew near, all at once there began a whizzing, whirring noise, which drowned the 'tic-tac; tic-tac' of the pendulum; and then loud and clear—too loud and too clear—sounded the great bell-hammer within, announcing that it was eleven o'clock.

'Ah!' growled Asher, as soon as the clock had struck; 'nice time for my job!' and then he pulled out another key, and prepared to open the great clock cupboard.

'Hallo?' said Asher, 'what now?' and he started back a step, for there was a tiny head and shoulders poked out of the keyhole, and two bright, glittering little eyes seemed to gaze at the clerk for a moment, and then popped in again.

Asher Skurge felt himself to be too old a bird to be caught with that sort of chaff—he only believed in four spirits, did

[52]

Asher; and, after gin, rum, brandy, and whisky had been named, the speaker would have got to the end of Asher's spiritual tether. So he put down his lantern and the key beside it; rubbed his eyes, lifted his hat, and scratched his head; and then began to warm himself by beating his hands against his breast.

'Gammon!' muttered Asher, taking up lantern and key, and going towards the cupboard again. 'Gammon!' he exclaimed aloud, and was about to put the key in the hole, when out popped the tiny head again, and remained looking at the astonished clerk, who stopped short and opened his mouth widely.

'It's the strong ale,' said Asher; and he made a poke at the keyhole with the key, when 'bang, crash'; the door flew open and struck him in the face, knocked him down and his lantern out; and of course, you'll say, 'there he lay in the dark!'

Not a bit of it. There lay Asher Skurge, certainly; but not in the dark; for shining out from the middle of the clock was a bright, glowing light, which filled the place, and made the bell-ropes shine as if made of gold. There was the great clock with all its works; but high and low, everywhere, it was covered with tiny figures similar to the one which gazed out of the keyhole, and all busily at work: there were dozens clinging to the pendulum and swinging backwards and forwards upon the great bob, while a score at each side gave it a push every time it swung within reach; dozens more were sliding down the long shaft to reach those upon the bob; while the weights seemed quite alive with the busy little fellows toiling and straining to push them down. Astride of the spindles; climbing up the cogs as though they were steps; clinging in, out, and about every wheel; and all, as it were, bent upon the same object—forcing on the clock—hurry and bustle—bustle and hurry—up and down—down and up—climbing, crawling, and leaping in the golden light were the tiny figures pushing on the wheels.

Asher Skurge sat up with his hair lifting on his head, but a staunch and obstinate man was he, and he wouldn't believe it a bit, and told himself in learned language it was a delusion; but for all that, he was very uncomfortable, and felt about for the old horn spectacles he had left in the room at home.

'I don't care; it's all gammon!' exclaimed the clerk; 'and if I was to say, "crafts and assaults of the devil, Good Lord, deliver us," they'd all vanish.'

'No, they wouldn't, Asher!' said a small voice close at his ear.

'Eh?' said Asher, starting.

'No, they wouldn't, Asher,' said the voice again; 'not till they've kept the clock going till your time's up. You wanted it to run down, but we didn't.'

Asher stared about him, and then saw that the tiny figure which first gazed at him from the keyhole was now squatted, nursing its knees, upon his lantern, and gazing fixedly at him.

'They wouldn't vanish, Asher,' said the tiny figure; 'and here they come.'

As it finished speaking, the little spirits came trooping towards Asher, and dragged out of his pocket a small key, which opened a padlock, and loosened a chain, and set at liberty the key of the great timepiece; for Asher was determined that no other hands should touch *his* clock, as he called it; but now he saw a couple of score of little figures seize the key, fit it in the hole, and then toil at it till they turned it round and round, and wound up first one and then the other weight.

'How much longer?' cried the little spirit upon the lantern.

'One hour,' cried all the other spirits in chorus; and the two words seemed to ring in Asher's ears, and then go buzzing round the place, and even up and amongst the bells, so that there was a sort of dumb pealing echo of the words.

'"One hour,"' cried Asher, at length; 'what's "one hour"?'

'One hour more for you,' said the little spirit, staring unwinkingly, with its little diamond eyes fixed upon Asher, while its mite of a chin rested upon its little bare knees.

'What do you mean,' said Asher, fiercely, 'with your one

more hour?' and then he tried to get up, but could not, for he found that a number of the little figures had busily tied him with the bell-ropes; and there he was fast, hand and foot.

'What do I mean?' said the little figure; 'lie still, and I'll tell you, Asher. I mean that your time's nearly up, and that you have now only fifty-six minutes left.'

'It must be the strong ale,' muttered Asher, turning hot all over, after vainly trying to loosen his bands. 'It must be the strong ale; but I think, perhaps, I'll let Mrs Bond stay another week.'

'Ha! ha! ha! she's all right. You see you didn't make a will, Asher.'

'How do you know?' cried the old man, now growing quite alarmed. 'Who says I didn't make a will?'

'I do,' said the little figure. 'But don't waste time, man. Only fifty minutes; and time's precious.'

'But who are you?' cried Asher, excitedly.

'Me?' said the little thing. 'Oh, I'm only a second, like those climbing about the clock; and I'm the last one in your hour. There's one beat off by the pendulum every moment. Don't you see fresh ones keep going down?'

'No!' growled Asher, savagely, 'I don't.' But he did though, for all that, though he would not own to it. There they were, clinging to the great round ball of the pendulum, and one dropping off at every beat, while fresh ones kept gliding down the long shaft into their places. What became of the others he could not tell, for, as they fell off, they seemed to dissolve in the glow which lit up the old clock's works.

It was of no use to struggle, for the efforts only made the ropes cut into his wrists and legs; and if it had not been that the rope which went round his neck was the part covered with worsted to save the ringers' hands, it seemed to him that he would have been strangled. He was horribly frightened, but he would not own to it, and, in spite of the fierce cold, he felt wet with perspiration.

'How slow the time goes,' said the little figure. 'I want to be off. You're about ready, I suppose.'

'No, I'm not,' cried Asher furiously, 'I've no end to do.'

'Turn out Widow Bond for one thing,' said the figure with a mocking leer. 'Never mind about that. Only forty-five more minutes now.'

'What a horrible dream,' cried Asher in agony.

''Tisn't a dream,' said the little figure. 'You pinch your leg and try now, or stop, I will,' and in a moment the tiny fellow leaped down and nipped the clerk's leg so vigorously that he shrieked with pain.

'Don't feel like a dream, does it?' said the spirit.

'Don't think it does,' said Asher, 'at least I never dreamed so loud before that I know of.'

'No, I shouldn't think you did, but you won't dream any more,' said the little spirit.

'You don't mean that?' said Asher in a pitiful voice.

'I shouldn't have said it if I had not,' said the spirit. 'Do you suppose we speak falsely?'

'Oh, I don't know,' groaned Asher. 'But, I say, let me go this time.'

'Thirty-five minutes,' said the little spirit; 'only thirty-five minutes more, and then my work's done, and yours too.'

Asher groaned again, and then gave a furious struggle, which only tightened the ropes and made one of the bells above give a sonorous clang, which sounded like a knell to the groaning clerk.

'How are you going to do it?' he cried at last.

'Going to do what?' said the spirit.

'Going to—to—to—make an end of me?' said Asher.

'Oh!' said the spirit, 'I shan't have anything to do with it. Some of those to come will do that; I shall be gone. I suppose they'll only put your head under the big hammer which strikes the hour, and it will do all that, so that people will say it was an accident. Only twenty-five minutes now.'

Asher turned as white as the parson's surplice, and his teeth chattered as he groaned out:—

'Oh! what for? what for?'

'Why, you see, you are no good,' said the spirit, 'and only in the way, so someone else may just as well be in your place. What do you know of love, or friendship, or affection, or anything genial? Why you're cold enough to chill the whole parish. Only a quarter of an hour now.'

Ten minutes later the little spirit told the trembling man that he had but five minutes more, and four of these were wasted in unavailing struggles and prayers for release, when all at once Asher felt himself seized by hundreds of tiny hands. The cords were tightened till their pressure was agonizing; and then he seemed to be floated up into the great open floor where the bells hung in the massive oaken framework, and though he could not see it, he knew well enough where the tenor bell was, and also how the great iron clock hammer was fixed, which would crush his skull like an egg-shell.

Asher struggled and tried to scream, but he felt himself impelled towards the bell, and directly after his cheek was resting upon the cold metal on one side, while the great hammer barely touched his temple on the other, and he knew when it was raised that it would come down with a fierce crash, and he shuddered as he thought of the splashed bell, and the blood, and brains, and hair clinging to the hammer.

'And they'll say it was an accident,' muttered Asher to himself, quoting the spirit's remark. 'They'll never give me credit for doing it myself. I'm the wrong sort.' And then the thoughts of a lifetime seemed crowded into that last minute, and he shuddered to see what little good he had done. Always money and self, and now what was it worth? He had pinched and punished all around him for the sake of heaping up riches, and now above all would come in those words—

'Thou fool, this night thy soul shall be required of thee.'

Thoughts crowded through the wretched man's brain thick

[57]

and fast. He seemed to be living his life through in these few remaining seconds, while above all there was the reproaching face of the poor widow whom he would have cast out that night homeless and friendless upon the bitter world. He could not explain it to himself, but it seemed that this face kept him down where he was more than anything else. There was no anger upon it, nothing but bitter sorrowful reproach, and though he would have closed his eyes he could not hide from his gaze that sad countenance. But now came the horror of death, for he seemed to see the little spirits glide down the pendulum far beneath him, rest for a moment upon the bob, and then as one was beaten off, up rose the hammer, and he felt its cold touch leave his temple. Up—up—higher—higher—and now it was about to come down and would dash out his brains. It was coming, and all was over, and for that second the agony he suffered was intense. Then down it came, after seeming to be poised in the air for an awful space of time, and at last came the fearful stroke.

'Clang,' and his brain rocked and reeled as the blow fell upon the sonorous metal close by his forehead. The piercing tones rang through him, but before he could collect his thoughts—'Clang' went the hammer again again, and yet his heart did not revive, for he felt that it would be the *last* stroke which would crush him.

'Clang—clang—clang—clang' came the solemn tones of the great bell; solemn, although they seemed to split his head with the noise, and now he had counted eleven, and the last blow was about to fall. The hammer was rising—slowly rising—and in less than a moment he felt that the blow would come. He could not struggle, though he was being impelled nearer and nearer. He could not cry. He could not move; and at last, after an agonising suspense, during which the widow's imploring, reproachful face was pressing closer and closer, down came the great hammer for the twelfth stroke—

'Crash!'

*

'The clock stopped; and the bells won't ring,' said a cheery voice; 'and on a Christmas-morning, too. Let me try.'

Asher Skurge heard the voice, and directly after he shrieked out with pain, for he felt something cutting into his leg, and this caused him to open his eyes, and to see that his lantern lay close beside him; that he was regularly wrapped, tied, and tangled with the bell-ropes, while the clock cupboard lay open before him—the clock at a standstill—probably from the cold; while, as for himself, he was quite at a lie-still, and there had been someone dragging at one of the ropes so as almost to cut his leg in two.

Directly after the head of young Harry Thornton appeared above the trap-door, and then at his call came the sexton; but more help was needed before Asher Skurge could be got down the ladders and across the churchyard to his cottage, where, what with rheumatics and lumbago, the old man is not so fond of winter night walks as of old.

But though Asher would as soon of thought of turning himself out as Widow Bond, he did not have her long for a tenant, for her husband's ship was not lost; and after three years' absence, Frank Bond came back safe and sound, but so weatherbeaten as hardly to be recognised.

But Asher Skurge was ever after an altered man, for it seemed to him that he had taken out a new lease of his life, and in spite of neighbourly sneers, he set heartily to work to repair his soul's tenement. You can see where it has been patched; and even now it is far from perfect, but there are much worse men in the world than Asher Skurge, even if he does believe in spirits, and you might have a worse man for a landlord than the obstinate old clerk, who so highly offended the new vicar because he would not go and wind up the clock after dark.

THE CHRISTMAS BANQUET

Nathaniel Hawthorne

Nathaniel Hawthorne (1804–64), best known for
his novels *The Scarlet Letter* and *The House of the
Green Gables*, was the most distinguished of the
New England school of literature. His best short
stories were collected as *Twice-Told Tales* and
Mosses from an old Manse.

'I have here attempted,' said Roderick, unfolding a few sheets
of manuscript, as he sat with Rosina and the sculptor in the
summerhouse—'I have attempted to seize hold of a person-
age who glides past me, occasionally, in my walk through life.
My former sad experience, as you know, has gifted me with
some degree of insight into the gloomy mysteries of the human
heart, through which I have wandered like one astray in a dark
cavern, with his torch fast flickering to extinction. But this
man, this class of men, is a hopeless puzzle.'

'Well, but propound him,' said the sculptor. 'Let us have an
idea of him, to begin with.'

'Why, indeed,' replied Roderick, 'he is such a being as I could
conceive you to carve out of marble, and some yet unrealized
perfection of human science to endow with an exquisite mockery

of intellect; but still there lacks the last inestimable touch of a divine Creator. He looks like man; and, perchance, like a better specimen of man than you ordinarily meet. You might esteem him wise; he is capable of cultivation and refinement, and has at least an external conscience; but the demands that spirit makes upon spirit are precisely those to which he cannot respond. When at last you come close to him you find him chill and unsubstantial—a mere vapour.'

'I believe,' said Rosina, 'I have a glimmering of idea what you mean.'

'Then be thankful,' answered her husband, smiling; 'but do not anticipate any further illumination from what I am about to read. I have here imagined such a man to be—what, probably, he never is—conscious of the deficiency in his spiritual organization. Methinks the result would be a sense of cold unreality wherewith he would go shivering through the world, longing to exchange his load of ice for any burden of real grief that fate could fling upon a human being.'

Contenting himself with this preface, Roderick began to read.

In a certain old gentleman's last will and testament there appeared a bequest, which, as his final thought and deed, was singularly in keeping with a long life of melancholy eccentricity. He devised a considerable sum for establishing a fund, the interest of which was to be expended, annually, forever, in preparing a Christmas Banquet for ten of the most miserable persons that could be found. It seemed not to be the testator's purpose to make these half a score of sad hearts merry, but to provide that the stern or fierce expression of human discontent should not be drowned, even for that one holy and joyful day, amid the acclamations of festival gratitude which all Christendom sends up. And he desired, likewise, to perpetuate his own remonstrance against the earthly course of Providence, and his sad and sour dissent from those systems of religion or philosophy which either find sunshine in the world or draw it down from heaven.

[61]

The task of inviting the guests, or of selecting among such as might advance their claims to partake of this dismal hospitality, was confided to the two trusteees or stewards of the fund. These gentlemen, like their deceased friend, were sombre humorists, who made it their principal occupation to number the sable threads in the web of human life, and drop all the golden ones out of the reckoning. They performed their present office with integrity and judgment. The aspect of the assembled company, on the day of the first festival, might not, it is true, have satisfied every beholder that these were especially the individuals, chosen forth from all the world, whose griefs were worthy to stand as indicators of the mass of human suffering. Yet, after due consideration, it could not be disputed that here was a variety of hopeless discomfort, which, if it sometimes arose from causes apparently inadequate, was thereby only the shrewder imputation against the nature and mechanism of life.

The arrangements and decorations of the banquet were probably intended to signify that death in life which had been the testator's definition of existence. The hall, illuminated by torches, was hung round with curtains of deep and dusky purple, and adorned with branches of cypress and wreaths of artificial flowers, imitative of such as used to be strewn over the dead. A sprig of parsley was laid by every plate. The main reservoir of wine was a sepulchral urn of silver, whence the liquor was distributed around the table in small vases, accurately copied from those that held the tears of ancient mourners. Neither had the stewards—if it were their taste that arranged these details—forgotten the fantasy of the old Egyptians, who seated a skeleton at every festive board, and mocked their own merriment with the imperturbable grin of a death's head. Such a fearful guest, shrouded in a black mantle, sat now at the head of the table. It was whispered, I know not with what truth, that the testator himself had once walked the visible world with the machinery of that same skeleton, and that it was one of the stipulations of his will, that he should thus be permitted to sit, from year to year, at the banquet which he had instituted. If so, it was perhaps covertly implied that he had cherished no hopes of bliss beyond the grave to compensate for the evils which he felt or imagined here. And if, in their bewildered conjectures as to the purpose of earthly existence, the banqueters should throw aside the veil, and cast an inquiring glance at this figure of death, as seeking thence the solution otherwise unattainable, the only reply would be a stare of the vacant eye caverns and a grin of the skeleton jaws. Such was the response that the dead man had fancied himself to receive when he asked of Death to solve the riddle of his life; and it was his desire to repeat it when the guests of his dismal hospitality should find themselves perplexed with the same question.

'What means that wreath?' asked several of the company, while viewing the decorations of the table.

They alluded to a wreath of cypress, which was held on high by a skeleton arm, protruding from within the black mantle.

'It is a crown,' said one of the stewards, 'not for the worthiest, but for the woefullest, when he shall prove his claim to it.'

The guest earliest bidden to the festival was a man of soft and gentle character, who had not energy to struggle against the heavy despondency to which his temperament rendered him liable; and therefore with nothing outwardly to excuse him from happiness, he had spent a life of quiet misery that made his blood torpid, and weighed upon his breath, and sat like a ponderous night fiend upon every throb of his unresisting heart. His wretchedness seemed as deep as his original nature, if not identical with it. It was the misfortune of a second guest to cherish within his bosom a diseased heart, which had become so wretchedly sore that the continual and unavoidable rubs of the world, the blow of an enemy, the careless jostle of a stranger, and even the faithful and loving touch of a friend, alike made ulcers in it. As is the habit of people thus afflicted, he found his chief employment in exhibiting these miserable sores to any who would give themselves the pain of viewing them. A third guest was a hypochondriac, whose imagination wrought necromancy in his outward and inward world, and caused him to see monstrous faces in the household fire, and dragons in the clouds of sunset and fiends in the guise of beautiful women, and something ugly or wicked beneath all the pleasant surfaces of nature. His neighbour at table was one who, in his early youth, had trusted mankind too much, and hoped too highly in their behalf, and, in meeting with many disappointments, had become desperately soured. For several years back this misanthrope had employed himself in accumulating motives for hating and despising his race—such as murder, lust, treachery, ingratitude, faithlessness of trusted friends, instinctive vices of children, impurity of women, hidden guilt in men of saintlike aspect—and, in short, all manner of black realities that sought to decorate themselves with outward grace or glory. But at every atrocious fact that was added to his catalogue, at every increase of the sad knowledge which he spent his life to collect, the native impulses of the poor man's loving and confiding heart made him groan with anguish. Next, with his heavy brown bent downward, there stole into the hall a man naturally earnest and impassioned, who, from his immemorial infancy, had felt the consciousness of a high message to the world; but essaying to deliver it, had found either no voice or form of speech, or else no ears to listen. Therefore his whole life was a bitter questioning of himself—'Why have not men acknowledged my mission? Am I not a self-deluding fool? What business have I on earth? Where is my grave?' Throughout the festival, he quaffed frequent draughts from the sepulchral urn of wine, hoping thus to quench the celestial fire that tortured his own breast and could not benefit his race.

Then there entered, having flung away a ticket for a ball, a gay gallant of yesterday, who had found four or five wrinkles in his brow, and more gray hairs than he could well number on his head. Endowed with sense and feeling, he had nevertheless spent his youth in folly, but had reached at last that dreary point in life where Folly quits us of her own accord, leaving us to make friends of Wisdom if we can. Thus, cold and desolate, he had come to seek Wisdom at the banquet, and wondered if the skeleton were she. To eke out the company, the stewards had invited a distressed poet from his home in the almshouse, and a melancholy idiot from the street corner. The latter had just the glimmering of sense that was sufficient to make him conscious of a vacancy, which the poor fellow, all his life long, had mistily sought to fill up with intelligence, wandering up and down the streets, and groaning miserably because his attempts were ineffectual. The only lady in the hall was one who had fallen short of absolute and perfect beauty, merely by the trifling defect of a slight cast of her left eye. But this blemish, minute as it was, so shocked the pure ideal of her soul, rather than her vanity, that she passed her life in solitude, and veiled her countenance even from her own gaze. So the skeleton sat shrouded at one end of the table and this poor lady at the other.

One other guest remains to be described. He was a young man of smooth brow, fair cheek, and fashionable mien. So far as his exterior developed him, he might much more suitably have found a place at some merry Christmas table, than have been numbered among the blighted, fate-stricken, fancy-tortured set of ill-starred banqueters. Murmurs arose among the guests as they noted the glance of general scrutiny which the intruder threw over his companions. What had he to do among them? Why did not the skeleton of the dead founder of the feast unbend its rattling joints, arise, and motion the unwelcome stranger from the board?

'Shameful!' said the morbid man, while a new ulcer broke out in his heart. 'He comes to mock us!—we shall be the jest of his tavern friends!—he will make a farce of our miseries, and bring it out upon the stage!'

'O, never mind him!' said the hypochondriac, smiling sourly. 'He shall feast from yonder tureen of viper soup; and if there is a fricassee of scorpions on the table, pray let him have his share of it. For the dessert, he shall taste the apples of Sodom. Then, if he likes our Christmas fare, let him return again next year!'

[65]

'Trouble him not,' murmured the melancholy man, with gentleness. 'What matters it whether the consciousness of misery comes a few years sooner or later? If this youth deem himself happy now, yet let him sit with us for the sake of the wretchedness to come.'

The poor idiot approached the young man with that mournful aspect of vacant inquiry which his face continually wore, and which caused people to say that he was always in search of his missing wits. After no little examination he touched the stranger's hand, but immediately drew back his own, shaking his head and shivering.

'Cold, cold, cold!' muttered the idiot.

The young man shivered too, and smiled.

'Gentlemen—and you, madam,'—said one of the stewards of the festival, 'do not conceive so ill either of our caution or judgment, as to imagine that we have admitted this young stranger—Gervayse Hastings by name—without a full investigation and thoughtful balance of his claims. Trust me, not a guest at the table is better entitled to his seat.'

The steward's guarantee was perforce satisfactory. The company, therefore, took their places, and addressed themselves to the serious business of the feast, but were soon disturbed by the hypochondriac, who thrust back his chair, complaining that a dish of stewed toads and vipers was set before him, and that there was green ditch water in his cup of wine. This mistake being amended, he quietly resumed his seat. The wine, as it flowed freely from the sepulchral urn, seemed to come imbued with all gloomy inspirations; so that its influence was not to cheer, but either to sink the revellers into a deeper melancholy, or elevate their spirits to an enthusiasm of wretchedness. The conversation was various. They told sad stories about people who might have been worthy guests at such a festival as the present. They talked of grisly incidents in human history; of strange crimes, which, if truly considered, were but convulsions of agony; of some lives that had been altogether wretched, and of others, which, wearing a general semblance of happiness, had yet been deformed, sooner or later, by misfortune, as by the intrusion of a grim face at a banquet; of death-bed scenes, and what dark intimations might be gathered from the words of dying men; of suicide, and whether the more eligible modes were by halter, knife, poison, drowning, gradual starvation, or the fumes of charcoal. The majority of the guests, as is the custom with people thoroughly and profoundly sick at heart, were anxious to make their own woes the theme of discussion, and prove themselves most excellent in anguish. The misanthropist went deep into the philosophy of evil, and wandered about in the darkness, with now and then a gleam of discoloured light hovering on ghastly shapes and horrid scenery. Many a miserable thought, such as men have stumbled upon from age to age, did he now rake up again, and gloat over it as an inestimable gem, a diamond, a treasure far preferable to those bright, spiritual revelations of a better world, which are like precious stones from heaven's pavement. And then, amid his lore of wretchedness, he hid his face and wept.

It was a festival at which the woeful man of Uz might suitably have been a guest, together with all, in each succeeding age, who have tasted deepest of the bitterness of life. And be it said, too, that every son or daughter of woman, however favoured with happy fortune, might, at one sad moment or another, have claimed the privilege of a stricken heart, to sit down at this table. But, throughout the feast, it was remarked that the young stranger, Gervayse Hastings, was unsuccessful in his attempts to catch its pervading spirit. At any deep, strong thought that found utterance, and which was torn out, as it were, from the saddest recesses of human consciousness, he looked mystified and bewildered; even more than the poor idiot, who seemed to grasp at such things with his earnest heart, and thus occasionally to comprehend them. The young man's conversation was of a colder and lighter kind, often brilliant, but lacking the powerful characteristics of a nature that had been developed by suffering.

[67]

'Sir,' said the misanthropist bluntly, in reply to some observation by Gervayse Hastings, 'pray do not address me again. We
have no right to talk together. Our minds have nothing in
common. But what claim you appear at this banquet I cannot
guess; but methinks, to a man who could say what you have just
now said, my companions and myself must seem no more than
shadows flickering on the wall. And precisely such a shadow are
you to us.'

The young man smiled and bowed, but drawing himself back
in his chair, he buttoned his coat over his breast, as if the
banqueting hall were growing chill. Again the idiot fixed his
melancholy stare upon the youth, and murmured, 'Cold! cold!
cold!'

The banquet drew to its conclusion, and the guests departed.
Scarcely had they stepped across the threshold of the hall when
the scene that had there passed seemed like the vision of a sick
fancy, or an exhalation from a stagnant heart. Now and then,
however, during the year that ensued, these melancholy people
caught glimpses of one another, transient, indeed, but enough
to prove that they walked the earth with the ordinary allotment
of reality. Sometimes a pair of them came face to face while
stealing through the evening twilight, enveloped in their sable
cloaks. Sometimes they casually met in churchyards. Once,
also, it happened that two of the dismal banqueters mutually
started at recognizing each other in the noonday sunshine of a
crowded street, stalking there like ghosts astray. Doubtless they
wondered why the skeleton did not come abroad at noonday too.

But whenever the necessity of their affairs compelled these
Christmas guests into the bustling world, they were sure to
encounter the young man who had so unaccountably been
admitted to the festival. They saw him among the gay and
fortunate; they caught the sunny sparkle of his eye; they heard
the light and careless tones of his voice, and muttered to
themselves with such indignation as only the aristocracy of
wretchedness could kindle—'The traitor! The vile impostor!

Providence, in its own good time, may give him a right to feast among us!' But the young man's unabashed eye dwelt upon their gloomy figures as they passed him, seeming to say, perchance with somewhat of a sneer, 'First, know my secret!—then measure your claims with mine!'

The step of Time stole onward, and soon brought merry Christmas round again, with glad and solemn worship in the churches, and sports, games, festivals, and everywhere the bright face of Joy beside the household fire. Again, likewise, the hall, with its curtains of dusky purple, was illuminated by the death torches gleaming on the sepulchral decorations of the banquet. The veiled skeleton sat in state, lifting the cypress wreath above its head, as the guerdon of some guest illustrious in the qualifications which there claimed precedence. As the stewards deemed the world inexhaustible in misery, and were desirous of recognizing it in all its forms, they had not seen fit to reassemble the company of the former year. New faces now threw their gloom across the table.

There was a man of nice conscience, who bore a blood stain in his heart—the death of a fellow-creature—which, for his more exquisite torture, had chanced with such a peculiarity of circumstances, that he could not absolutely determine whether his will had entered into the deed or not. Therefore, his whole life was spent in the agony of an inward trial for murder, with a continual sifting of the details of his terrible calamity, until his mind had no longer any thought, nor his soul any emotion, disconnected with it. There was a mother, too—a mother once, but a desolation now—who, many years before, had gone out on a pleasure party, and, returning, found her infant smothered in its little bed. And ever since she has been tortured with the fantasy that her buried baby lay smothering in its coffin. Then there was an aged lady, who had lived from time immemorial with a constant tremor quivering through her frame. It was terrible to discern her dark shadow tremulous upon the wall; her lips, likewise, were tremulous; and the expression of her eye

[69]

seemed to indicate that her soul was trembling, too. Owing to the bewilderment and confusion which made almost a chaos of her intellect, it was impossible to discover what dire misfortune had thus shaken her nature to its depths; so that the stewards had admitted her to the table, not from any acquaintance with her history, but on the safe testimony of her miserable aspect. Some surprise was expressed at the presence of a bluff, red-faced gentleman, a certain Mr Smith, who had evidently the fat of many a rich feast within him, and the habitual twinkle of whose eye betrayed a disposition to break forth into uproarious laughter for little cause or none. It turned out, however, that with the best possible flow of spirits, our poor friend was afflicted with a physical disease of the heart, which threatened instant death on the slightest cachinnatory indulgence, or even that titillation of the bodily frame produced by merry thoughts. In this dilemma he had sought admittance to the banquet, on the ostensible plea of his irksome and miserable state, but, in reality, with the hope of imbibing a life-preserving melancholy.

A married couple had been invited from a motive of bitter humour, it being well understood that they rendered each other unutterably miserable whenever they chanced to meet, and therefore must necessarily be fit associates at the festival. In contrast with these was another couple still unmarried, who had interchanged their hearts in early life, but had been divided by circumstances as unpalpable as morning mist, and kept apart so long that their spirits now found it impossible to meet. Therefore, yearning for communion, yet shrinking from one another and choosing none beside, they felt themselves companionless in life, and looked upon eternity as a boundless desert. Next to the skeleton sat a mere son of earth—a hunter of the Exchange—a gatherer of shining dust—a man whose life's record was in his ledger, and whose soul's prisonhouse the vaults of the bank where he kept his deposits. This person had been greatly perplexed at his invitation, deeming himself one of the most fortunate men in the city; but the stewards persisted in

demanding his presence, assuring him that he had no concep-
tion how miserable he was.

And now appeared a figure which we must acknowledge as our
acquaintance of the former festival. It was Gervayse Hastings,
whose presence had then caused so much question and criticism,
and who now took his place with the composure of one whose
claims were satisfactory to himself, and must needs be allowed
by others. Yet his easy and unruffled face betrayed no sorrow.
The well-skilled beholders gazed a moment into his eyes and
shook their heads, to miss the unuttered sympathy—the count-
ersign, never to be falsified—of those whose hearts are cavern
mouths, through which they descend into a region of illimitable
woe, and recognize other wanderers there.

'Who is this youth?' asked the man with a blood stain on his
conscience. 'Surely he has never gone down into the depths! I
know all the aspects of those who have passed through the dark
valley. By what right is he among us?'

'Ah, it is a sinful thing to come hither without a sorrow,'
murmured the aged lady, in accents that partook of the eternal
tremor which pervaded her whole being. 'Depart, young man!
Your soul has never been shaken; and, therefore, I tremble so
much the more to look at you.'

'His soul shaken! No; I'll answer for it,' said bluff Mr Smith,
pressing his hand upon his heart, and making himself as
melancholy as he could, for fear of a fatal explosion of laughter.
'I know the lad well; he has as fair prospects as any young man
about town, and has no more right among us miserable creatures
than the child unborn. He never was miserable, and probably
never will be!'

'Our honoured guests,' interposed the stewards, 'pray have
patience with us, and believe, at least, that our deep veneration
for the sacredness of this solemnity would preclude any willful
violation of it. Receive this young man to your table. It may not
be too much to say that no guest here would exchange his own
heart for the one that beats within that youthful bosom!'

[71]

'I'd call it a bargain, and gladly, too,' muttered Mr Smith, with a perplexing mixture of sadness and mirthful conceit. 'A plague upon their nonsense! My own heart is the only really miserable one in the company; it will certainly be the death of me at last!'

Nevertheless, as on the former occasion, the judgment of the stewards being without appeal, the company sat down. The obnoxious guest made no more attempt to obtrude his conversation of those about him, but appeared to listen to the table talk with peculiar assiduity, as if some inestimable secret, otherwise beyond his reach, might be conveyed in a casual word. And in truth, to those who could understand and value it, there was rich matter in the upgushings and outpourings of these initiated souls to whom sorrow had been a talisman, admitting them into spiritual depths which no other spell can open. Sometimes out of the midst of densest gloom there flashed a momentary radiance, pure as crystal, bright as the flame of stars, and shedding such a glow upon the mysteries of life that the guests were ready to exclaim, 'Surely the riddle is on the point of being solved!' At such illuminated intervals the saddest mourners felt it to be revealed that mortal griefs are but shadowy and external; no more than the sable robes voluminously shrouding a certain divine reality, and thus indicating what might otherwise be altogether invisible to mortal eye.

'Just now,' remarked the trembling old woman, 'I seemed to see beyond the outside. And then my everlasting tremor passed away!'

'Would that I could dwell always in these momentary gleams of light!' said the man of stricken conscience. 'Then the bloodstain in my heart would be washed clean away.'

This strain of conversation appeared so unintelligibly absurd to good Mr Smith, that he burst into precisely the fit of laughter which his physicians had warned him against, as likely to prove instantaneously fatal. In effect, he fell back in his chair a corpse, with a broad grin upon his face, while his ghost, perchance, remained beside it bewildered at its unpremeditated exit. This catastrophe, of course, broke up the festival.

'How is this? You do not tremble?' observed the tremulous old woman to Gervayse Hastings, who was gazing at the dead man with singular intentness. 'Is it now awful to see him so suddenly vanish out of the midst of life—this man of flesh and blood, whose earthly nature was so warm and strong? There is a never-ending tremor in my soul, but it trembles afresh at this! And you are calm!'

'Would that he could teach me somewhat!' said Gervayse Hastings, drawing a long breath. 'Men pass before me like shadows on the wall; their actions, passions, feelings, are flickerings of the light, and then they vanish! Neither the corpse, nor yonder skeleton, nor this old woman's everlasting tremor can give me what I seek.'

And then the company departed.

We cannot linger to narrate, in such detail, more circumstances of these singular festivals, which, in accordance with the founder's will, continued to be kept with the regularity of an established institution. In process of time the stewards adopted the custom of inviting, from far and near, those individuals whose misfortunes were prominent above other men's, and whose mental and moral development might, therefore, be supposed to possess a corresponding interest. The exiled noble of the French Revolution, and the broken soldier of the Empire, were alike represented at the table. Fallen monarchs, wandering about the earth, have found places at that forlorn miserable feast. The statesman, when his party flung him off, might, if he chose it, be once more a great man for the space of a single banquet. Aaron Burr's name appears on the record at a period when his ruin—the profoundest and most striking, with more of moral circumstance in it than that of almost any other man—was complete in his lonely age. Stephen Girard, when his wealth weighed upon him like a mountain, once sought admittance of his own accord. It is not probable, however, that these men had any lesson to teach in the lore of discontent and misery which might not equally well have been studied in the common walks of life. Illustrious unfortunates attract a wider sympathy, not because their griefs are more intense, but because, being set on lofty pedestals, they the better serve mankind as instances and bywords of calamity.

It concerns our present purpose to say that, at each successive festival, Gervayse Hastings showed his face, gradually changing from the smooth beauty of his youth to the thoughtful comeliness of manhood, and thence to the bald, impressive dignity of age. He was the only individual invariably present. Yet on every occasion there were murmurs, both from those who knew his character and position, and from them whose hearts shrank back as denying his companionship in their mystic fraternity.

'Who is this impassive man?' had been asked a hundred times. 'Has he suffered? Has he sinned? There are no traces of either. Then wherefore is he here?'

'You must inquire of the stewards or of himself,' was the constant reply. 'We seem to know him well here in our city, and know nothing of him but what is creditable and fortunate. Yet hither he comes, year after year, to this gloomy banquet, and sits among the guests like a marble statue. Ask yonder skeleton, perhaps that may solve the riddle!'

It was in truth a wonder. The life of Gervayse Hastings was not merely a prosperous, but a brilliant one. Everything had gone well with him. He was wealthy, far beyond the expenditure that was required by habits of magnificence, a taste of rare purity and cultivation, a love of travel, a scholar's instinct to collect a splendid library, and, moreover, what seemed a magnificent liberality to the distressed. He had sought happiness, and not vainly, if a lovely and tender wife, and children of fair promise, could insure it. He had, besides, ascended above the limit which separates the obscure from the distinguished, and had won a stainless reputation in affairs of the widest public importance. Not that he was a popular character, or had within him the mysterious attributes which are essential to that species of success. To the public he was a cold abstraction, wholly destitute of those rich hues of personality, that living warmth, and the peculiar faculty of stamping his own heart's impression on a multitude of hearts by which the people recognize their favourites. And it must be owned that after his most intimate associates had done their best to know him thoroughly and love him warmly, they were startled to find how little hold he had upon their affections. They approved, they admired, but still in those moments when the human spirit most craves reality, they shrank back from Gervayse Hastings, as powerless to give them what they sought. It was the feeling of distrustful regret with which we should draw back the hand after extending it, in an illusive twilight, to grasp the hand of a shadow upon the wall.

As the superficial fervency of youth decayed, this peculiar effect of Gervayse Hastings's character grew more perceptible. His children, when he extended his arms, came coldly to his knees, but never climbed them of their own accord. His wife wept secretly, and almost adjudged herself a criminal because she shivered in the chill of his bosom. He, too, occasionally appeared not unconscious of the chillness of his moral atmosphere, and willing, if it might be so, to warm himself at a kindly fire. But age stole onward and benumbed him more and more. As the hoarfrost began to gather on him, his wife went to her grave, and was doubtless warmer there; his children either died or were scattered to different homes of their own; and old Gervayse Hastings, unscathed by grief—alone, but needing no companionship—continued his steady walk through life, and still on every Christmas day attended at the dismal banquet. His privilege as a guest had become prescriptive now. Had he claimed the head of the table, even the skeleton would have been ejected from its seat.

Finally, at the merry Christmas tide, when he had numbered fourscore years complete, this pale, high-browed, marble-featured old man once more entered the long-frequented hall, with the same impassive aspect that had called forth so much dissatisfied remark at his first attendance. Time, except in matters merely external, had done nothing for him, either of good or evil. As he took his place, he threw a calm, inquiring glance around the table, as if to ascertain whether any guest had yet appeared, after so many unsuccessful banquets, who might impart to him the mystery—the deep, warm secret—the life within the life—which, whether manifested in joy or sorrow, is what gives substance to a world of shadows.

'My friends,' said Gervayse Hastings, assuming a position which his long conversance with the festival caused to appear natural, 'you are welcome! I drink to you all in this cup of sepulchral wine.'

The guests replied courteously, but still in a manner that proved them unable to receive the old man as a member of their sad fraternity. It may be well to give the reader an idea of the present company at the banquet.

One was formerly a clergyman, enthusiastic in his profession, and apparently of the genuine dynasty of those old puritan divines whose faith in their calling, and stern exercise of it, had placed them among the mighty of the earth. But yielding to the speculative tendency of the age, he had gone astray from the firm foundation of an ancient faith, and wandered into a cloud region, where everything was misty and deceptive, ever mocking him with a semblance of reality, but still dissolving when he flung himself upon it for support and rest. His instinct and early training demanded something steadfast; but, looking forward, he beheld vapours piled on vapours, and behind him an impassable gulf between the man of yesterday and today, on the borders of which he paced to and fro, sometimes wringing his hands in agony, and often making his own woe a theme of scornful merriment. This surely was a miserable man. Next, there was a theorist—one of a numerous tribe, although he deemed himself unique since the creation—a theorist who had conceived a plan by which all the wretchedness of earth, moral and physical, might be done away, and the bliss of millennium at once accomplished. But the incredulity of mankind debaring him from action, he was smitten with as much grief as if the whole mass of woe which he was denied the opportunity to remedy were crowded into his own bosom. A plain old man in black attracted much of the company's notice, on the supposition that he was no other than Father Miller, who, it seemed, had given himself up to despair at the tedious delay of the final conflagration. Then there was a man distinguished for native pride and obstinacy, who, a little while before, had possessed immense wealth, and held the control of a vast moneyed interest which he had wielded in the same spirit as a despotic monarch would wield the power of his empire, carrying on a tremendous moral warfare, the roar and tremor of which was felt at every fireside in the land. At length came a crushing ruin—a total overthrow of fortune, power, and character—the effect of which on his imperious and, in many respects, noble and lofty nature, might have entitled him to a place, not merely at our festival, but among the peers of Pandemonium.

There was a modern philanthropist, who had become so deeply sensible of the calamities of thousands and millions of his fellow-creatures, and of the impracticableness of any general measures for their relief, that he had no heart to do what little good lay immediately within his power, but contented himself with being miserable for sympathy. Near him sat a gentleman in a predicament hitherto unprecedented, but of which the present epoch probably affords numerous examples. Ever since he was of capacity to read a newspaper, this person had prided himself on his consistent adherence to one political party, but, in the confusion of these latter days, had got bewildered and knew not whereabouts his party was. This wretched condition, so morally desolate and disheartening to a man who has long accustomed himself to merge his individuality in the mass of a great body, can only be conceived by such as have experienced it. His next companion was a popular orator who had lost his voice, and—

as it was pretty much all that he had to lose—had fallen into a state of hopeless melancholy. The table was likewise graced by two of the gentler sex—one, a half-starved, consumptive seamstress, the representative of thousands just as wretched; the other, a woman of unemployed energy, who found herself in the world with nothing to achieve, nothing to enjoy, and nothing even to suffer. She had, therefore, driven herself to the verge of madness by dark broodings over the wrongs of her sex and its exclusion from a proper field of action. The roll of guests being thus complete, a side table had been set for three or four disappointed office seekers, with hearts as sick as death, whom the stewards had admitted partly because their calamities really entitled them to entrance here, and partly that they were in especial need of a good dinner. There was likewise a homeless dog, with his tail between his legs, licking up the crumbs and gnawing the fragments of the feast; such a melancholy air as one sometimes sees about the streets without a master, and willing to follow the first that will accept his service.

In their own way, these were as wretched a set of people as ever had assembled at the festival. There they sat, with the veiled skeleton of the founder holding aloft the cypress wreath, at one end of the table, and at the other, wrapped in furs, the withered figure of Gervayse Hastings, stately, calm, and cold, impressing the company with awe, yet so little interesting their sympathy that he might have vanished into thin air without their once exclaiming, 'Whither is he gone?'

'Sir,' said the philanthropist, addressing the old man, 'you have been so long a guest at this annual festival, and have thus been conversant with so many varieties of human affliction, that, not improbably, you have thence derived some great and important lessons. How blessed were your lot could you reveal a secret by which all this mass of woe might be removed!'

'I know of but one misfortune,' answered Gervayse Hastings, quietly, 'and that is my own.'

'Your own!' enjoined the philanthropist. 'And, looking back

on your serene and prosperous life, how can you claim to be the sole unfortunate of the human race?'

'You will not understand it,' replied Gervayse Hastings, feebly, and with a singular inefficiency of pronunciation, and sometimes putting one word for another. 'None have understood it—not even those who experience the like. It is a chillness—a want of earnestness—a feeling as if what should be my heart were a thing of vapour—a haunting perception of unreality! Thus seeming to possess all that other men have—all that men aim at—I have really possessed nothing, neither joy nor griefs. All things, all persons—as was truly said to me at this table long and long ago—have been like shadows flickering on the wall. It was so with my wife and children—with those who seemed my friends: it is so with yourselves, whom I see now before me. Neither have I myself any real existence, but am a shadow like the rest.'

'And how is it with your views of a future life?' inquired the speculative clergyman.

'Worse than with you,' said the old man, in a hollow and feeble tone; 'for I cannot conceive it earnestly enough to feel either hope or fear. Mine—mine is the wretchedness! This cold heart—this unreal life! Ah! it grows colder still.'

It so chanced that at this juncture the decayed ligaments of the skeleton gave way, and the dry bones fell together in a heap, thus causing the dusty wreath of cypress to drop upon the table. The attention of the company being thus diverted for a single instant from Gervayse Hastings, they perceived on turning again towards him that the old man had undergone a change. His shadow had ceased to flicker on the wall.

'Well, Rosina, what is your criticism?' asked Roderick, as he rolled up the manscript.

'Frankly, your success is by no means complete,' replied she. 'It is true, I have an idea of the character you endeavour to describe; but it is rather by dint of my own thought than your expression.'

'That is unavoidable,' observed the sculptor, 'because the characteristics are all negative. If Gervayse Hastings imbibed one human grief at the gloomy banquet, the task of describing him would have been infinitely easier. Of such persons—and we do meet with these moral monsters now and then—it is difficult to conceive how they came to exist here, or what there is in them capable of existence hereafter. They seem to be on the outside of everything; and nothing wearies the soul more than an attempt to comprehend them within its grasp.

THE WOLVES OF CERNOGRATZ

'Saki'

An unusual tale by the celebrated short story
writer 'Saki' (Hector Hugh Munro, 1870–1916).
His tales of *Beasts and Super-Beasts* and *The
Chronicles of Clovis* are perennial favourites, being
regularly dramatised on radio. A weaver of 'fairy-
tales grimmer than Grimm', he was a master of
satire and the uncanny.

'A re there any old legends attached to the castle?' asked
Conrad of his sister. Conrad was a prosperous Hamburg
merchant, but he was the one poetically-dispositioned
member of an eminently practical family.

The Baroness Gruebel shrugged her plump shoulders.

'There are always legends hanging about these old places.
They are not difficult to invent and they cost nothing. In this
case there is a story that when anyone dies in the castle all the
dogs in the village and the wild beasts in the forest howl the
night long. It would not be pleasant to listen to, would it?'

'It would be weird and romantic,' said the Hamburg merchant.

'Anyhow, it isn't true,' said the Baroness complacently; 'since
we bought the place we have had proof that nothing of the sort

happens. When the old mother-in-law died last springtime we all listened, but there was no howling. It is just a story that lends dignity to the place without costing anything.'

'The story is not as you have told it,' said Amalie, the grey old governess. Everyone turned and looked at her in astonishment. She was wont to sit silent and prim and faded in her place at table, never speaking unless someone spoke to her, and there were few who troubled themselves to make conversation with her. Today a sudden volubility had descended on her; she continued to talk, rapidly and nervously, looking straight in front of her and seeming to address no one in particular.

'It is not when *anyone* does in the castle that the howling is heard. It was when one of the Cernogratz family died here that the wolves came from far and near and howled at the edge of the forest just before the death hour. There were only a few couple of wolves that had their lairs in this part of the forest, but at such a time the keepers say there would be scores of them, gliding about in the shadows and howling in chorus, and the dogs of the castle and the village and all the farms round would bay and howl in fear and anger at the wolf chorus, and as the soul of the dying one left its body a tree would crash down in the park. That is what happened when a Cernogratz died in his family castle. But for a stranger dying here, of course no wolf would howl and no tree would fall. Oh, no.'

There was a note of defiance, almost of contempt, in her voice as she said the last words. The well-fed, much-too-well-dressed Baroness stared angrily at the dowdy old woman who had come forth from her usual and seemly position of effacement to speak so disrespectfully.

'You seem to know quite a lot about the von Cernogratz legends, Fräulein Schmidt,' she said sharply; 'I did not know that family histories were among the subjects you are supposed to be proficient in.'

The answer to her taunt was even more unexpected and astonishing than the conversational outbreak which had provoked it.

'I am a von Cernogratz myself,' said the old woman, 'that is why I know the family history.'

'You a von Cernogratz? You!' came in an incredulous chorus.

'When we became very poor,' she explained, 'and I had to go out and give teaching lessons, I took another name; I thought it would be more in keeping. But my grandfather spent much of his time as a boy in this castle, and my father used to tell me many stories about it, and, of course, I knew all the family legends and stories. When one has nothing left to one but memories, one guards and dusts them with especial care. I little thought when I took service with you that I should one day come with you to the old home of my family. I could wish it had been anywhere else.'

There was silence when she finished speaking, and then the Baroness turned the conversation to a less embarrassing topic than family histories. But afterwards, when the old governess had slipped away quietly to her duties, there arose a clamour of derision and disbelief.

'It was an impertinence,' snapped out the Baron, his protruding eyes taking on a scandalized expression; 'fancy the woman talking like that at our table. She almost told us we were nobodies, and I don't believe a word of it. She is just Schmidt and nothing more. She has been talking to some of the peasants about the old Cernogratz family, and raked up their history and their stories.'

'She wants to make herself out of some consequence,' said the Baroness; 'she knows she will soon be past work and she wants to appeal to our sympathies. Her grandfather, indeed!'

The Baroness had the usual number of grandfathers, but she never, never boasted about them.

'I dare say her grandfather was a pantry boy or something of the sort in the castle,' sniggered the Baron; 'that part of the story may be true.'

The merchant from Hamburg said nothing; he had seen tears in the old woman's eyes when she spoke of guarding her memories—or, being of an imaginative disposition, he thought he had.

'I shall give her notice to go as soon as the New Year festivities are over,' said the Baroness; 'till then I shall be too busy to manage without her.'

But she had to manage without her all the same, for in the cold biting weather after Christmas, the old governess fell ill and kept to her room.

'It is most provoking,' said the Baroness, as her guests sat round the fire on one of the last evenings of the dying year; 'all the time that she has been with us I cannot remember that she was ever seriously ill, too ill to go about and do her work, I mean. And now, when I have the house full, and she could be useful in so many ways, she goes and breaks down. One is sorry for her, of course, she looks so withered and shrunken, but it is intensely annoying all the same.'

'Most annoying,' agreed the banker's wife sympathetically; 'it is the intense cold, I expect, it breaks the old people up. It has been unusually cold this year.'

'The frost is the sharpest that has been known in December for many years,' said the Baron.

'And, of course, she is quite old,' said the Baroness; 'I wish I had given her notice some weeks ago, then she would have left before this happened to her. Why, Wappi, what is the matter with you?'

The small, woolly lapdog had leapt suddenly down from its cushion and crept shivering under the sofa. At the same moment an outburst of angry barking came from the dogs in the castle-yard, and other dogs could be heard yapping and barking in the distance.

'What is disturbing the animals?' asked the Baron.

And then the humans, listening intently, heard the sound that had roused the dogs to their demonstrations of fear and rage; heard a long-drawn whining howl, rising and falling, seeming at one moment leagues away, at others sweeping across the snow until it appeared to come from the foot of the castle walls. All the starved, cold misery of a frozen world, all the relentless hunger-fury of the wild, blended with other forlorn and haunting melodies to which one could give no name, seemed concentrated in that wailing cry.

'Wolves!' cried the Baron.

Their music broke forth in one raging burst, seeming to come from everywhere.

'Hundred of wolves,' said the Hamburg merchant, who was a man of strong imagination.

Moved by some impulse which she could not have explained, the Baroness left her guests and made her way to the narrow, cheerless room where the old governess lay watching the hours of the dying year slip by. In spite of the biting cold of the winter night, the window stood open. With a scandalized exclamation on her lips, the Baroness rushed forward to close it.

'Leave it open,' said the old woman in a voice that for all its weakness carried an air of command such as the Baroness had never heard before from her lips.

'But you will die of cold!' she expostulated.

'I am dying in any case,' said the voice, 'and I want to hear their music. They have come from far and wide to sing the death-music of my family. It is beautiful that they have come; I am the last von Cernogratz that will die in our old castle, and they have come to sing to me. Hark, how loud they are calling!'

The cry of the wolves rose on the still winter air and floated round the castle walls in long-drawn piercing wails; the old woman lay back on her couch with a look of long-delayed happiness on her face.

'Go away,' she said to the Baroness; 'I am not lonely any more. I am one of a great old family . . .'

'I think she is dying,' said the Baroness when she had rejoined her guests; 'I suppose we must send for a doctor. And that terrible howling! Not for much money would I have such death-music.'

'That music is not to be bought for any amount of money,' said Conrad.

'Hark! What is that other sound?' asked the Baron, as a noise of splitting and crashing was heard.

It was a tree falling in the park.

There was a moment of constrained silence, and then the banker's wife spoke.

'It is the intense cold that is splitting the trees. It is also the cold that has brought the wolves out in such numbers. It is many years since we have had such a cold winter.'

The Baroness eagerly agreed that the cold was responsible for these things. It was the cold of the open window, too, which caused the heart failure that made the doctor's ministrations unnecessary for the old Fräulein. But the notice in the news-papers looked very well—

'On December 29th, at Schloss Cernogratz, Amalie von Cernogratz, for many years the valued friend of Baron and Baroness Gruebel.'

GANTHONY'S WIFE

E. Temple Thurston

Ernest Temple Thurston (1879–1933) achieved
enormous success with his novels *The Apple of
Eden* (1905), *The City of Beautiful Nonsense*
(1909), *The Greatest Wish in the World* (1910),
and a trilogy of the life of Richard Furlong. Often
mixing humour with pathos, he was particularly
adept with his insights into the psychology of the
feminine soul. 'Ganthony's Wife' is taken from his
collection *The Rossetti, and Other Tales* (1926).

The custom of telling stories round the fire on Christmas
Eve is dying out, like letterwriting and all the amateur
domestic arts of the last century. Our stories are told us
by professionals and broadcast to thousands by the printing
machine. We give our letters to a dictaphone or a stenographer.
The personal touch is going out of life, if it has not already
gone. In an age where every conceivable machine is invented
to save time and labour, we have no time to spare for these
things. We are too exhausted from working our machines to
give them our attention.

We were saying all this last year as we sat round a blazing
wood fire at that little house party the Stennings give every

Christmas in that Tudor house of theirs on the borders of Kent and Sussex.

The children had gone to bed. There were five of us grown-ups left round the broad open fire-place where huge oak logs were burning on the glowing heart of a pile of silver ashes that had been red-hot for a week or more.

Miss Valerie Brett, the actress, was sitting inside the chimney corner warming first one toe, then the other. She comes there every Christmas. The children love her. She can make funny noises with her mouth. Also by facial contortion, she can look like Queen Victoria on the heads of all the pennies that ever were minted. In a semi-circle outside we sat, the rest of us, Stenning and his wife, Northanger and myself, smoking our various smokes and sipping that punch, the secret of which Stenning learnt from an old wine merchant in Winthrop Street, Cork. I think he relies on it to secure the few select guests he always has at his Christmas parties.

'Come down for Christmas. Punch.'

This is a common form of his invitation.

We had been playing games with the children, hide-and-seek being the most popular. We were all a bit exhausted. It was Mrs Stenning who opened the discussion by complaining that there was no one qualified to tell children ghost stories nowadays.

'We had a man here last Christmas,' she said, 'and he began one, but the children guessed the end of it before it was half-way through.'

'Bless 'em,' said Miss Brett.

'It was a rotten story, anyhow,' said Stenning. 'You can't make a mystery now by just rattling a chain and slamming a door and blowing out the candle. When the candle went out, young John said, "Why didn't he shut the window?" Our amiable story teller assured John that he did, but he wasn't convincing about it, because Emily said, "'Spect it was like that window up in my bedroom. The wind comes through there when it's shut and blows the curtains about."'

Mrs Stenning sighed.

'I suppose they know too much,' she said—'and all I've done, you don't know, to try and keep them simple.'

'They don't know too much,' said Northanger. 'It's more likely we who know too little. We don't believe in the rattling chain and the extinguished candle ourselves. We've been laughing at them for the last twenty years, and they've caught up with us.'

'Do you mean this civilization's at the end of its evolution?' I asked.

'Either that,' said he, 'or we're in one of those hanging pauses, like a switchback when it gets to the top of a crest and just crawls over the top till it gathers a fresh impetus to rise to a higher crest. It's only pessimists who say we're finished. Shedding an old skin is a proper process of nature. There are signs of the old skin going.'

Northanger is a queer chap. He talks very little. This was voluble for him. As usually happens with a man like that, we listened.

'What signs?' asked Miss Brett.

'All sorts,' said he. 'There's even a new ghost. I saw one last Christmas.'

'You saw one?'

Two or three of us spoke at once.

'I saw one,' he repeated.

If a man like Northanger admits to seeing a ghost, we felt there must be something in it. It would not be a mere turnip head with a candle inside.

'Why didn't you tell us when the children were here?' asked Mrs Stenning immediately.

'It's not a story for children,' he replied. 'Though I don't know why it shouldn't be. They wouldn't understand it, and that's the first quality required of a ghost story.'

'Tell us.'

This was practically simultaneous from everybody. Miss Brett pulled her feet up on to the chimney-corner seat. Stenning slipped over to the table and brought round the punch bowl to fill our glasses. I say 'slipped over' because he moved like a man who does not want to disturb an atmosphere. Somehow that chap Northanger had put a grip on us. We felt he knew that what he was going to tell us was unknowable. He had indeed created an atmosphere, the atmosphere that Stenning was careful not to disturb. There was the proper sort of hush in the air while he was filling our glasses. No one had lit the lights since we had been playing at hide-and-seek. We were all grouped around the light of the fire. Then Northanger began.

'Do any of you know Ganthony—Ganthony's a tea planter in Ceylon?'

None of us did.

'Well—that makes it better,' said he. Then he looked across at Miss Brett. 'You and I haven't met before, Miss Brett,' he said, 'till our good friends brought us together this Christmas. I've seen you on the stage, but not being one of those admirers who have the courage to offer their congratulations without introduction, you haven't seen me till now.'

In that prelude, I suddenly had a glimpse of Northanger's way with women, an odd sardonic sort of way, too subtle for most of them, but conveying with it an impression that he was not unsusceptible.

She smiled as he continued:

'In case our good friends haven't told you then,' he went on, 'it's necessary to say I'm a bachelor. I have rooms in Stretton Street, Piccadilly. I've been there seventeen years. When they pull down Devonshire House, they pull me off my perch. That'll be the end of Stretton Street. I don't mean my going. But without the restraining influence of the Baroness Burdett-Coutts and the Duke of Devonshire, Stretton Street will become anybody's street. A cinema theatre in those new buildings they are going to put up on the site of Devonshire House will send Stretton Street to the dogs. It's like that with people.

Ninety per cent of us live by example. However, my story's about Ganthony.

'It was last Christmas. I mean 1923. I was staying in town. I often do. I like London on Christmas Day.'

Miss Brett shuddered.

"Yes—I know,' said Northanger. 'London seems dead to lots of people when the shops are shut, and the theatres are closed. It doesn't get me like that. It seems alive to me.'

'What with?' It was Mrs Stenning who asked this.

'With the spirits of people. We were talking about ghosts. Well, how could you expect a ghost to clank a chain when the rattle of motor buses would drown the noise of it out of existence? What's the good of blowing out candles when the streets are daylight with night signs? There's one thing I always do when I'm in London on Christmas Day. I go to my club. It used to be one of the old gaming houses before the Regency. Modern interior decoration has hidden all that, but on Christmas Day, when some of the rooms are absolutely empty, they come back, the old gamesters. You can feel them about you. Imagination, I know—but who has properly defined what imagination is? Memory's impulse of association isn't good enough. Where does the impulse come from?

'I always go to my club. I went there that afternoon and to my amazement found Ganthony in the smoking-room writing letters. Ganthony is one of those men who belong to a London club and appear in it, somewhat like a comet, at rare intervals. Suddenly he walks in, gets his letters from the hall porter, fills a waste-paper basket with the accumulated rubbish, and writes a pile of answers. For the next week or so you can find him practically at any moment on the premises. Then one day, you say to the hall porter, "Mr Ganthony in the club?" "Mr Ganthony, sir? He's gone."

'Perhaps as much as three years go by before you see him again. That Christmas Day I hadn't seen him for four years at least. He was surrounded with letters and was writing for all he was worth. I think he was as glad to see me as I was to see him. He'd just come home from Ceylon—didn't know how long he was going to stay. He never does. I picked out a comfortable chair and we talked. Presently I inquired about his wife, whether he'd brought her with him—how she was. His eyes went like pebbles when the water's dried off them.

'"My wife died nearly a year ago," said he.

'I must tell you about Ganthony's wife. He had met and married her during the War. But the War had nothing to do with it. We've got into the habit of putting those hurried marriages down to the War. Whenever they'd met, Ganthony would have married her. It was the case of a man meeting the fate that was in store for him and rushing to it like a bit of steel to a magnet. What he had meant to her I've never been able to quite satisfy my mind about. The relationships that circumstance contrives between individuals must have some sort of scheme about them. But I'm blowed if it's possible to begin to think what it is or how it's regulated.

'Ganthony met her in a restaurant. He'd just come out of hospital. Been knocked out by a shell burst on Vimy Ridge. His face had been cut about and was still all wrapped in bandages. One side of his face was fairly clear—on the other, his eye just peeped out of a mass of lint. He didn't care what he looked like. In fact I think it rather amused him to go and dine in public. He went alone.

'She was dining at a table a few yards away with a man. Like everyone else she was attracted by the sight of this bandaged face of Ganthony's. She drew her companion's attention. I had all this from Ganthony himself just before he was married. It was as though she said, "They've been knocking him about— haven't they?"

'The man looked at him for a moment or two. Wounded men were pretty common those days. He was a soldier himself. He was in khaki. He took no more notice. But the woman went on looking. Every other second Ganthony caught her eye. More than that, he could see she didn't want her companion to notice it. Something about it intrigued Ganthony. The scheme, whatever it is, was beginning to work. The fate was beginning to draw him. He smiled—so far as that was possible with half his face in bandages. She smiled in return—one of those smiles a woman can hide from everyone but the person for whom it is intended. In a few minutes they were talking to each other with their eyes, that sort of conversation that isn't hampered with the expression and meaning of mere words.

'Ganthony cut a course out and finished his meal before they did. He ordered his bill when she was looking at him. He paid it, looked at the door, then at her, then he got up and went out. He hadn't to wait more than two seconds before she was outside on the pavement beside him. She'd made some excuse to her companion. She had for decency's sake to go back and finish her dinner. They arranged to meet later.

'They were married in a week. No need to tell you more than that. You can put it down to the War if you like. But Ganthony wasn't the sort of man to marry that sort of woman just because there was a war on. He did it with his eyes open even if his face was bandaged. He knew the kind she was. He knew he wasn't the first, but I suppose he may have thought that when he took her out to Ceylon after he was quit of the War, he would be the last. I never thought so. But it was no good telling him that. When a man runs into his fate as he did, platitudes and speculations about morals don't stop him. He has to find things out for himself. God disposes sometimes, it seems to me before and after a man's proposal.

'Anyhow that's as much as it has to do with this story. Ganthony had married and now his wife was dead. I confess to a feeling of satisfaction when I heard it. She was a beautiful woman no doubt—intensely attractive. I had never seen her, but he had sent me a snapshot of himself and her from Ceylon after they got out there. However, attraction isn't everything. It invites, but it doesn't always entertain.'

[93]

'It doesn't sound very much like a ghost story,' said Mrs Stenning.

Northanger apologized.

'I warned you it wasn't a ghost story for children,' said he. 'I told you they wouldn't understand it. I doubt if I understand it myself.'

'Shove a log on, Valerie,' said Stenning, 'and don't interrupt him, Grace. The man's earning his punch with me anyhow. Go on, Northanger. You tell it your own way. Women always want to see the last page. Ganthony's wife was dead.'

'Yes—dead,' Northanger went on. 'Ganthony saw her dead. They had lived in Colombo for the first six or eight months and apparently in that short time, he came to know how attractive she was. And yet, it was not only her physical attraction for men, he told me, as a sort of fatality about her that drew them as it had drawn him.

'Apparently he knew nothing in fact. She was not so much secretive about it, as almost mysterious. As far as I can make out, it was as though she had a vocation for that sort of life, like the sacred women in the temple of Osiris at Thebes. I can imagine her having been extraordinarily mysterious with that other man in the restaurant when she first met Ganthony. She must have just slipped away from him when that dinner was over. At one moment he may have thought she was his for the evening. The next she was gone.

'It was the beginning of that feeling in Ganthony that at any moment he might lose her, made him leave Colombo and take her up country to a spot close to his plantations. She made no complaint. It was not as though she were a gay woman and were being torn away from her gaiety. She went without a word. He was terribly fond of her. Any fool could have seen that. Notwithstanding the way he had met her, it had not continued to be promiscuous with him. She was a sacred women to him right enough. He told me about her death, in that slow, measured sort of way as a man walks at the end of a journey.

Whatever she'd been, her death had left a wound in his life that wouldn't heal in a hurry.'

'Are we to hear how she did die?' I asked.

'Yes—I want to hear how she died,' said Miss Brett.

'I'm coming to that,' said Northanger. 'Away there up country, Ganthony felt she was safe. Except down at the plantations, there were no Englishmen about. After a few months up there, when she seemed to be quite contented, Ganthony had to go down to Colombo on business. He was gone three days. When he came back, she was gone. The native servants were in a panic. He scoured the country for two days. They'd heard nothing of her down at the plantations. She'd vanished—slipped away. On the third day, coming back after a fruitless search, he found a Buddhist priest waiting for him at his bungalow. All the man would say was, "I've come to bring you to see the memsahib." Ganthony followed him. Again and again he asked the fellow what was the matter, threatened him, tried to frighten him, but he'd say nothing except—"You shall see the memsahib."

'On the side of a hill about three miles from Ganthony's bungalow, there was a Buddhist monastery. He was taken there, and there on a rough sort of bed in one of the rooms—it was a rest place—he found his wife lying—dead. There was no question of getting a doctor. There was not a doctor within miles.

'I asked him if he was sure she was dead, and he turned those stone eyes of his on me.

'"You have to be your own doctor out there," said he, "and there are one or two things you can't fail to recognize. Death's one of 'em. She'd been dead some time. She was quite cold. There's no mistaking when the spirit's gone out of the body. Hers was gone. I could feel it had. She lay there, just a dead body, and I felt I couldn't touch her then—it seemed repulsive without her spirit."

'I asked him how she got there, what he thought she'd died

of, how long he imagined she'd been dead. None of his answers were very elaborate. He made it out to be fever. She had walked by herself into the monastery. She must have been dead two days. He arrived at that decision apart from what the monks told him.

'Then he said an extraordinary thing which made me realize the repulsion he had felt for that body bereft of its spirit.

'"I left her there," he said—"they buried her."

'Well, that was Ganthony's story as he told it me that Christmas afternoon in the club. We had tea together while we talked. After that he went back to finish his letters. I went into the reading-room till about a quarter to seven. It was snowing then, coming down like a white fog over the black darkness outside. There was hardly a taxi moving in the streets. I'd ordered my dinner for eight o'clock at my rooms. I went out of the reading-room to make a move towards Stretton Street and then I thought of Ganthony, probably dining there in the club by himself. I looked into the smoking-room and asked him to come along. He pushed his hand through his bundle of letters.

'"Only half finished," said he.

'"Finish 'em to-morrow."

'"No," he said, "I'll get 'em done now while I'm at it. If I get finished before ten, I'll look in and have a drink with you. But no more raising from the dead. That's buried."

'I nodded my head. It was plain he wasn't coming. When a man wants to do a thing, he does it without ifs and buts. Those are feminine prerogatives. I left him to his letters. I walked out of the club, pushed my way through that white storm across the black gape of Trafalgar Square, up the Haymarket, and turned off into Jermyn Street.

'I always think Jermyn Street is a queer street. I've known odd men living there, in little rooms over little shops. It keeps an atmosphere about it which the rest of London is losing as fast as a woman loses self-respect directly she takes to drink. It has dark, sunken doorways. The houses are so close together that you hardly ever look up at the windows as you pass along its narrow thoroughfare. I never used to think of the existence of those windows till an odd chap I knew invited me to his rooms there. There was something so queer about them that after that, I spent a morning walking along the north side of Jermyn Street looking up at the houses on the opposite side. They're nearly all of them funny. They're hiding places. And the street itself has got that feeling. So much has it got it, that it is one of the favourite walking places of that band of sisters who count the world well lost for—why shouldn't they call it love?

'I never expected to see one of them that night. There wasn't a soul anywhere. The snow was coming down like a muslin curtain of a big design. A policeman passed me. His footsteps and mine were silent in the snow. I wished him a happy Christmas as I went by. His answer was like the voice of a man with a respirator on. The snow had dressed him in white. He just appeared and disappeared.

'I was getting near the St James's end, just about where old Cox's Hotel used to stand when through that muslin curtain of snow, just as through the curtains you can dimly see someone moving about inside a room, I saw a figure coming towards me. I felt a moment's surprise. It was a woman.

'There were not many steps for us to approach each other before we met. With that snow the whole of London was cramped up into the dimensions of a narrow, little room. As we passed, it was just as though she had pulled the curtains for an instant and looked through the window at me. Then, like the policeman, she was gone.'

It might have been the instinct of a raconteur to heighten the suspense, but here Northanger stopped and looked at Valerie Brett.

'Go on,' we said.

'Well,' said he, 'I'm considering this young lady's feeling. To give you the proper impression of what happened, I have to be what the novelists call—psychological here. Will she mind?'

'Don't be an ass,' said Stenning. 'You know jolly well you're only trying to tantalize us. Go on with your psychology. She's on the stage. They're full of psychology there.'

'I only felt it necessary,' said Northanger, 'to describe a man's attitude towards encounters like this. Perhaps it would be more accurate to say my own towards this particular one. Because though, as far as the story is, she'd gone by, there had been that half-instant's pause—the moment as I said when she seemed to have pulled the muslin curtains and looked at me out of the window. That pause was indescribable. It was an encounter. Most often a woman like that says something—a fatuous word of endearment—a challenge—a salute as if you were old friends. This woman didn't say anything. She just looked through that pause at me, and though I could not have described her for the life of me, I felt clearly conscious of her personality.

'I don't know what a woman feels like about her own sex of that class. I expect most men would have felt what I did then, a sort of demand for consideration, quite unsupported by the conscience or moral standards of a county councillor. Christmas Day and that snow-storm when most people were sitting beside a warm fire awaiting the announcement of a comfortable meal! I felt pretty sorry for her. I suppose it was this and that consciousness of her personality made me turn. If she had said anything I should have walked straight on. She had gone by in silence, and I turned.

'She had not only turned as well. She had stopped. With all that snow on the ground I hadn't heard her. We stood there looking at each other and then she came back.

'"Going to your club?" she said.

'"Coming from it," said I.

'"Going home, I suppose?"

'I nodded my head.

'"And all the family expecting you back to dinner?"

'I told her there was no family—merely dinner.

'"Alone?" she asked.

'"Quite alone," said I.

'That didn't deter her. She started walking in my direction. I should have looked a fool if I had refused to accompany her. Besides that, there's a considerable excitement of interest in talking to an absolute stranger of the other sex. Men and women too would indulge more frequently in that kind of adventure if they weren't so afraid of appearances. Probably the snow-storm gave me courage. We walked into St James's Street together and up into Piccadilly.

'"I live just in Stretton Street," said I. "If you come much farther, a mere common politeness will compel me to ask you in to dinner."

'"If you did," said she, "a mere common appetite for a comfortable meal would compel me to accept."

'The human voice is an extraordinary thing. It is an unfailing indication of character and personality. You can't really fake it. The best actor or actress in the world'—he made a sweep of his hand excluding Valerie Brett—'can only make up their face. They can't make up their voice. They can imitate. But that's not the same thing. There was something in this woman's voice that guaranteed me against feeling ashamed of myself before my man, Charles. Charles is essentially a diplomat, but he has taste. How she was dressed didn't matter so much. How she was dressed I couldn't see, covered as she was with the snow that was falling. I don't know anything about women's dress, but I was conscious of the impression that she was what a man calls—all right.

'"Allow me to invite you then," said I, and when she accepted I felt I had done a thing which you do, not so much because you want to, as because of some arrangement of things which needs a certain act from you at a certain given moment. I felt that Ganthony's refusal to come and dine with me was an essential part of that whole arrangement. I felt that my will was not concerned in the matter. I walked up the steps and opened the door with my latchkey, and it seemed as though it were a mere act of obedience on my part. When she passed me into the hall it was as though she had the control of the situation, not I.

'I am trying to convey my impressions to you in the light of what happened, yet I don't want to exaggerate those impressions because, up to the last moment, there was no reason why it should not have appeared absolutely natural. A little unconventional perhaps—but that's all.

'I have only four rooms at Stretton Street—a dining-room, a sitting-room and two bedrooms. Charles showed her along to the spare bedroom to take her coat off and tidy up. It was ten minutes off dinner. And here is another impression I'm sure I don't exaggerate. Charles's manner from the moment he saw her was by no means that of the incomparable diplomat. It was not that he objected to her coming to a meal in the flat so much as that he would have avoided the situation if he could. When I taxed him with it afterwards, he said:

'"I make my apologies, sir, if I showed anything.'

'"You disapproved, Charles?" I asked him.

'"No, sir—why should I disapprove?"

'"Then what was it?"

'"I just felt awkward, sir—I felt as though the lady knew more about things than what I did, which is an uncomfortable feeling, sir, when it's a woman."

'Well—that's that. Charles has no reason to exaggerate his impressions, because I've never told him anything. Anyhow, we don't matter. She's the centre of the tale. She came into the sitting-room in about five minutes with her coat and hat off. I suppose she was well-dressed. I can only tell you there was nothing of Jermyn Street about her appearance. At the same time, there she was, unmistakably the courtesan. I don't mean that she was rouged or dyed. I don't mean that she made advances to me. I don't mean that her conversation was anything but what any woman's might have been who found herself dining with a man completely strange to her. She was perfectly natural, and yet there was this extraordinary suggestion about her that she was not just one of a type, but the type itself embodied in one person.

'Added to this was the impression I received directly she entered the room, that I had seen her before. Again and again through dinner, stealing glances, because I had a strong reluctance to show how interested I was, I tried to place her somewhere in my life. I failed so completely that for a time I gave it up. We just talked—oh, about all sorts of things. It came to jewellery. She was wearing a big cabochon ruby in a ring. It was the only bit of jewellery she had. I admired it and asked her where it came from.

'"I got that in Ceylon," said she.

'Suddenly my memory quickened. I held my tongue till we got into the sitting-room. Then, while we were drinking coffee, I looked straight at her and said: "Did you know a man named Ganthony in Ceylon?"

'If I had expected any flutter of surprise I was disappointed. Very serenely she looked at me and she said:

'"Are you trying to place me?"

'I admit for the moment I was disconcerted. I didn't know whether to apologize—or frankly agree that I was.

'"My inquisitiveness is not as rude as it appears," I said. "I have a reason for asking."

'She inquired quite placidly what it was.

'For answer I went straight across to my desk. Somewhere in one of the drawers was that snapshot Ganthony had sent me from Ceylon. I fished it out, satisfied myself first, and then brought it across to her. So far as a snapshot can be said to be a likeness in its minute dimensions and unposed effect, that picture of Ganthony's wife was the picture of the woman who was sitting there in my room. I'll swear to that.

'She took it from my hand. For quite a long while she sat there looking at it, a slow smile spreading over her face as I watched her. At the sound of the door-bell of my flat, she looked up, straight at me.

'"Does this man named Ganthony come here?" she asked.

'Then it suddenly occurred to me. This was Ganthony. It couldn't be anyone else—and somehow she knew it. I hurried out of the room before Charles could open the door. It was Ganthony. Despite his ifs and buts he'd come. And all this seemed part of the arrangement—part of some scheme of things which none of us could have prevented. I caught his arm as he passed through the door.

'"Are you prepared for a shock?" I said as quietly as I could.

'I don't know why he should have looked distressed so quickly, but he did.

'"What is it?" he asked.

'I pointed to my sitting-room door.

'"Your wife's in there," said I.

'"My wife's dead," he said, and there was a sharp note of anger in his voice. "I told you she was dead. I saw her dead"—and thrusting my arm away before I could stop him, he strode to the door, opened it and went in. For a moment I wondered whether I should follow. There's a sound principle about not interfering between a husband and wife. I was just about to go into the dining-room when the sense of an odd silence got me. There were no voices. I followed him. Ganthony was standing in the middle of the room staring at the little photograph of her. There was no one else there.

'Without a word to him I went to the little bedroom that opened off the sitting-room. Her hat and coat were gone. I came back and walked across to the window. My flat is on the ground floor. I opened the window. There were no signs of her having gone that way, though certainly the snow was falling so fast that if there had been, her footsteps outside would have been covered by them.

'I turned back and looked at Ganthony.

'"I'll swear," I began.

'He just smiled at me, a thin sort of a smile, the smile of a man who has plumbed the depths of suffering and knows that nothing more can hurt him.

'"Don't bother," said he. "I've seen her myself. Nearly a year ago it was, at Monte Carlo. Last September I was in London. Just for three days. I saw her then. She's dead," he added, "I saw her dead—as dead as that sort of women ever dies."'

Northanger passed his glass to Stenning to be replenished. All our minds were battling through the subsequent silence to ply him with our questions.

'It's no good asking me any more about it,' said he—'that's all I know and I don't pretend to understand.'

MR HUFFAM

Hugh Walpole

Sir Hugh Walpole (1884–1941) is best known for
his novels of cathedral life, and the popular
'Herries' lakeland saga. This entrancing ghost
story was originally written for the *Strand*
Christmas Number, December 1933.

i

Once upon a time (it doesn't matter when it was except
that it was long after the Great War) young Tubby
Winsloe was in the act of crossing Piccadilly just below
Hatchard's bookshop. It was three days before Christmas and
there had been a frost, a thaw, and then a frost again. The roads
were treacherous, traffic nervous and irresponsible, while against
the cliff-like indifference of brick and mortar a thin, faint snow
was falling from a primrose-coloured sky. Soon it would be dusk
and the lights would come out. Then things would be more
cheerful.

It would, however, take more than lights to restore Tubby's
cheerfulness. Rubicund of face and alarmingly stout of body
for a youth of twenty-three, he had just then the spirit of
a damp face-towel, for only a week ago Diana Lane-Fox had

refused to consider for a moment the possibility of marrying him.

'I like you, Tubby,' she had said. 'I think you have a kind heart. But marry you! You are useless, ignorant and greedy. You're disgracefully fat, and your mother worships you.'

He had not known, until Diana refused him, how bitterly alone he would find himself. He had money, friends, a fine roof above his head; he had seemed to himself popular wherever he went.

'Why, there's old Tubby!' everyone had cried.

It was true that he was fat, it was true that his mother adored him. He had not, until now, known that these were drawbacks. He had seemed to himself until a week ago the friend of all the world. Now he appeared a pariah.

Diana's refusal of him had been a dreadful shock. He had been quite sure that she would accept him. She had gone with him gladly to dances and the pictures. She had, it seemed approved highly of his mother, Lady Winsloe, and his father, Sir Roderick Winsloe, Bart. She had partaken, again and again, of the Winsloe hospitality.

All, it seemed to him, that was needed was for him to say the word. He could choose his time. Well, he *had* chosen his time— at the Herries dance last Wednesday evening. This was the result.

He had expected to recover. His was naturally a buoyant nature. He told himself, again and again, that there were many other fish in the matrimonial sea. But it appeared that there were not. He wanted Diana and only Diana.

He halted at the resting-place half-way across the street, and sighed so deeply that a lady with a little girl and a fierce-looking Chow dog looked at him severely, as though she would say:

'Now this is Christmas time—a gloomy period for all concerned. It is an unwarranted impertinence for anyone to make it yet more gloomy.'

There was someone else clinging to this small fragment of

security. A strange-looking man. His appearance was so unusual that Tubby forgot his own troubles in his instant curiosity. The first unusual thing about this man was that he had a beard. Beards were then very seldom worn. Then his clothes, although they were clean and neat, were most certainly old-fashioned. He was wearing a high sharp-pointed collar, a black stock with a jewelled tie-pin, and a most remarkable waistcoat, purple in colour, and covered with little red flowers. He was carrying a large, heavy-looking brown bag. His face was bronzed and he made Tubby think of a retired sea captain.

But the most remarkable thing of all about him was the impression that he gave of restless, driving energy. It was all that he could do to keep quiet. His strong, wiry figure seemed to burn with some secret fire. The traffic rushed madly past, but, at every moment when there appeared a brief interval between the cars and the omnibuses, this bearded gentleman with the bag made a little dance and once he struck the Chow with his bag and once nearly thrust the small child into the road.

The moment came when, most unwisely, he darted forth. He was almost caught by an imperious, disdainful Rolls-Royce. The lady gave a little scream and Tubby caught his arm, held him, drew him back.

'That nearly had you, sir!' Tubby murmured, his hand still on his arm. The stranger smiled—a most charming smile that shone from his eyes, his beard, his very hands.

'I must thank you,' he said, bowing with old-fashioned courtesy. 'But damn it, as the little boy said to the grocer, "there's no end to the dog," as he saw the sausages coming from the sausage machine.'

At this he laughed very heartily and Tubby had to laugh, too, although the remark did not seem to him very amusing.

'The traffic's very thick at Christmas-time,' Tubby said. 'Everyone doing their shopping, you know.'

The stranger nodded.

'Splendid time, Christmas!' he said. 'Best of the year!'

'Oh, do you think so?' said Tubby. 'I doubt if you'll find people to agree with you. It isn't the thing to admire Christmas these days.'

'Not the thing!' said the stranger, amazed. 'Why, what's the matter?'

This was a poser because so many things were the matter, from Unemployment to Diana. Tubby was saved for the moment from answering.

'Now there's a break,' he said. 'We can cross now.' Cross they did, the stranger swinging his body as though at any instant he might spring right off the ground.

'Which way are you going?' Tubby asked. It astonished him afterwards when he looked back and remembered this question. It was not his way to make friends of strangers, his theory being that everyone was out to 'do' everyone, and in these days especially.

'To tell you the truth I don't quite know,' the stranger said. 'I've only just arrived.'

'Where have you come from?' asked Tubby.

The stranger laughed.

'I've been moving about for a long time. I'm always on the move. I'm considered a very restless man by my friends.'

They were walking along very swiftly, for it was cold and the snow was falling fast now.

'Tell me,' said the stranger, '—about its being a bad time. What's the matter?'

What was the matter? What a question!

Tubby murmured:

'Why, everything's the matter—unemployment—no trade—*you* know.'

'No, I don't. I've been away. I think everyone looks very jolly.'

'I say, don't you feel cold without an overcoat?' Tubby asked.

'Oh, that's nothing,' the stranger answered. 'I'll tell you when I *did* feel cold though. When I was a small boy I worked in a factory putting labels on to blacking-bottles. It was cold *then*. Never known such cold. Icicles would hang on the end of your nose!'

'No!' said Tubby.

'They did, I assure you, and the blacking-bottles would be coated with ice!'

By this time they had reached Berkeley Street. The Winsloe mansion was in Hill Street.

'I turn up here,' said Tubby.

'Oh, do you?'

The stranger looked disappointed. He smiled and held out his hand.

Then Tubby did another extraordinary thing. He said:

'Come in and have a cup of tea. Our place is only five yards up the street.'

'Certainly,' the stranger said. 'Delighted.'

As they walked up Berkeley Street, he went on confidentially:

'I haven't been in London for a long time. All these vehicles are very confusing. But I like it—I like it immensely. It's so lively, and then the town's so quiet compared with what it was when I lived here.'

'Quiet!' said Tubby.

'Certainly. There were cobbles, and the carts and drays screamed and rattled like the damned.'

'But that's years ago!'

'Yes. I'm older than I look.'

Then, pointing, he added:

'But that's where Dorchester House was. So they've pulled it down. What a pity!'

'Oh, everything's pulled down now,' said Tubby.

'I acted there once—a grand night we had. Fond of acting?'

'Oh, I'd be no good,' said Tubby modestly, 'too self-conscious.'

'Ah, you mustn't be self-conscious,' said the stranger. 'Thinking of yourself only breeds trouble, as the man said to the hangman just before they dropped him.'

'Isn't that bag a terrible weight?' Tubby asked.

'I've carried worse things than this,' said the stranger. 'I carried a four-poster once, all the way from one end of the Marshalsea to the other.'

They were outside the house now and Tubby realized for the first time his embarrassment. It was not his way to bring anyone into the house unannounced, and his mother could be very haughty with strangers. However, here they were and it was snowing hard and the poor man was without a coat. So in they went. The Winsloe mansion was magnificent, belonging in all its features to an age that was gone. There was a marble staircase and up this the stranger almost ran, carrying his bag like a feather. Tubby toiled behind him but was, unhappily, not in time to prevent the stranger from entering through the open doors of the drawing-room.

Here, seated in magnificent state, was Lady Winsloe, a roaring fire encased with marble on one side of her, a beautiful tea-table in front of her, and walls hung with magnificent imitations of the great Masters.

Lady Winsloe was a massive woman with snow-white hair, a bosom like a small skating rink, and a little face that wore a look of perpetual astonishment. Her dress of black-and-white silk fitted her so tightly that one anticipated with pleasure the moment when she would be compelled to rise. She moved as little as possible, she said as little as possible, she thought as little as possible. She had a very kind heart and was sure that the world was going straight to the devil.

The stranger put his bag on the floor and went over to her with his hand outstretched.

'How are you?' he said. 'I'm delighted to meet you!'

By good fortune, Tubby arrived in the room at this moment.

'Mother,' he began, 'this is a gentleman——'

'Oh, of course,' said the stranger, 'you don't know my name. My name's Huffam,' and he caught the small white podgy hand and shook it. At this moment, two Pekinese dogs, one brown and one white, advanced from somewhere violently barking. Lady Winsloe found the whole situation so astonishing that she could only whisper:

'Now, Bobo—now, Coco!'

'You see, Mother,' Tubby went on, 'Mr Huffam was nearly killed by a motor-car and I rescued him and it began to snow heavily.'

'Yes, dear,' Lady Winsloe said, in her queer husky little voice that was always a surprise coming from so vast a bosom. Then she pulled herself together. For some reason Tubby had done this amazing thing, and whatever Tubby did was right.

'I do hope you'll have some tea, Mr——?' She hesitated.

'Huffam, ma'am. Yes, thank you. I *will* have some tea!'

'Milk *and* sugar?'

'All of it!' Mr Huffam laughed and slapped his knee. 'Yes, milk *and* sugar. Very kind of you indeed. A perfect stranger as I am. You have a beautiful place here, ma'am. You are to be envied.'

'Oh, do you think so?' said Lady Winsloe, in her husky whisper. 'Not in these days—not in these terrible days. Why, the taxes alone! You've no idea, Mr——?'

'Huffam.'

'Yes. How stupid of me! Now, Bobo! Now, Coco!'

Then a little silence followed and Lady Winsloe gazed at her strange visitor. Her manners were beautiful. She never looked *directly* at her guests. But there was something about Mr Huffam that *forced* you to look at him. It was his energy. It was his obvious happiness (for happy people were so very rare). It was his extraordinary waistcoat.

Mr Huffam did not mind in the least being looked at. He smiled back at Lady Winsloe, as though he had known her all his life.

'I'm so very fortunate,' he said, 'to find myself in London at Christmas-time. And snow, too! The very thing. Snowballs,

Punch and Judy, mistletoe, holly, the pantomime—nothing so good in life as the pantomime!'

'Oh, do you think so?' said Lady Winsloe faintly. 'I can't, I'm afraid, altogether agree with you. It lasts such a *very* long time and is often so exceedingly vulgar!'

'Ah, it's the sausages!' said Mr Huffam, laughing. 'You don't like the sausages! For my part I dote on 'em. I know it's silly at my age, but there it is—Joey and the sausages. I wouldn't miss them for anything.'

At that moment a tall and exceedingly thin gentleman entered. This was Sir Roderick Winsloe. Sir Roderick had been once an Under Secretary, once a Chairman of a Company, once famous for his smart and rather vicious repartees. All these were now glories of the past. He was now nothing but the husband of Lady Winsloe, the father of Tubby, and the victim of an uncertain and often truculent digestion. It was natural that he should be melancholy, although perhaps not so melancholy as he found it necessary to be. Life for him was altogether without savour. He now regarded Mr Huffam, his bag and his waistcoat, with unconcealed astonishment.

'This is my father, said Tubby.

Mr Huffam rose at once and grasped his hand.

'Delighted to meet you, sir,' he said.

Sir Roderick said nothing but 'Ah'—then he sat down. Tubby was suffering now from a very serious embarrassment. The odd visitor had drunk his tea and it was time that he should go. Yet it seemed that he had no intention of going. With his legs spread apart, his head thrown back, his friendly eyes taking everyone in as though they were all his dearest friends, he was asking for his second cup.

Tubby waited for his mother. She was a mistress of the art of making a guest disappear. No one knew quite how she did it. There was nothing so vulgarly direct as a glance at the clock or a suggestion as to the imminence of dressing for dinner. A cough, a turn of the wrist, a word about the dogs, and the thing was done. But *this* guest, Tubby knew, was a little more difficult than the ordinary. There was something old-fashioned about him. He took people naïvely at their word. Having been asked to tea, he considered that he *was* asked to tea. None of your five minutes' gossip and then hastening on to a cocktail-party. However, Tubby reflected, the combination of father, mother *and* the drawing-room, with its marble fireplace and row of copied Old Masters, was, as a rule, enough to ensure brief visitors. On this occasion also it would have its effect.

And then—an amazing thing occurred! Tubby perceived that his mother *liked* Mr Huffam, that she was smiling and even giggling, that her little eyes shone, her tiny mouth was parted in expectation as she listened to her visitor.

Mr Huffam was telling a story—an anecdote of his youth. About a boy whom he had known in his own childhood, a gay, enterprising, and adventurous boy who had gone as page-boy to a rich family. Mr Huffam described his adventures in a marvellous manner, his *rencontre* with the second footman, who was a snob and Evangelical, of how he had handed biscuits through the pantry window to his little sister, of the friendship that he had made with the cook. And, as Mr Huffam told these things, all these people lived before your eyes, the pompous mistress with her ear-trumpet, the cook's husband who had a wooden leg, the second footman who was in love with a pastrycook's daughter. The house of this young page-boy took on life, and all the furniture in it, the tables and chairs, the beds and looking-glasses, everything down to the very red woollen muffler that the footman wore in bed, because he was subject to colds in the neck. Then Lady Winsloe began to laugh and Sir Roderick Winsloe even laughed, and the butler, a big, red-faced man, coming in to remove the tea, could not believe his parboiled eyes, but stood there, looking first of all at his mistress, then at his master, then at Mr Huffam's bag, then at Mr Huffam himself, until he remembered his manners and, with a sudden apologetic cough, set sternly (for himself this disgraceful behaviour of his employers was no laughing matter) about his proper duties.

But best of all perhaps was the pathos at the end of Mr Huffam's story. Pathos is a dangerous thing in these days. We so easily call it sentimentality. Mr Huffam was a master of it. Quite easily and with no exaggeration he described how the sister of the little page-boy lost some money entrusted to her by her only too bibulous father, of her terror, her temptation to steal from her aged aunt's purse, her final triumphant discovery of the money in a band-box!

How they all held their breaths! How vividly they saw the scene! How real was the sister of the little page-boy! At last the story was ended. Mr Huffam rose.

'Well, ma'am, I must thank you for a very happy hour,' he said.

Then the most remarkable thing of all occurred, for Lady Winsloe said:

'If you have not made any other arrangements, why not stay here for a night or two—while you are looking about you, you know? I'm sure we should be delighted—would we not, Roderick?'

And Sir Roderick said:

'Ah—ah—certainly.'

ii

On looking back, as he so often did afterwards, into the details of this extraordinary adventure, Tubby was never able to arrange the various incidents in their proper order. The whole affair had the inconsequence, the coloured fantasy, of a dream—one of those rare and delightful dreams that are so much more true and reasonable than anything in one's waking life.

After that astounding invitation of Lady Winsloe's, in what order did the events follow—the cynical luncheon-party, the affair of Mallow's young woman (Mallow was the butler), the extraordinary metamorphosis of Miss Allington? All of these were certainly in the first twenty-four hours after Mr Huffam's arrival. The grand sequence of the Christmas Tree, the Mad Party, the London Vision, were all parts of the tremendous climax.

At once, Tubby realized, the house itself changed. It had never been a satisfactory house; always one of those places rebelliously determined not to live. Even the rooms most often inhabited—the drawing-room, the long, dusky dining-room, Sir Roderick's study, Tubby's own bedroom—sulkily refused to play the game. The house was too large, the furniture too heavy, the ceilings too high. Nevertheless, on the first evening of Mr Huffam's visit, the furniture began to move about. After dinner on that evening there was only the family present. (Miss Agatha Allington, an old maid, a relation with money to be left, an unhappy old woman, suffering from constant neuralgia, had not yet arrived.) There they were in the drawing-room and, almost at once, Mr Huffam had moved some of the chairs away from the wall, had turned the sofa with the gilt, spiky back more cosily towards the fire. He was not impertinent nor officious. Indeed, on this first evening, he was very quiet, asking them some questions about present-day London, making some rather odd social enquiries about prisons and asylums and the protection of children. He was interested, too, in the literature of the moment and wrote down in a little note-book an odd collection of names, for Lady Winsloe told him that Ethel M. Dell, Warwick Deeping, and a lady called Wilhelmina Stitch who wrote poetry, were her favourite writers, while Tubby suggested that he should look into the work of Virginia Woolf, D. H. Lawrence and Aldous Huxley. They had, in fact, a quiet evening which ended with Mr Huffam having his first lesson in Bridge. (He had been, he told them, when he had last 'tried' cards, an enthusiastic whist player.) It was a quiet evening, but, as Tubby went up the long, dark staircase to his room, he felt that, in some undefined way, there was excitement in the air.

[114]

Before undressing he opened his window and looked out on to the roofs and chimney-pots of London. Snow glittered and sparkled under a sky that quivered with stars. Dimly he heard the recurrent waves of traffic, as though the sea gently beat at the feet of the black, snow-covered houses.

'*What* an extraordinary man!' was his last thought before he slept. Before he had known that he would have Mr Huffam as his guest, Tubby had invited a few of his clever young friends to luncheon—Diana, Gordon Wolley, Ferris Band, Mary Polkinghorne. Gathered round the Winsloe luncheon-table, Tubby regarded them with new eyes. Was it because of the presence of Mr Huffam? He, gaily flaunting his tremendous waistcoat, was in high spirits. He had, all morning, been revisiting some of his old haunts. He was amazed. He could not conceal, he did not attempt to conceal, his amazement. He gave them, as they sat there, languidly picking at their food, a slight notion of what East London had once been—the filth, the degradation, the flocks of wild, haggard-eyed, homeless children—Mary Polkinghorne, who had a figure like an umbrella-handle, an Eton crop and an eye-glass, gazed at him with bemused amazement.

'But they say our slums are awful. I haven't been down there myself, but Bunny Carlisle runs a Boys' Club and *he* says . . .!'

Mr Huffam admitted that he had seen some slums that morning, but they were nothing, nothing at all, to the things he had seen in his youth.

'Who *is* this man?' Ferris Band whispered to Diana.

'I don't know,' she answered. 'Someone Tubby picked up. But I like him.'

And then this Christmas!

'Oh dear,' young Wolley sighed, 'here's Christmas again! Isn't it awful! I'm going to bed. I shall sleep, and I hope dream, until this dreadful time is over.'

Mr Huffam looked at him with wonder.

'Hang up your stocking and see what happens,' he said.

[115]

Everyone screamed with laughter at the idea of young Wolley hanging up his stocking. Afterwards, in the drawing-room, they discussed literature.

'I've just seen,' Ferris Band explained, 'the proofs of Hunter's new novel. It's called *Pigs in Fever*. It's quite marvellous. The idea is, a man has scarlet fever and it's an account of his ravings. Sheer poetry.'

There was a book on a little table. He picked it up. It was a first edition of *Martin Chuzzlewit* bound in purple leather.

'Poor old Dickens,' he said. 'Hunter has a marvellous idea. He's going to rewrite one or two of the Dickens books.'

Mr Huffam was interested.

'Rewrite them?' he asked.

'Yes. Cut them down to about half. There's some quite good stuff in them hidden away, he says. He'll cut out all the sentimental bits, bring the humour up to date, and put in some stuff of his own. He says it's only fair to Dickens to show people that there's something there.'

Mr Huffam was delighted.

'I'd like to see it,' he said. 'It will make quite a new thing of it.'

'That's what Hunter says,' Band remarked. 'People will be surprised.'

'I should think they will be,' Mr Huffam remarked.

The guests stayed a long time. Mr Huffam was something quite new in their experience. Before she went, Diana said to Tubby:

'What a delightful man! Where *did* you find him?'

Tubby was modest. She was nicer to him than she had ever been before.

'What's happened to you, Tubby?' she asked. 'You've woken up suddenly.'

During the afternoon, Miss Agatha Allington arrived with a number of bags and one of her worst colds.

'How are you, Tubby? It's kind of you to ask me. What

horrible weather! What a vile thing Christmas is! You won't expect me to give you a present, I hope?'

Before the evening, Mr Huffam made friends with Mallow the butler. No one knew quite how he did it. No one had ever made friends with Mallow before. But Mr Huffam went down to the lower domestic regions and invaded the world of Mallow, Mrs Spence, the housekeeper, Thomas the footman, Jane and Rose the housemaids, Maggie the scullery-maid. Mrs Spence, who was a little round woman like a football, was a Fascist in politics, said that she was descended from Mary Queen of Scots, and permitted no one, except Lady Winsloe, in her sitting-room. But she showed Mr Huffam the photographs of the late Mr Spence and her son, Darnley, who was a steward on the Cunard Line. She laughed immeasurably at the story of the organ-grinder and the lame monkey. But Mallow was Mr Huffam's great conquest. It seemed (no one had had the least idea of it) that Mallow was hopelessly in love with a young lady who assisted in a flower shop in Dover Street. This young lady, apparently, admired Mallow very much and he had once taken her to the pictures. But Mallow was shy. (No one had conceived it!) He wanted to write her a letter, but simply hadn't the courage. Mr Huffam dictated a letter for him. It was a marvellous letter, full of humour, poetry and tenderness.

'But I can't live up to this, sir,' said Mallow. 'She'll find me out in no time.'

'That's all right,' said Mr Huffam. 'Take her out to tea tomorrow, be a little tender. She won't worry about letters after that!'

He went out after tea and returned powdered with snow, in a taxi-cab filled with holly and mistletoe.

'Oh dear,' whispered Lady Winsloe, 'we haven't decorated the house for years. I don't know what Roderick will say. He thinks holly so messy.'

'I'll talk to him,' said Mr Huffam. He did, with the result that Sir Roderick came himself and assisted. Through all this, Mr

Huffam was in no way dictatorial. Tubby observed that he had even a kind of shyness—not in his opinions, for here he was very clear-minded indeed, seeing exactly what he wanted, but he seemed to be aware, by a sort of ghostly guidance, of the idiosyncrasies of his neighbours. How did he know, for instance, that Sir Roderick was afraid of a ladder? When he, Mallow, Tubby and Sir Roderick were festooning the hall with holly, he saw Sir Roderick begin timidly, with trembling shanks, to climb some steps. He went to him, put his hand on his arm, and led him safely to ground again.

'I know you don't like ladders,' he said. 'Some people can't stand 'em. I knew an old gentleman once terrified of ladders, and his eldest son, a bright, promising lad, *must* become a steeple-jack. Only profession he had a liking for.'

'Good heavens!' cried Sir Roderick, paling. 'What a horrible pursuit! Whatever did his father do?'

'Persuaded him to be a diver instead,' said Mr Huffam. 'The lad took to it like a duck to water. Up or down, it was all the same to him, he said.'

In fact, Mr Huffam looked after Sir Roderick as a father his child, and, before the day was out, the noble Baronet was asking Mr Huffam's opinion on everything—the right way to grow carnations, the Gold Standard, how to breed dachshunds, and the wisdom of Lord Beaverbrook. The Gold Standard and Lord Beaverbrook were new to Mr Huffam, but he had his opinions all the same. Tubby, as he listened, could not help wondering where Mr Huffam had been all these years. In some very remote South Sea island surely! So many things were new to him. But his kindness and energy carried him forward through everything. There was much of the child about him, much of the wise man of the world also, and behind these a heart of melancholy, of loneliness.

'He has, it seems,' thought Tubby, 'no home, no people, nowhere especially to go.' And he had visions of attaching him to the family as a sort of secretarial family friend. Tubby was no sentimentalist about his own sex, but he had to confess that he was growing very fond of Mr Huffam. It was almost as though he had known him before. There were, in fact, certain phrases, certain tones in the voice that were curiously familiar and reminded Tubby in some dim way of his innocent departed childhood.

And then, after dinner, there was the conquest of Agatha Allington. Agatha had taken an instant dislike to Mr Huffam. She prided herself on her plain speech.

'My dear,' she said to Lady Winsloe, 'what a ruffian! He'll steal the spoons.'

'I don't think so,' said Lady Winsloe with dignity. 'We like him very much.'

He seemed to perceive that Agatha disliked him. He sat beside her at dinner—he wore a tail-coat of strange, old-fashioned cut, and carried a large gold fob. He was, as Tubby perceived, quite different from Agatha. He was almost, you might say, an old maid himself—or, rather, a confirmed old bachelor. He discovered that she had a passion for Italy—she visited Rome and Florence every year—and he described to her some of his own Italian journeys, taken many years ago: confessed to her that he didn't care for frescoes, which he described as 'dim virgins with mildewed glories'. But Venice! Ah! Venice! with its prisoners and dungeons and lovely irides-cent waters! All the same, he was always homesick when he was out of London, and he described the old London to her, the fogs and the muffin-bells and the 'growlers,' and enchanted her with a story about a shy little bachelor, and how he went out one evening to dine with a vulgar cousin and be kind to a horrible godchild. Indeed they all listened spellbound: even Mallow stood, with a plate in his hand and his mouth open, forgetting his duties. Then, after dinner, he insisted that they should dance. They made a space in the drawing-room, brought up a gramophone, and set about it. Then how Mr Huffam laughed when Tubby showed him a one-step.

[119]

'Call that dancing!' he cried. Then, humming a polka, he caught Agatha by the waist and away they polkaed! Then Lady Winsloe, who had adored the polka once, joined in. Then the Barn Dance. Then, few though they were, Sir Roger.

'I know!' Mr Huffam cried. 'We must have a party!'

'A party!' almost screamed Lady Winsloe. 'What kind of a party?'

'Why, a children's party, of course. On Christmas night.'

'But we don't know any children! And children are bored with parties. And they'll all be engaged anyway.'

'Not the children *I'll* ask!' cried Mr Huffam. 'Not the party *I'll* have! It shall be the best party London has seen for years!'

iii

It is well known that good-humoured, cheerful, and perpetually well-intentioned people are among the most tiresome of their race. They are avoided by all wise and comfort-loving persons. Tubby often wondered afterwards why Mr Huffam was *not* tiresome. It was perhaps because of his childlikeness; it was also, most certainly, because of his intelligence. Most of all it was because of the special circumstances of the case. In ordinary daily life, Mr Huffam *might* be a bore—most people are at one time or another. But on this occasion no one was a bore, not even Agatha.

It was as though the front wall of the Hill Street House had been taken away and all the detail and incidents of these two days, Christmas Eve and Christmas Day, became part of it. It seemed that Berkeley Square was festooned with crystal trees, that candles—red and green and blue—blazed from every window, that small boys, instead of chanting 'Good King Wenceslas' in the usual excruciating fashion, carolled with divine voices, that processions of Father Christmases, with snowy beards and red gowns, marched from Selfridges and Harrods and Fortnum's, carrying in their hands small Christmas trees, and even attended by reindeer, as though brown-paper parcels tied with silver bands and decorated with robins fell in torrents through the chimney, and gigantic Christmas puddings rolled on their own stout bellies down Piccadilly, attended by showers of almonds and raisins. And upon all this, first a red-faced sun, then a moon, cherry-coloured and as large as an orange, smiled down, upon a world of crusted, glittering snow, while the bells pealed and once again the Kings of the East came to the stable with gifts in their hands . . .

Of course, it was not like that—but most certainly the Winsloe house was transformed. For one thing, there was not the usual present-giving. At breakfast on Christmas Day, everyone gave everyone else presents that must not by order cost more than sixpence apiece. Mr Huffam had discovered some marvellous things—toy dogs that barked, Father Christmases glistening with snow, a small chime of silver bells, shining pieces of sealing-wax.

Then they all went to church at St James's, Piccadilly. At the midday meal Sir Roderick had turkey and Christmas pudding, which he hadn't touched for many a day.

In the evening came the Party. Tubby had been allowed to invite Diana—for the rest the guests were to be altogether Mr Huffam's. No one knew what was in his mind. At 7.15 exactly came the first ring of the door-bell. When Mallow opened the portals, there on the steps were three very small children, two girls and a boy.

'Please, sir, this was the number the gentleman said,' whispered the little girl, who was very frightened. Then up Hill Street the children came, big children, little children, children who could scarcely walk, boys as bold as brass, girls mothering their small relations, some of them shabby, some of them smart, some with shawls, some with mufflers, some with collars, some brave, some frightened, some chattering like monkeys, some silent and anxious—all coming up Hill Street, crowding up the stairs, passing into the great hall.

[121]

It was not until they had all been ushered up the stairs by Mallow, were all in their places, that Sir Roderick Winsloe, Bart., Lady Winsloe, his wife, Tubby Winsloe, their son, were permitted to see their own drawing-room. When they did they gasped with wonder. Under the soft and shining light the great floor had been cleared, and at one end of the room all the children were gathered. At the other end was the largest, the strongest, the proudest Christmas Tree ever beheld, and this Tree shone and gleamed with candles, with silver tissue, with blue and gold and crimson balls, and so heavily weighted was it with dolls and horses and trains and parcels that it was a miracle that, Tree as it was, it could support its burden. So there it was, the great room shining with golden light, the children massed together, the gleaming floor like a sea, and only the crackle of the fire, the tick of the marble clock, the wondering whispers of the children for sound.

A pause, and from somewhere or other (but no one knew whence) Father Christmas appeared. He stood there, looking across the floor at his guests.

'Good evening, children,' he said, and the voice was the voice of Mr Huffam.

'Good evening, Father Christmas,' the children cried in chorus.

'It's all his own money,' Lady Winsloe whispered to Agatha. 'He wouldn't let me spend a penny.'

He summoned them then to help with the presents. The children (who behaved with the manners of the highest of the aristocracy—even *better* than that, to be truthful) advanced across the shining floor. They were told to take turn according to size, the smallest first. There was no pushing, no cries of 'I want *that!*' as so often happens at parties, no greed and satiety. At last the biggest girl (who was almost a giantess), and the biggest boy (who might have been a heavyweight boxing champion) received their gifts. The Tree gave a little quiver of relief at its freedom from its burden, and the candles, the silver tissue, the red and blue and golden balls shook with a shimmer of pleasure because the present-giving had been so successful.

Games followed. Tubby could never afterwards remember what the games had been. They were no doubt Hunt the Slipper, Kiss in the Ring, Cross-your-Toes, Last Man Out, Blind Man's Buff, Chase the Cherry, Here Comes the Elephant, Count Your Blessings, and all the other games. But Tubby never knew. The room was alive with movement, with cries of joy and shouts of triumph, with songs and kisses and forfeits. Tubby never knew. He only knew that he saw his mother with a paper cap on her head, his father with a false nose, Agatha beating a child's drum—and on every side of him children and children and children, children dancing and singing and running and sitting and laughing.

There came a moment when Diana, her hair dishevelled, her eyes shining, caught his arm and whispered:

'Tubby, you are a dear. Perhaps—one day—if you keep this up—who knows?'

And there was a sudden quiet. Mr Huffam, no longer Father Christmas, arranged all the children round him. He told them a story, a story about a circus and a small child who, with her old grandfather, wandered into the company of those strange people—of the fat lady and the Living Skeleton, the jugglers and the beautiful creatures who jumped through the hoops, and the clown with the broken heart and how his heart was mended.

'And so they all lived happily ever after,' he ended. Everyone said good-night. Everyone went away.

'Oh dear, I *am* tired!' said Mr Huffam. 'But it has been a jolly evening!'

Next morning when Rose the housemaid woke Lady Winsloe with her morning cup of tea she had startling news.

'Oh dear, my lady, the gentleman's gone!'

'What gentleman?'

'Mr Huffam, my lady. His bed's not been slept in and his bag's gone. There isn't a sign of him anywhere.'

[123]

Alas, it was only too true. Not a sign of him anywhere. At least one sign only.

The drawing-room was as it had always been, every chair in its proper place, the copied Old Masters looking down solemnly from the dignified walls.

One thing alone was different. The first edition of *Martin Chuzzlewit* in its handsome purpose binding was propped up against the marble clock.

'How very strange!' said Lady Winsloe. But, opening it, she found that on the fly-leaf these words were freshly written:

> For Lady Winsloe
> with gratitude
> from her Friend
> the Author—

And, under this, the signature, above a scrawl of thick black lines, 'Charles Dickens'.

JEREMIAH

Jessica Amanda Salmonson

Jessica Amanda Salmonson is one of the busiest
writers in the new generation of American horror
writers, with many novels and short stories to
her credit including *The Swordswoman, Ou Lu
Khen and the Beautiful Madwoman*, and *Anthony
Shriek* (1992). 'Jeremiah' is one of a number of her
tales featuring (and narrated by) occult detective
Penelope Pettiweather, collected in a limited
edition booklet *Harmless Ghosts* (Haunted
Library, 1990).

'Je suis dégoûté de tout.'
. . . René Crevel, 1935.

To: Jane Bradshawe
   Oundle, Northants,
   England

My dear Jane,

I'm glad you received that copy of *Satan's Circus* by Lady Eleanor
Smith. One frets about the overseas mail. You'll note that while
the spine says the publisher is 'Doran', the title page says 'Bobbs
Merrill', yet both purport to be the first edition. I'm told that
Doran had a habit, in those days, of purchasing unbound sheets of
other publishers' overruns and reissuing them under their own
imprint. So you see, it isn't really the first edition except on the
inside! I was also delighted by your perceptive comments on the
outstanding story 'Whittington's Cat'. The compiler of *Giddy's
Ghost Story Guide* completely misunderstood that one, didn't he?

Thank you for that perfect copy of *Stoneground Ghost Tales*. I could never have afforded it over here. You'd pale at the American prices for old British books! The stories struck me as quaintly amusing rather than horrific, but there is a lot more to them than meets the eye, though once more the compiler of *Giddy's* failed to see much in them. There's so much to the central protagonist's character that could be further explored if some talented and enterprising fellow ever wished to add new episodes about the haunted vicar and his parish.

But, enough of mere fictional ghosts. I was chilled to the bone by your recent experience with those two paintings you were restoring. If you wrote that one up as a 'fictional' adventure you could certainly sell it to one of the fantasy magazines. They needn't know it actually happened. But what a shame the paintings had ultimately to be covered up. Not that I blame you; still, I'd like to have seen the one of Death on my next trip abroad, and that won't be possible now that it's safely 'preserved' under whitewash.

Did my colleague Mrs Byrne-Hurliphant bother you *that* much on her English journey? She can be a pest, certainly. Please forgive my giving her your address. Now, at least, you'll know exactly what I'm on about!

Yes, yes, I did promise to tell you what happened over Christmas if you'd tell me that horrid adventure with the paintings of the 'Gravedigger' and 'Death'. Well, a bargain is a bargain, so now I suppose I must. It's much more terrible than any of the little accounts I've sent Cyril for his antiquarian journal. So brace yourself, and remember—you asked.

It was three weeks to Christmas. I planned holidays alone. All my friends would be off to other states to visit kin. And while Christmas is no big thing to me—growing up with both East European Jews and Southeast Asian Buddhists in one's motley family helps to weaken the impact of Christian holidays—it can yet be gloomy and sad when one's options are unexpectedly restricted. I can't count a couple of pre-Christmas parties I would probably attend. The fact that people are so fantastically tedious makes the *doing* sometimes as depressing as the *not*, so you can see I was just in no mood for anything.

I'd finished some early grocery shopping and was coming up the backstairs out of a bleak afternoon rain, two bags squashed in my arms, when I heard the phone ringing. You just know when you hurry, things take longer. I dropped the keys. Then I tried the wrong key. Then I tried the right key upside down. By the time I'd tossed the torn bags and their contents across the kitchen table and grabbed the receiver, all I heard was a faint 'click'. Surprising how discouraging that click can be at times.

But before I'd put all the groceries away, and pulled together the majority of the bulk beans I'd scattered, the phone rang again.

It was the feeblest voice I'd ever heard.

'Miss Pettiweather?'

'Absolutely,' I replied, affecting the prim and the resolute.

'I beg your pardon?' said the faint, elderly voice of a woman who must have been a hundred and fifty-eight if her age matched such a sad, rasping, tired timbre.

'Yes, this is Miss Pettiweather,' I said, donning a more conservative aspect.

'I read your article in the Seattle *Times*,' said the cracked old voice, 'The one about the haunted houses.'

I winced. It hadn't been an article but an interview. And while the reporter tried her best to be straight-faced about it, it was so garbled and misquoted that even I had to wonder if the interviewee weren't a lunatic.

'Did you?' I said affably.

The feeble voice said, 'If it happens to me again, I don't think I can make it.'

It seemed she was on the verge of tears.

'What happened?' I asked, worried that some wretched woman was truly in need of my special talents, but so old it would be difficult for her to communicate her problem. 'Who am I speaking to?'

'Gretta Adamson,' she said. 'My heart isn't as good as it was. If he does it again, I'll die. I tried to tell the doctor but he said not to excite myself. He doesn't believe me. Do you believe me, Miss Pettiweather? Won't anyone believe me?'

[127]

'Oh I can believe just about anything; but I don't know anything about it as yet, Miss . . . Mrs?'

'I'm widowed.'

'Mrs Adamson. You haven't told me . . .'

'It's Jeremiah,' she said. 'He comes back.'

'Is it bad?' I asked. That was the simplest way I could put the question. And she answered even more simply.

'It's terrible.'

Then very quietly, very sadly, she added:

'Every Christmas. But . . . but . . .' She broke down at that point and could barely finish. 'He isn't the same.'

She lived alone in a small run-down house in a run-down part of the city. The house hadn't been repainted in a full generation, for even curls and flakes had long since come loose and disappeared, so that the whole gray structure looked as though it had never been painted at all. Most of the windows were cracked; some of the cracks were taped; and a few small panes had been replaced with wood or plastic.

The lawn was a miniature meadow for inner city fieldmice. A wooden fence set her small property apart from the surrounding houses and cheap lowrise apartment buildings. The fence was falling down in places. The front gate was held closed with a length of rope, which had been woven about in a curious manner, as though the inhabitant beyond had a secret method no one else could duplicate, thereby making it possible to tell whenever someone had tinkered with it. I retied the gate in a much simpler manner, then strode a broken stone walkway between the two halves of her little meadow of frozen, brittle grass.

When Mrs Adamson opened the door, her white, creased face looked up at me from so far down, it made me feel like I was a giant. In her gaze was a world of pitiful hope, worry and despair. Her head was cocked completely on its side, resting on a shoulder in a spectacularly unnatural posture.

'I'm Miss Pettiweather,' I said, hoping my ordinary demeanor and harmless, frumpy middle-agedness would be enough to reassure her. In such a neighborhood, it was no wonder she was leery of opening her own front door.

She was badly hunchbacked and the spinal deterioration caused her obvious pain. The smell of medicine assured me she had a doctor's care at least. Her neck was so twisted that her left ear was pressed against her shoulder and she could by no method straighten her head. But it was a kind soul inside that ruined body, and they were kind eyes that glared up at me.

I followed her into the dimly lit, grubby interior. Her shuffling gait was slow and awkward, as it was difficult to walk with such a horribly calcium-leached spinal column. For her own part, she seemed to count herself lucky to be able to walk, and bore up boldly.

She was eighty-five.

'Jeremiah died when I was seventy,' she said in her familiar cracked voice. I sat with her at her kitchen table. 'Fifteen years ago. Christmas Eve, in Swedish Hospital.'

'What did he die of?' I asked, moving my rickety chair closer to Mrs Adamson, to better hear her thin, distant voice.

'He was old,' she said.

'Yes, I know, but, well, it will help me to know more. Was he in his right mind? I'm sorry to be so blunt about it, Mrs Adamson, but it's only a few days to Christmas. I assure you I *can* help, but I'll need as much information beforehand as you can give me. Was he able to think clearly until close to the end?'

'Lord, no,' she said, her sideways head staring with the brightest, sharpest, bluest eyes. 'He had Alzheimer's.'

I sighed. I would have to grill her a bit more, to find out what Mr Adamson's final days were like. But I could already guess, and later, after an interview at Swedish Hospital, I would be certain. The raving last moments, the delusions—in this case, the delusion that he had gotten into such a state because his wife had poisoned him. It was often the case with the more malignant spirits that they had died in abject confusion, anger, and horror, hence they could not go on to a better existence elsewhere.

The tea kettle whistled and though I insisted I could make it myself, Mrs Adamson obviously wished to entertain me. She got up, for all the agony of motion, and toddled weirdly round the vile kitchen. A moldy pork chop sat in hard grease in a rusty pan on the stove. A garbage bag was filled with tuna fish and Chef Boyarde spaghetti cans. Something totally beyond recognition reposed on a plate upon the counter, and, though it was days old, whatever it was appeared to have been nibbled on that very morning, whether by Mrs Adamson or some rat I didn't want to speculate.

In some ways she was sharp as could be. In others, she was indubitably senile. I kept her company the long afternoon. She rambled on about all kinds of things, mostly pretty dull, but was so terribly lonesome I couldn't allow myself to leave. Fifteen years a widow! And all those years, she had spent Christmases alone in that crumbling house—every year awaiting . . . Jeremiah. The toughness of someone that frail is really surprising, though such stoicism had left its mark.

She was cheered no end when I promised to spend Christmas Eve with her. I think her relief wasn't entirely because I convinced her I could lay Jeremiah to rest. Fifteen years is a lot of Christmases spent alone. Such loneliness is hard to bear, even had there not been the terror of a ghost. So it seemed as though Mrs Adamson was more interested in our Christmas Eve together than in the laying of a ghost. Indeed, she took for granted that I could save her from the long-endured horror, and was more worried about the months or years she might have yet to live by whatever means available.

Later that evening, at home in my own warm bed, I was filled with sorrow to think of her. I fought back my tears as I pondered that wreck of a body, the years of desperation, the terrible thing she faced year in and year out, darkening her whole life. What will *our* last years be like, Jane? Who will come to visit us? Who will keep us company when we've lost even the skill to write our letters?

I was so involved with the pitifulness of her material situation, I was not preparing myself sufficiently for my encounter with Jeremiah. What could be worse than a sick old age, separated from the rest of the world? Well, Jane, something *can* be worse, as you and I have learned and relearned in our explorations. But I wasn't thinking so on the day I met Gretta Adamson.

Her odd, sad sort of strength was the other thing that left me unprepared, and the simple way she took for granted that I would put an end to the horrors. She had looked so frail, and had endured so long, how could I have expected her particular demon to be a bad one? I wasn't ready, that's all, though I did do my research, and never imagined there were surprises waiting.

I visited Mrs Adamson on two other occasions before the holiday in question, and reassured her about my research at the hospital where her husband died. She hadn't known the worst of his last hours, as she had been ill herself, and unable to be constantly at his side. The day he died, she had been with him only a short time in the morning, thus was spared the worst of his venomous accusations, hallucinations, and the screaming hatred that preluded his death-rattle.

I had talked to a head-nurse, who had been a night nurse at the beginning of her career fifteen years before; she gave me a vivid, startling account of Jeremiah Adamsons's raging thirst for revenge against a wife he imagined to be his murderess. I certainly wasn't going to fill in Mrs Adamson at this late date, and was therefore careful to avoid telling her too much of what I had discovered.

That that head-nurse remembered so much should have been a warning to me, as death is too common in hospitals for a nurse to recall one old man in detail. But I chalked it up to her youthfulness at the time—we all remember our first encounters with grotesque tragedy—and Jeremiah *had* been memorably inventive in his repellent promises, given his otherwise impaired faculties.

So I had learned all too well Jeremiah's state of mind in his last moments of senile dementia. Mrs Adamson was able to tell me a bit more, and remembered other things piece by piece whenever I probed as gently as the situation allowed. But I couldn't delve far at a time, for some of it was too much for her to bear recalling, and much else, I presumed, was genuinely lost through her own age-related difficulties with memory.

'I would like to see Jeremiah's personal papers, whatever you may have,' I asked a couple of days before Christmas Eve. Mrs Adamson was aghast, for she herself had never interfered with his privacy, had never sorted through his personal letters and what-nots in the fifteen years since his death. This should have been another clue informing me that Jeremiah's tyranny began well before senility set in. But I continued to be blind. I thought only to convince Mrs Adamson of what was essential.

'You see,' I explained, 'I have to find out more about him. You mustn't think of it as really being Jeremiah. It's only a shadow of him, and a shadow of his darkest mood at that. The afterlife mentality is very simple compared to life. It fixes on a few things. In his private papers, there may be some clue to the thing that he most feared, or most wanted, and whatever it is can become a tool to erase his lingering shade.'

'He wouldn't like us to know those things about him,' Mrs Adamson insisted, protecting her husband with a peculiar devotion, and looking at me sadly with those sharp blue eyes in her sideways expression.

'Do you know the meaning of an exorcism, Mrs Adamson?' She wasn't Catholic and wouldn't know much, but of course everyone knows a little. 'There are many ways to lay a ghost, but exorcism is the cruellest. It is a real fight. It's a terrible thing for the exorcist and for the ghost. But there are other means. Sometimes you can reason with them, but it is like reasoning with a child, and you have to be careful. But think a minute, Mrs Adamson, about the classic type of exorcism you may have heard about, with holy water and the cross of Jesus. To tell the truth, such a procedure is worthless unless the individual had some personal belief in these things while living. The cross of Jesus is a powerful amulet against the ghost of a Catholic. But if he wasn't mindful of holy things in life, then his ghost won't care about them either.

'But other things can become equally significant. Once I got rid of a ghost by showing it a rare postage stamp it had never been able to get when living. A pretty rotten spirit it was, too, but gentle as a lamb when it saw that postage stamp. And the ghost never showed up again.

'Only by careful research can I find out what that special item might be. The more personal the papers, Mrs Adamson, the better it will be.'

She sat like a collapsed rag doll in a big overstuffed chair, pondering all that I had told her, her bright eyes expressing what a dreadful decision I was forcing her to make. At length I helped her stand, reassuring her the whole while, and she led me to a musty closet in which we were able to dig out two shoeboxes held together with rubber-bands so old they had melted into the cardboard of the boxes.

Inside these shoeboxes were faded photographs and mementoes and yellowed letters and a lock of baby's hair in a red envelope labeled 'Jeremiah'.

'I recollect that,' said Mrs Adamson. 'Jeremiah showed it to me. He had a lot of hair when he was a baby. Lost it all.'

And her dry, horrible old voice managed a sweet laugh as she fumbled the envelope open and gazed at the little curl of hair tied with a piece of thread.

She told me, as best she could, who were the people in the family photos.

[133]

She became very silent on discovering, for the first time in her whole long life, that Jeremiah had once been unfaithful; the evidence being a love-letter written by her rival several years *after* Jeremiah had married Gretta.

I patted her liver-spotted hand and assured her, 'It is sometimes just this sort of thing that brings them back. He may have wanted to spare you knowing.'

But that kind of haunting was rarely menacing, so I kept sorting through the two boxes. Jeremiah kept no diaries—it is usually women who do that, and they're the most easily laid ghosts as a result—and it didn't seem there were going to be many clues to the sort of thing it would take to lay Jeremiah come Christmas Eve.

In the bottom of the second box I found an old black and white photograph of the handsome young man and the strikingly good-looking woman I'd learned were Gretta and Jeremiah when they were courting. What a smile he had! He wore a soldier's bloomers. Her hair was short and little curls hung out from under a flowered hat. Very modern, both of them, in their day. As I looked at this photograph a long time, the bent old woman beside me leaned to one side to see what I had, and she went misty-eyed at once.

In the photo, Gretta was holding a round Japanese fan. The camera had focused well enough that I could make out a floral design painted upon it.

'Jeremiah gave me that fan,' she said. 'I still have it.'

And she rose painfully from the chair beside me and tottered back into her bedroom. She returned with the antique fan, dusty and faded from having been displayed in countless ways over countless years. To see that crooked old lady holding that fan, and to see the young beauty holding it in the photo in my hand; well, I cannot tell you how I felt. And she was so moony and oddly happy in her expression. I was once again convinced Jeremiah's ghost couldn't be all that bad, or she couldn't still think of him tenderly.

[134]

'It was the day we were engaged, that picture was taken. He'd been to fight in Asia and for all we knew might fight somewhere else soon, and die. He gave me this fan and I've always kept it.'

'It's our Cross of Jesus,' I said, somehow overawed by the loving emanations from the woman as she held the fan.

'Do you think so?' she asked.

'Jeremiah died with the delusion that you wanted to hurt him, Gretta.'

I told her this as unhurtingly as possible.

'That fan will remind him that such a delusion couldn't have been true.'

I'd been doing this sort of thing a long time, Jane. I really thought I had it worked out.

On Christmas Eve I came early and brought a chicken casserole and a small gift. Gretta was overwhelmed and wept for joy. And we did not mention Jeremiah during our humble repast, for it would have put a pall upon our cross-generational friendship and Gretta's first holiday with anyone in many a long year.

She tittered pleasantly and made her usual horrible tea in dirty cups. The Christmas spirit was so much upon me that I actually drank the terrible stuff without worrying if her tea were infected with beetles. She opened the smartly wrapped present—nothing special, just an old Chinese snuff bottle that I'd had for years and been quite fond of. It had roses carved on two sides and it had seemed appropriate because we'd talked about roses a few days before.

Then to my surprise, Gretta came up with a box as well—wrapped in some quaint faded, crinkled paper recycled from two decades before, and crookedly taped all over with yellowing, gooey, transparent tape.

In the box was a tiny ceramic doll that must have been fifty or sixty years old if it was a day, and far more valuable than the

[135]

bottle I'd wrapped for Gretta. I raved about the beauty of the tiny doll, coddled it tenderly, and really didn't have to put on an act, I was honestly overwhelmed.

'It was my grandmother's,' said Gretta, at which my jaw dropped open, realizing my guess of 'fifty or sixty years' was off by a full century.

'You shouldn't part with it!' I exclaimed. 'It must be terribly valuable.'

'I won't need it any longer, Penelope. In fact, I haven't needed it for years. I almost couldn't find it for you. So you be pleased to take it and don't go thinking it's too much.'

Our eyes held one another a long while. How ashamed I was of what I thought of that neck-bent, hunchbacked woman when first I laid eyes on her. Not that I ever thought ill. But it wasn't her humanity that struck me at the start. The things I had first noticed were her crippled pitifulness, her loneliness, her wretched old age, and the decades of accumulating dirt and clutter that surrounded her fading existence. Somewhere down the list of impressions, I must have noted her own unique individuality, but it hadn't been the first thing.

And now, despite that she looked at me with her head fused to one side, with her face turned upward from her permanently crooked posture, I could see, how clearly I could see, that *this* was indeed the young beauty of that old photograph.

We sang carols out of tune and reminisced about our childhood winters; we laughed and we bawled and had a grand day together. She remembered her youth with far greater clarity than she could recall her widowed years. Then long about nine-thirty, she was terribly worn out. Though she ordinarily didn't require a lot of sleep, this had been quite an exciting day. I could see she could barely keep her eyes open.

'Gretta,' I said, 'we've got to put you to bed. No, don't argue. If you're thinking of waiting up for Jeremiah, there's no need. I've got your fan right here, and with it I will lay him flat; you won't even have to be disturbed. When you wake up in the morning, I'll be there on your sofa, and we'll celebrate a peaceful Christmas Day.'

It was a half-hour more before I actually got her to bed, somewhat after ten. Though she insisted she would be wide awake if I needed her at midnight, she was snoring in homely fashion even before I closed her bedroom door.

I walked down the hall, passed the kitchen, and entered the dining room. I surveyed the room and began quietly to push Gretta's furniture against one wall. She had told me in one of our earlier interviews that Jeremiah would first appear at the living room window and make his way to the kitchen and thence to her bedroom. I went into the living room to move that furniture out of the way also. Such precautions were probably excessive, but I didn't want to stumble into anything if for some unforeseen reason I had to move quickly.

It was still some while to midnight, so I turned on Gretta's radio very quietly and listened to a program on change-ringing. The day had been tiring for me as well. Like Gretta, I thought I would be wide awake until midnight. But the next thing I knew, the radio station was signing off the air, and I was startled awake by a change in the house's atmosphere.

I was not immediately alert. The realization that it was suddenly midnight, coupled with a vague movement beyond the front room window, caused me to stand abruptly from where I'd set napping. The sudden movement made my head swim. A black cloud swirled around me. The brittle old paper fan had fallen from my lap onto the floor. I bent to pick it up and nearly lost consciousness. I was forcing my mind to be more fully awake, slowly realizing my dizziness wasn't the natural cause of standing too quickly, but was imposed upon me by something *other*.

As I picked up the fan and moved toward the window, I was brought up short by Jeremiah's sudden appearance there. His black gums were bared, revealing a lack of teeth and reminding me of a lamprey. His eyes were fogged white, as though he were

[137]

able to see only what he imagined and not what was. It was a very complete materialization and he might easily have been taken for a mad peeping tom. He raised both his hands, which were bony claws, and shoved them writhing toward the glass. I expected it to shatter, but instead, the spectre vanished.

By the increasing chill, I knew he was in the house.

I hurried toward the kitchen, recovering my senses more than not, holding the paper fan before me. I was shaking frightfully, beginning to comprehend the depth of his malignancy.

There he was, in the kitchen, bent down, scrabbling wildly but noiselessly at the door under the sink. The cupboard opened under his insistence, and he tried to grasp a little faded blue carton, but his clawed hands only passed through it.

Then he slowly stood, his back to me. He sensed my presence, and his very awareness gave me the shivers. His shoulders stiffened and he began slowly to turn about. I took a strong posture and held the paper fan in front of me, so that it would be the first thing he saw.

He turned and, for a moment, was no longer a spidery old man. He was a young soldier, and he looked at me with sharp but unseeing eyes. I can only describe it thus, because, although his gaze fell directly on me and was no longer clouded white, he seemed to see something infinitely more pleasing to him than I could have been. I supposed he thought I was Gretta, and he was imposing upon my form his memory of her when she was as young as he himself now appeared to be.

He came forward with such a look of love and devotion that in spite of my persisting alarm, and due I'm sure to some occult influence rather than my own nature, I was momentarily terribly aroused. He reached outward to clasp his youthful hands at the sides of my shoulders. I held my ground, certain that my humane exorcism was having its intended effect.

When his ghostly fingers touched me, I felt a warming vibration, as though my whole upper body were encased in fine electrical wire, the voltage slowly increasing. The fan began to shine so brightly that I felt I risked blindness if I failed to close my eyes, but close them I could not.

Before my gaze, the young Jeremiah's angelic face grew sinister by rapid degrees. Simultaneously, the electricity that held me in anguished thrall became more painful. His perfect smile became twisted; his white teeth yellowed and grew long as his gums receded; and then there was only that toothless maw yelling at me without making a sound, dreadful threats I blessedly could not hear. The young soldier had withered and wizened; it was evil rather than years that aged him; and the claws that gripped my shoulders drew blood.

When he let go of me, the light of the fan went out, and I collapsed upon the floor, half sitting against the door jamb. Jeremiah loomed over me with menace, yet my rattled thoughts were pondering in a distant, withdrawn place. I wondered idly if the electrical shock had stopped my heart. I was dimly aware that my lips were wet with froth and drool, and for a moment I was concerned mainly with the nuisance of being unable to move my arm to wipe my mouth.

If these sorts of things were the usual result of my investigations, I should not be so in love with haunted places. I have occasionally felt real danger, but this was the first time I had been so insufficiently prepared that physical harm became inevitable.

His blackening claw grasped me anew and he dragged me across the kitchen floor. His other hand wound into my hair as he pushed my face under the sink, so that I saw before my eyes a thirty or forty year old package of poison—a brand from the days when it was still possible to purchase strychnine to kill rats or even wolves—a damp-stained blue package with skull and crossbones printed in black.

And I realized at that moment what it had to have been that I had overlooked: the critical information without which I was helpless before so malignant a spirit. *Gretta had indeed poisoned her husband*, out of love I do not doubt, and to end his awful suffering. It explained why, on that Christmas Eve fifteen years before, she had spent only a few minutes with him. There would have been no reason for the physicians to suspect such a thing; but Jeremiah had known, though he lacked the capacity to understand it as an act of mercy.

And now my face was shoved hard against the open package of poisonous salts. I clamped my eyes and mouth shut. Jeremiah's ghost was trying to kill me, and at that moment I felt he had a good chance at success.

Then a sad, raspy voice came from the kitchen doorway, saying, 'Let her go, Jeremiah. It's me you want.'

The calm resignation in her voice was heartbreaking.

The black claws let go of my arm and hair. I pushed myself away from under the sink. I was still smarting from the shock of Jeremiah's first touch. I could barely see, and when I tried to focus, it looked to me as though a young woman was moving toward me in a dressing gown. She reached across my shoulder and removed the strychnine from under the sink. A sweet, youthful voice said, 'I guess I should have told you all of it, Penelope, but I thought you could stop him from coming without knowing everything. I'm sorry. Now it's left to me to finish, and there's only one thing that will give my poor Jeremiah peace.'

'No, Gretta, no,' I said, struggling to rise, reaching outward and trying to grab the package from her hand. But I fell back all but senseless, still gripped by the paralysis of the electric shock. I watched as from a dream as Gretta moved about the kitchen, heating water on the stove, calmly making herself a cup of tea, and heaping into it a spoon of strychnine as though it were sugar.

Standing beside her the whole while was the young soldier. She talked to him in loving terms, and addressed me from time to time as well. She thanked me for a lovely Christmas Eve while I strove uselessly to break the paralysis, tears streaming from my eyes.

Then Gretta and her soldier left the kitchen. I heard her footsteps, inexplicable spritely, echoing down the hall. I heard her shut her bedroom door.

And that, Jane, is the gist of a sad adventure. It was over. Oh, I had to suffer interviews with police and coroner. But it didn't take long, because, unfortunately, suicide is the commonest thing among the elderly. I was not pressed to tell the whole story, which they certainly would not have believed. As to myself, I suffered no ill after-effects of the spiritual electrocution, which was, after all, less dangerous than actual electricity. In fact, if you will believe it, the next day I felt partially rejuvenated, and seem since that night to have gotten over my mild arthritis.

And now you may open the gift box I sent along, and which said on it not to open until after you read my letter. As you will see, it is Gretta's paper fan. I bought it at the estate sale, together with a few other small mementoes of a brief friendship.

You will observe that the fan, for all its simplicity, is of the finest craftsmanship, completely hand-made in a manner not seen in over half a century. When I first saw it, it was faded, dusty, and tattered to thinness as though occasionally sampled by moths. And the fan I've sent you *is* the same one, miraculously restored, as though cut and pasted recently, the classic floral design as bright as though painted yesterday.

I take this surprising restoration as evidence that Gretta is forgiven by Jeremiah and that they are now happily reunited—out there in the 'somewhere' we're all destined one day and eternally to know.

Yours,
Penelope

TWO RETURNS

Terry Lamsley

'Two Returns' is taken from Terry Lamsley's new
collection, *Under the Crust* (Wendigo, 1993), six
memorable supernatural tales of dark fantasy and
terror set in and around present-day Buxton, the
author's home town.

After carefully lowering his bags of Christmas shopping on to the platform Mr Rudge shook his wrist out of his overcoat to reveal his watch. Noting that he had a wait of nine minutes before his train was due to arrive, he looked about him for a seat. He had had an exhausting day, and the half mile walk just completed had left him limp and sweating under his thick winter clothes. When he had set out in the morning it had been a cold, bright day promising snow, and he had dressed for that. Later, misty rain had brought an evening of muggy warmth that seemed to draw the energy out of him. He longed for the short rest the train journey home would provide.

He spotted a single bench at the end of the platform, lugged his bags over to it, and sat down.

The position offered no protection from the weather, but the seat was wide and comfortable. He drew his head down into his coat collar, regretting that he had not brought a hat, and tried to lull himself into a cosy frame of mind. The persistent, almost invisible rain blowing into his face made this state impossible to achieve however, and he presently found himself gazing at the bricked-up windows, graffitied-over walls, and snaggle tiled roof of the redundant ticket office and waiting room on the platform opposite him across the line.

The whole station was lit by a few crude lamps of unbreakable glass set in tight metal cages about ten feet up the walls. These gave merely adequate illumination, and the quality of the light was garish and alarming, splashing the wet platforms with puddles and streams of orange, like sticky juice. There were no shadows, only intensities and absences of this golden glow, and drifting veils of drizzle, shining and fading, increased the illusion of insubstantiality adopted for the evening by the stolid, utilitarian railway buildings.

Mr Rudge tried to remember the station as it had been years ago, before it had been all but closed down, but the details that had made it individual had been stripped away, leaving it as featureless as a child's drawing of a barn.

'The "*genius loci*" has deserted this place,' he mused, depressed by the dereliction and air of used-up emptiness.

He was not surprised that there were no other people waiting with him for the train. The little town the station served had almost forgotten the existence of its rail link with Manchester, and few of the population would care to risk the long, dark, crumbling Station Approach Road on a winter evening. It would have been pleasant if there had been others with him to give the place a human presence, as long as they were the right sort of people, of course. Company was not always companionship.

The last time he had been waiting on a lonely station at night he had been stranded with a couple who seemed to be holding each other up against a wall. He had turned his back on what he assumed was lovemaking, and dismissed them from his mind

[143]

so successfully that, wandering up and down a few minutes later, he suddenly found himself face to face with them. They were both men, looked drunk or drugged, and were watching him with an intensity of greed that had scared him. They had made him feel his age, his vulnerability, and, foolishly, with his hand, the place above his heart where his wallet was buttoned into the inside pocket of his obviously expensive suit. Luckily his train had arrived seconds later, and saved him from the mugging he had been sure he was about to get.

He looked at his watch again and was sorry to see that only four minutes had passed since he had last referred to it. He yawned. His neck was stiff, so he waggled it from side to side.

As he did so, he caught a movement at the far end of the platform, at the down-line end. A dark, rectangular shape opened out of a wall against the liquid light. It wavered, and faded away at once. He assumed a door had been swiftly opened and shut; or had it? Perhaps it had been opened all the way, flat against the wall. He squirmed round in his seat, took off his rain-misted glasses to wipe them, and screwed up his eyes to see as best he could.

For some moments there was no further movement, and he was just replacing his spectacles onto his nose and settling back again, when he caught a glimpse of something, a single motion, down where he thought the door had opened. He could see more clearly now, and thought he must have been right about the door, as a shape like the top half of a human torso, the outline of a head, one shoulder, and part of the second, now protruded out of the wall, some three feet from the ground.

The form was silhouetted against the light from a lamp situated immediately behind and above it. Because of the position of this light it was not possible to determine any features on the face of the individual, but he was sure that it was turned towards him, as he felt himself stared at.

[144]

Or even glared at, he corrected himself uncomfortably, as he sensed that he was subject to a most intense scrutiny.

'Why doesn't the beggar move?' he thought, 'and why is he standing like that, as though he were peering round from behind a tree?'

He found himself staring back with his chin jutting out and his mouth gaping childishly open. He turned to look behind him to check that some other person had not silently joined him on the platform, and could therefore be the object of his distant observer's attention, but the end of the platform was as empty as it had been when he had stepped onto it. It stretched away, quite desolate, into the murky dark.

'Well, you'll know me when you see me again,' he thought, aware that his own face was lit by a light some five feet ahead of him.

Then, for what seemed a long time, but was probably less that a minute, the two of them watched each other.

Mr Rudge was beginning to think that he had been mistaken, and that what he had taken for a head and shoulders was in fact some broken thing, part of a door that had blown open in the wind and become stuck, when the figure moved.

It stepped out.

It took one stride, quick and purposeful, giving him a glimpse of a pale face and shining black hair, then turned towards him and stood quite motionless again.

Mr Rudge was convinced that he had been—identified.

The figure was that of a tall man, above six foot. He stood with his legs apart, and seemed to have his arms folded across his chest. He wore, as far as Mr Rudge was able to make out, some kind of cape slung over his shoulders.

Mr Rudge began to recall that the building from which the door had opened, and from which the figure had emerged, was the old, original part of the station. That section had long ago been vandalized and declared unsafe. It had been due for demolition, but enough local people and lovers of railway history had objected to this to save the basic structure. As a compromise, to preserve what was left, all the doors and windows had been bricked up. The building was sealed tight.

Mr Rudge stood up and walked a little way down the platform towards the figure. He wanted to say something, if only to hear the sound of his own voice.

When he did speak, he was surprised to hear himself say, in a high, almost pleading voice, 'Is everything alright? Can I help you at all?'

He stood and waited for some response. None came.

The two of them stared at each other in static silence until a distant clanking rumble announced that the train Mr Rudge was waiting for was about to arrive. Behind the dark figure, the lights of the driver's cabin swung round a curve in the line, and the little toy-like train began to slow down as it approached the platform.

'Now I shall get a look at you,' muttered Mr Rudge, whose gaze had momentarily been diverted by the train.

But the man, whoever he was, moved again.

He stepped back against the wall and, as he did so, his arms and legs appeared to fold into himself, like blades returning to the handle of a knife. Mr Rudge blinked, and the figure was gone. A shadow remained against the wall, fading in the light from the windows of the train.

Mr Rudge snatched up his shopping bags and ran down the length of the station. When he got to the place where the figure had disappeared, something of the shadow still hung upon the wall. Sure enough, it suggested, in vague outline, the figure he had seen; but nothing stood near to cast such a shadow.

He reached out to touch the darkness against the wall as, behind him, the doors of the train slid open, and a tiny quantity of passengers disembarked.

The wall felt just as a wall should.

Confused, Mr Rudge took a few steps backward. Close to him

a peevish child complained to its parents, saying it was tired, and begging to be carried. Its father growled a 'No.'

Hardly able to take his eyes off the dark place on the wall, Mr Rudge backed towards the carriage closest to him, sidled through one of the doors, and tumbled into a seat.

There was plenty of room on the train. He sank back, clutching his bags on his lap, and pressed his face against the grimy window to look out.

He saw the back of someone—a late arrival, perhaps?—dashing for the carriage in front of his.

He wondered if the doors had closed in time to shut whoever it was out.

He hoped they had; but feared they had not.

Mr Rudge used the time the train took to haul itself up the long, steep incline towards Buxton to try to reconnect with normalcy, or was it reality?

His bags of shopping had received a bashing as he had stumbled into the train. To occupy his mind, he checked the contents of each. The fact that one of the sparsely populated yet costly boxes of chocolates that he had purchased for his family was badly dented was no catastrophe, and he was much relieved to see that the two bottles of Laphroaig Malt, one of which was his present to himself, were undamaged. However, the plastic bag containing these items had begun to split. He stood up and began transferring its contents to the pockets of his overcoat. Not everything would fit, so he had to juggle some of the gifts from bag to bag.

Doing this in his highly nervous state was perplexing. He put one bag in the aisle for a moment, satisified that it was as full as he could get it, and at once kicked it over. Bending down to retrieve it, he became aware of eyes upon him. Not surprising, considering all the fuss he was making, but whose eyes were they?

He turned his attention to the other occupants of the carriage.

[147]

A few seats away a bloated, pink-faced man with wild corkscrews of yellow hair blinked slowly back at him from under drink-weighted lids. Beyond him sneered a small tribe of adolescents in outfits of cake-icing pinks and greens. One of them, hairless as a baby rat, made a gesture at him with his finger that the others at once copied. Its significance escaped Mr Rudge, who looked away at a figure close to them.

All he could see of this passenger was his dark hair above the back of his seat. He was lolling against the window, and something about him, perhaps only the fact that he was obviously a tall man, made Mr Rudge uneasy. He tried to manoeuvre himself into a position from which he could get sight of the man's reflection in the window, and must have made himself look absurd in doing so, as the teenagers began to laugh aloud at him. This caused the tall man to turn to see what the noise was about.

The pasty, gaunt face that twisted towards him made Mr Rudge's heart skip once, before he recognized it to be that of a man whom he had seen about on the streets of Buxton for years. He nodded in embarrassed recognition, and hastily sat down again, satisfied that, if his fellow passengers were not the most attractive examples of humanity, they were at least that human.

With that thought, his mind returned to the consideration of what he had seen, or thought he had seen, back at the station. Somewhere inside him was an urge to walk into the next carriage, perhaps under the pretext of searching for the toilet, just to reassure himself about who might be travelling there, but it was an urge he found he was easily able to resist. Instead, he turned his attention to what he would do when he got to Buxton, assuming that whoever it was who may have got on with him happened to be heading for the same destination.

Being a methodical man, Mr Rudge began to devise a stratagem, in case such a situation should arise.

He decided he would be first off the train at Buxton Station. To put his mind at rest he would wait on the platform until all the other passengers had disembarked, and he was satisfied that the train was empty. Then, although it was less than a ten minute walk to his flat, he would ring for a taxi to take him home.

When the train was half a mile from Buxton Mr Rudge rose up, with his bags and his bulging pockets, and placed himself at the centre of the sliding doors. He was somewhat shamefaced about his fears by now, but determined to proceed with his plan. Nevertheless, as the train drew to a halt, he was nervous; his teeth were dry, and his tongue tasted of iron.

He pressed through the doors the instant they opened.

As his feet touched the platform, out of the corner of his eye, he noticed that the doors of the carriage in front of him were still moving apart. He planned to stand by the station's only exit, and made towards it as, behind him, other passengers tumbled out into the damp night air.

When he had almost reached the exit a long shape strode past him very quickly. Like a shadow in the lights of a moving car, it rose and fell in one smooth, swift motion, and passed out of sight through the exit door.

Baffled at that moment, Mr Rudge forgot his plan. He hurried after the figure.

He passed into the waiting room where a guard lurked, intending to collect tickets. The man was staring out into the car-park at the front of the station, looking uneasy, dismayed.

Mr Rudge knew that he could have passed through without showing his ticket, and was tempted to do so, but a lifetime of orderly conduct could not be denied. This transaction took precious seconds. As he left the station he saw a figure moving away beyond the road outside, on the far side of the pedestrian crossing.

The crossing light was red. He waited while cars slid by on the slick velvet tarmac, and jabbed at the button to get the green man walking.

He noticed that it was raining harder. His glasses were mottled with large drops, warping his vision.

To his right, squatting on its hill, the vast citadel that was the Palace Hotel hunched its padded shoulders against the wind and blinked down at the town through dozens of lighted windows. Ahead of him and to his left, a lumination which had no single source hung low over Spring Gardens, the main shopping centre, open late that night for the pre-Christmas rush. Hundreds of spots of light from the outer residential districts encircled him on the hills that surrounded the town. Previously he had found this sight a comfort; it had pleased him to be part of a small community that could be taken in with one circular gaze, but tonight he felt somehow engulfed by it all. He felt that he had walked into something inexplicable, and that he had no alternative but to go in deeper.

He crossed the road and hurried down the slope towards the town.

It was almost nine o'clock and the shops were beginning to close. Few people remained to brave the weather. By the taxi rank and phone booths a large Christmas tree, scantily decorated with cheerless lights, drooped its arms under the weight of rain. Next to it a crib stood empty and unblessed due to the depredations of hooligans who had run off with the statues of the Holy Family and their guests. The ululation of seasonal pop music nagged away out in the darkness.

His way home led him past The Crescent, Buxton's major claim to architectural distinction, and he took advantage of the sheltered promenade at the front of the building to get out of the rain. The many small arches, dimly lit, the boarded-up windows along the first floor of the empty, decaying building, made Mr Rudge, who had once been taken to an exhibition of Di Chirico's work, feel that he had walked into one of that painter's sinister, vacant, echoing canvases.

Twice, through the arches curving to the left ahead of him, he thought—no, he was sure—he saw the dark figure hurrying along. The fact that he, Mr Rudge, now found himself trailing behind whoever it was that he had first feared had been following him, was particularly distasteful to him. The figure could almost have been leading him back to his own home!

He was reluctant to consider the implications of this, indeed he felt a general dullness throughout his system, a numbness blanketing a core feeling of dread that had come to occupy the base of his consciousness.

As he was passing the 'Old Hall Hotel', his favourite local eating and drinking place, he had what was almost his last glimpse of the figure that he had first seen less than forty minutes earlier, on the otherwise empty station. He had just come in sight of the front of his flat, on the first floor of a block that overlooked the parklands of the Pavilion Gardens, when he clearly saw the tall, caped form, now almost familiar, crossing the road ahead of him.

It was running.

It took the road that forked behind the buildings along the Broadwalk, the pedestrianized lane that fronted Mr Rudge's flat. That was the road that he would have to take, as the only entrance to the flat was from the rear.

Feeling in his pocket for his key, Mr Rudge went in pursuit.

The door of his flat was safely locked when he reached it. He had feared that it would not be. He had a vision of it hanging open wide, perhaps smashed off its hinges.

Inside all was quiet.

He cautiously ventured through into his kitchen and switched on his electric kettle. He took off his soaked overcoat, took the gifts out of its pockets, and draped it over the back of a chair. He pulled a clean towel out of a drawer and set about drying his face and what little remained of his hair. He put his bags in a corner, intending to deal with them later, and made a pot of tea. His hands were shaking so he made his drink in a mug with a big handle.

He discovered he had a headache and took two paracetamol.

After half an hour he felt better, but very tired. Despite the fact that his mind was full of the events of the evening, he decided he would go to bed and try to sleep. He picked up his overcoat, and went into the hallway to hang it on its customary peg.

Someone had beaten him to it.

In the place where he always hung his coat was a dark cape that did not belong to him. It looked old. Its surface shone with damp. It had a drawstring of faded yellow cord around the neck.

It was some time before Mr Rudge could bring himself to go near it. He watched it intently, as though he expected it to move, to jump down, or run off. It did none of these things. When at last he did come close to it, he noticed at once its smell. It stank of soot, hot coal, and steam. And age; it smelled of old sweat and decay.

It was somehow both disgusting and deeply intimidating.

Close up, he could see the collar of the cape was frayed with use. Otherwise, it was undamaged except for a number of sharp tears, or cuts, a few inches long on the left front.

Mr Rudge, who had fought in a war, had never felt panic charge up inside him with such force before. Panic and loathing!

He absent-mindedly touched his lips with a finger that had touched the cape, in a gesture of bewilderment, and there was a flavour like acid on his tongue. He spat grossly, and scrubbed his mouth with his sleeve, to be rid of the taste.

Angry now, he stepped over to a large brass pot where he kept his collection of walking sticks and a few umbrellas. He selected his biggest stick and swiped out at the cape as though he was being assailed by it. He hit it again and again. The cape swung to and fro until at last it fell off the peg. Mr Rudge gave a grunt of satisfaction, kicked it into a ball, then kicked the ball away down the hall towards the door. He leaned against the wall, gasping from the violence he had done, and watched the cape, waiting for something to happen.

He waited a long time, and nothing did happen. Satisifed, he hung his coat on the peg, and went back into the kitchen.

Thirsty, he made more tea. He drank two cups slowly, washed his mug, and went back through the hallway towards his bedroom.

In the hall, the cape was back on the peg and his coat, torn to shreds where it had been pulled down, lay on the floor.

Mr Rudge snatched the cape and ran with it into the kitchen. Holding it firmly under his arms, he found a roll of plastic sacks and tore one off. He thrust the cape inside the sack with the vigour of a man trying to drown a large animal. He tied a tight knot at the top of the bag and flung it to the ground. He went out of the kitchen and into his study, closing the door behind him. He waited there for almost an hour, then went back into the kitchen.

To his surprise, the bag was just as he had left it.

He looked out into the hallway. The coat also lay where he had left it, and the peg was empty.

Feeling almost cheerful, Mr Rudge returned to the kitchen and prodded the bin bag with his foot. He could feel the cape inside it. For some reason he felt the need to put a weight on the bag. He found a wooden box, placed it on the bag, and filled it with the heaviest items he could find.

Then he went to bed and tried to sleep with the light on.

Next morning, tired and timorous after his nightmarish night, Mr Rudge stepped gingerly into his kitchen at just after nine o'clock.

The box had not been moved and the plastic sack remained under it. He knew the cape was still inside the bag because the shape of its surface had not changed.

There were tears in his eyes as he made his breakfast. He was scared that he was going mad or senile.

He forced fried food into himself, in spite of a total lack of appetite, then imagined that he felt much better. He left the bin bag under the box and kept himself busy all day with various non-urgent tasks about the flat. At nine in the evening he sat down in front of the TV and drank two inches of whisky from a bottle of Bells; not his favourite, but cheaper than broaching the Laphroaig.

Then, when his dander was well and truly up, as he would have phrased it, he went into the kitchen and hauled the box off the black plastic bag. He lifted the bag, feeling with satisfaction the weight of the cape inside, and slung it into a cupboard under the stairs that led to the flat above his.

Then he went to bed and slept for twelve hours.

During the next couple of days Mr Rudge found it difficult to settle to anything but, on the third morning, he woke up feeling more like his old, calm, clear and capable self.

With a shock he realised that it was less than a week to Christmas.

He spent the morning wrapping presents and signing and addressing cards. After a trip to the Post Office to send them off, he returned to the flat with the determination to dig out his box of Christmas decorations. It was time to brighten things up a bit.

Though he never did much about Christmas, he had discovered that it was better, since his wife had died and he had been living alone, to make some concessions to the festive season, rather than try to turn his back and ignore it. It was his habit on Christmas Day to eat a turkey dinner at the Old Hall Hotel then, if the weather permitted, to take a turn or two round the Pavilion Gardens. He would then return to his flat and, sitting under strips and chains of coloured paper, and with a bottle of Malt by his side, he would read or watch television until his eyes drooped shut. It was the only sensible way to deal with Christmas.

On Boxing Day he would visit his daughter in Derby, staying overnight and returning next day. He never lingered longer. His daughter's toleration of him only lasted twenty-four hours at most.

*

The Christmas decorations he kept on a shelf at the back of the cupboard under the stairs.

He opened the door and paused for some seconds before switching on the light.

The air smelt stale in there.

'No,' he thought, poking his head inside, 'it smells downright unpleasant; it stinks!'

He had noticed a smell in the flat for a few days now.

He flicked the switch on. The low-powered bulb lit with a pallid light tidy piles of bags and boxes and orderly shelves stacked with household equipment and cleaning materials. The only object in there that had not been placed with neat precision was the plastic bag containing the cape. It sprawled at an angle up against a wall. Mr Rudge, who had not visited the cupboard since he had flung it there, noticed that it had become—fuller. The bag now looked as though it had something in it other than, or as well as, the cape, because it was bulging where it had once been flat.

Mr Rudge decided to throw it out.

He reached down, grabbed the knotted part, and gave a tug. It was surprisingly heavy; very heavy, in fact. He felt the plastic stretch as he pulled it.

'God, don't let it burst!' he thought, and let go of it.

He stood considering the situation for some moments. He thought of untying the knot to look inside the bag but dismissed the idea because he was sure the smell was coming from inside there, and he thought it would be best to leave it undisturbed. He bent down closer and gave it a prod with the tip of a tin of wax spray polish. It was only a gentle prod, but something hard inside fell away, or did it move away? It almost looked as though something had—retreated.

He stood up and, as he did so, whatever he had moved swiftly slid back in place. There was a soft sound in the cupboard, the kind of noise an old, sick dog might make when it was dreaming. It could only have come from inside the sack.

[155]

Mr Rudge flicked off the light and slammed the door shut with a speed remarkable for a man his age.

It was hours before he remembered why he had gone to the cupboard. Then he decided he would do without Christmas decorations for once that year.

The incident in the cupboard brought back thoughts about his homeward journey three days previously, which he was just beginning to hope he had put at the back of his mind for ever. Now, he had to confront them.

He sat in the classic posture of a deeply troubled man, with his elbows on his knees and his head in his hands, and went over and over the events that had occurred while he had been waiting on the station and, after that, when he had returned home.

Particularly he had in mind the image of the figure he had seen then, of the man in the cape. Memories began to stir, fugitive, fragmentary, and trivial, of something he had seen or done, perhaps years ago, that had some connection with the figure. He remembered how quickly the shape of it had become almost familiar to him that night, and he began to think that somewhere, somehow, he had seen the figure before. Then, for no apparent reason, his mind filled with reminiscences of his working life.

He had been a junior school teacher until he had retired at sixty, nine years before. Out of a haze of general impressions of that time, he began to recall some of the work he had so enthusiastically done. He had been a very good teacher, and it had been a pleasure for him to organize extracurricular activities and projects for the children in his classes, because he had the knack of stirring their interest, and because they responded so well, and produced sometimes quite remarkable work for him. Some of the projects had unearthed facts and information of such high quality he had thought them worth preserving and even, in some cases, publishing, if only in a very small, limited way. He had never actually got round to this, but he still kept a lot of work from those years, meaning to take a look at it again someday. He had piles of such stuff in his little study.

Then he remembered a particular project; one he had set the older children in the top form.

It had been called, not very excitingly, 'The Story of my Home'.

He had asked his pupils to research back as far as they could go to discover what they could about the places where they lived. Some of them, with the aid of their mothers and fathers, aunts and uncles, came up with some astonishing facts, amounting almost to family histories. To set an example of what he hoped to achieve from the project, he had compiled a history of his own home; the flat he now occupied, but had then been living in for little more than a year.

Suddenly, disturbed by some foreboding, Mr Rudge jumped up.

He went into his study and began sifting through boxes of files. It took some finding, but at last he had it; a dingy green folder, faded across the top by sunlight, and stuffed full to bursting.

The photographs he wanted were close to the top, in the opening section of the project. They were both of the same man; Mr Rudge remembered his name as he lifted them out; George Nathan-Dyson, Architect and Engineer. A 'Great Man' of the Victorian period. He had designed and built a huge range of buildings in his brief life, but he was in Mr Rudge's file because he had built the house where he, Mr Rudge, now lived. Nathan-Dyson had put the place up with his own money and had lived in the very same apartment that Mr Rudge had moved into over one hundred years later. He had lived there until the time of his death.

The first photograph had been taken at an extensive building site, at the early, excavational stage of the work. Men with shovels toiled in deep mud in the background while, in the left foreground, others hauled cumbersome equipment into place. A little right of centre of the picture, also in the foreground, a tall, imperious, youngish looking man was watching the work in progress. He stood with his legs apart, with one hand on his hip while the other, clenched into a fist, hung by his side. The photographer had got the focus slightly wrong, bringing out more detail in the middle distance than in the foreground so the central figure's features were indistinct, but there was no mistaking his body language; his posture was quite unambiguous. Here was an arrogant, egotistical, merciless man who would have his own way, no matter what. Here was George Nathan-Dyson.

Mr Rudge studied the picture for a long time. He noted that Nathan-Dyson wore the tight, tapered trousers of the period and that he wore a cape over his shoulders. Also, the picture was not so blurred that Mr Rudge could not, with the aid of a magnifying glass, make out the loops of a pale cord tied under the man's chin to hold the cape in place.

The other picture was a formal portrait of Nathan-Dyson taken at home in his study. This was not the small room that Mr Rudge called his study, but the larger one next to it.

At first glance, the picture was of little interest. Nathan-Dyson, his pose as wooden as the chair he sat in, stared at the photographer and, down the years, at Mr Rudge, with an expression of tight lipped, self-satisfied contempt.

He was surrounded by tables almost invisible under masses of bric-a-brac. Glass-fronted cases, full of more of the same, stood in the background. To Mr Rudge it looked as though anyone who took two steps in any direction would send dozens of ornaments and artifacts tumbling. *He* certainly would have done. It was hard to imagine a man the size of Nathan-Dyson moving amongst them without accident, but the ability to do so was plainly one of his many skills and talents.

Mr Rudge was interested in the details of the room. It was fascinating to compare the way it had looked then to the way it was now. His eyes wandered from window to fireplace, from fireplace to door, and he noticed the door behind Nathan-Dyson was open. He could see out into the hall. A beam of light shone, as it still did on sunny days, through the window above the main door, making every detail of the hall's interior astonishingly clear.

'Some of those Victorian photographers produced remarkable results with what must have been quite primitive equipment', mused Mr Rudge, as he explored details revealed in the hall with his magnifying glass.

It was then he saw the cape, hanging on its peg.

It was clearly to be seen, even without the aid of the glass, hanging where he had found it a few days earlier, in the place where he had used to hang his own coat in recent years. The cape in the photograph was the one that he had stuffed into the plastic sack and hidden under the stairs; he knew it, and dark clouds, present at the back of his mind for days, began to roll forward.

He threw the photograph down and pushed the file away from him.

Facts he had forgotten about Nathan-Dyson, products of his researches into the life of the man, returned to Mr Rudge out of nowhere. Facts so unpleasant he had decided not to include them in a project that children would read.

Nathan-Dyson had a reputation for cruelty. His wife had left him after only two months of marriage and there had been a national scandal when she had revealed details of his treatment of her in court. Prostitutes had come forward to support her allegations against him, and to add their own. Mrs Nathan-Dyson got her divorce, and the man escaped prison by a hair's breadth.

Nathan-Dyson used and abused the people who worked for him without scruple. That had finally caused his downfall. The wife of a man who had died in an accident caused by Nathan-Dyson's negligence stabbed him in the heart. The woman had waited on a station for him to arrive by train. There was a story that he had pulled the knife out of his heart and stabbed the woman in the face and arms in the moments before he died.

The murder had taken place on the platform where Mr Rudge had been waiting a few nights earlier.

The clouds in Mr Rudge's mind stormed forwards thick and fast.

They became a tempest.

Two days later Mr Rudge visited the library to do some research.

He was dressed in a bizarre collection of sweaters, jackets, and scarves topped by an overcoat that hung in shreds about his shoulders. He had not shaved, his eyes were vivid red, and there was a ghastly smell about him.

He tottered as he walked, and he tumbled over a chair in the Local History section.

An almost empty bottle of expensive malt whisky slid from his pocket and smashed on the floor as he tried to get up.

To the librarian's question concerning any assistance she could provide, he gave no reply. He talked to himself, however. As he pulled rare and valuable volumes from the shelves and, after glancing at them, tossed them aside, he was heard to mutter the name Nathan-Dyson again and again. It was a name that the knowledgeable librarian recognized at once.

'We do have books on that subject,' she said, 'but not on the open shelves. If you'd like to take a chair and wait, I can get them for you.' She had no intention of doing this. She was going to call the police.

'Get what out?' stormed Mr Rudge. 'You won't get me out! That's what he wants to do, but he won't. He wants his old place back, that's what he's after, the bastard. And he's been dead all that time; all those years!'

A couple who knew Mr Rudge slightly, and were aghast at the state he was in, and who happened to be browsing in the library, stepped in to help. They took him by the arms and led him out to their car.

Surprisingly, he offered no resistance.

They drove him home.

They tried to get a social worker to look in on Mr Rudge. They described the conditions he was living in, the chaotic state of his flat, and how foul it smelt in there, but were told nobody would be available to visit him until after Christmas.

On the afternoon of Christmas Eve Mr Rudge, dressed in most of his clothing as he had been for his visit to the library (he kept all his windows open all the time now because of the smell, and it was well below freezing outside), drank the last drop of whisky he had in the house, lurched up out of his chair, and stumbled towards the cupboard under the stairs.

Because his fingers were very cold he had trouble with the catch on the door. When it did lift, and the door flew open, he flicked on the light switch with a jab of the side of his hand, and peered inside through watery eyes.

The big plastic bag was full now.

He had thought once that the cape might have been rotting away in there, and producing a gas. That would account for the swelling and the smell, but gasses cause things to swell like balloons. The bag was full of lumps and bumps and angles. Parts of it moved from time to time.

No, it wasn't gas.

Mr Rudge looked very sad as he reached out to untie the top of the sack. He sighed as his stiff fingers refused to do their business again, and the job was made even harder because pressure inside the bag had forced the knot tighter.

But, at last, it unravelled, and the top of the bag gaped open.

'Right,' said Mr Rudge, leaning forward to see inside. 'Let's have a look at you.'

And he did get one brief glimpse of a familiar face as the contents of the sack unfolded and extended around him, silently and swiftly.

He seemed to go a very long way in a very short time. When he got to the end of his journey, there was nothing there.

Nothing at all.

When her father did not turn up as expected on Boxing Day, and did not phone her with an excuse, Mr Rudge's daughter, who worried guiltily about him sometimes, called the Buxton police and asked them to check his flat.

The constable who was sent on the job noticed the open windows and went for a ladder.

He climbed through the window into the stinking rooms. After looking round, he reported his findings back to base.

'It's a bad one,' he said, in a shocked voice. 'There's a corpse, I think, in a jumbo bin bag. Been dead a while from the stench. Get a team round. As soon as you can. It's very nasty.'

When the police untied the knot at the top of the plastic sack they discovered Mr Rudge inside. He had been strangled by a yellow cord that was still around his neck. The police believed the cord had been taken from a cape that was discovered hanging on a peg in the hallway; an antique item.

The cape was taken away for use as evidence, but did not prove to be at all helpful in the hunt for the murderer.

The cape's owner was not much disturbed by his loss. He had no further use for it because, as the unfortunate couple who moved into the flat to replace Mr Rudge some weeks later were to discover, this time he was home to stay.

BILLY DROPS IN

Jill Drower

Jill Drower is the author of *Good Clean Fun—
The Story of Britain's First Holiday Camp*. She
divides her time between writing, training
teachers and looking after her two children.

'Well, well. If it isn't Billy Squirrel. What's the matter?
You going straight or something?'
'That's right.' Behind his scratchy false beard,
Billy's face was burning with rage, as crimson as his ill-fitting
costume. Then, almost inaudibly, he muttered, 'I ain't doing no
more bird. I ain't never goin' back in the stir.'
Constable Stammers had apparently not heard him, for he
needled on relentlessly. He nodded at the Santa's sack. 'I could
nab you for going equipped. Plenty of room for swag in there,
I'll bet.'
'I've been goin' straight, honest.' Billy's expression was now
desperate. Panic gripped him as he realized that Kershaw, the
floor walker, was well within earshot. That bastard Kershaw
kept going on about how Christmas was nothing but trouble.
He was always hovering around the grotto, eagle-eyed, waiting
for Billy to put a foot wrong.
It was not as though Billy even liked the job—all those runny

nosed little blighters. He'd wanted to box their ears, most of them.

Stammers was now moving out of the Toy Department, his son by his side. Even in civvies, he was unmistakeably a rozzer— unmistakeably out to get you.

It was 5.15 pm and the toy department of Holdrons was emptying. Billy moved into his grotto and came face to face with Kershaw. 'You've got a criminal record, haven't you?' He narrowed his eyes and gave Billy an I-always-knew-it stare. 'You and your war service. Where did you serve? In the glasshouse I suppose. Well, you're out! Collect your things and get your pay from the staff office, now!'

'I've been going straight, truly I have,' Billy pleaded. 'The kiddies love me. Please give me another chance.'

'How do I know you haven't already stolen our goods?'

'Honest, I haven't. Please give me a chance.'

Kershaw had already turned his back and was off to tell the assistant manager.

Billy slumped down into the seat of his ornately carved sleigh. A small hand tugged at his long red gown. He looked down at the child. 'Get bleedin' lost, we're closed' he snarled.

When Sarah had finished off the final stitches, she broke the cotton between her teeth. She held the finished article out to admire. It was a red and green quilted festive garland for the mantel shelf. She was a real sucker for Christmassy things. She had even threaded ribbon through home-baked biscuits to hang on the tree. This year they'd splashed out on a Caucasian fir instead of the usual spruce that dropped fistfuls of needles the moment you brought it inside. They'd hacked off the bottom branches and spent much of the afternoon trying to wedge it into an old enamel bucket with the help of some bricks.

Robert had gone upstairs to the attic to hunt around for the box of glass icicles. Sarah curled up on the sofa, admiring her handiwork. She saw herself as an Xmas-oholic. Why not? When they started a family she knew they'd never have time for all this cosiness.

This was her favourite room in the house. There was an elegant simplicity about it and a brightness, despite the under-sized leaded casement windows. It just felt quaint—no, not quaint, homely, that was the word—it was as if the room had trapped all the happy experiences of those who had been before and preserved them for future generations.

'Robert, You're taking your time up there', she called up through the bannisters as she went through to the kitchen to put the kettle on.

Kershaw had told Billy to collect his things and get out. As a parting V-sign, Billy had wrapped up the Santa's cloak in a copy of the Daily Sketch and tucked it under his jacket. 'You want me to nick something,' he thought, 'I'll be happy to oblige.'

Outside the staff entrance, Billy tore open his pay packet. It was a bitter blow. He checked the copperplate handwriting on the manilla envelope. Fifty-five shillings: they'd underpaid him by two days. He knew that if he went back in to complain, they'd only turf him out again. He started down the High Street towards the nearest Lyons Tea Shop.

The rain spat into his face adding to his bitterness and humiliation. 'What's the use? What's the bleedin' use if they don't want me to go straight?' At the kerbside a huddle of shoppers was boarding a double-decker. An impulse made him join them.

'On top only now,' the conductor rang twice and the bus shook its way towards Tooting.

Billy lit up a Woodbine and exhaled slowly. He stared through the smeary glass down at all the cheer that was not his. As a child, he had been the institution-grown lad gazing with envy at the fathers and sons flying kites on the common; he had been the ragamuffin staring through the sweet shop window at the children who had pocket money to spend, studying their

[165]

delicious indecision as they chose between bulls' eyes and gobstoppers. This was no different.

The rain had stopped and the evening was clear. Billy got off the bus at the first pub he saw. It wasn't until he was staring into his third pint of Ramrod and Special that his anger softened.

'I'll bleedin show 'em.' After another two pints he'd cheered up sufficiently to be able to face the hostile world outside.

Sarah managed to push the door open with her hip so that she didn't have to put the tray down. She placed the tea things on the occasional table and poured some Lapsang into two identical yule mugs.

'Where's he got to?' The decorations were in a neatly labelled cardboard box. How could he possibly miss them? But then he could never find his gloves, however many times she told him they were in the second drawer down.

Sarah helped herself to a Garibaldi biscuit.

They'd lived there three years now—she loved telling the story at dinner parties, how they were walking arm in arm and had come across this ruin of a place in Wisteria Drive, and had put an offer on it straight away. She'd say how it had shot up in value soon after they'd exchanged contracts (they could never afford it if it were on the market now). Then Robert would chip in with the story about the old lady who died of flu during that terrible winter after the war leaving a lawyer's dream of a will, which, once it had been deciphered read, 'And I leave the house to whichever of my daughters will look after it best.' The resulting litigation meant the house lay empty for seventeen years while the two sisters battled it out. The argument was only resolved by the death of the elder of the two in an accident involving a trolley bus. The triumphant younger sister had moved into Wisteria Drive and had survived a score more years.

The house—more of a folly than a proper building—was a cross between the gatehouse on a large estate and the cottage

Hansel and Gretel came across in the middle of the wood. Whoever dreamt this one up had more money than consistency of style, but this in itself gave the house an eclectic charm all its own. The sitting room had been overhauled at the turn of the century and been fitted out with a low frieze rail around the room, a window seat and an overmantel above the fireplace complete with display shelves and ornamental hinges.

As Sarah leant over for another Garibaldi, all the lights in the house went out.

Outside the pub, the temperature was down a couple of degrees. Above the entrance, the pub sign jerked frantically backwards and forwards. It read, 'The Green Man' and had obviously been done on the cheap as the lettering was crooked. Billy put on the crimson Santa's cloak to keep out the wind. It made him feel comfortable. He looked back over his shoulder at the sign. The green man looked more like a devil, jumping up and down with arms above his head, gleefully egging Billy on.

As people gazed from buses they now smiled at him as though he were suddenly likeable afterall. Passers-by no longer gave him sidelong suspicious glances but looked him full in the face. Someone even called out laughingly, 'Season's Greetings.'

Billy decided not to go straight back to his digs. Instead he turned a corner into a wide quiet avenue of detached houses. He was protected from suspicion by his rosy, Father Christmas glow.

A new cloud of bitterness settled on Billy as he walked along in the electric lamplight. He thought of how he'd fought for his King and country, and how he'd hardly been out of the army a week before that magistrate had banged him up. He'd done two stretches since the War. He missed his pals in the slammer. Just now he felt he wanted to be back there. Inside, he was respected by his mates—he kept them all entertained with stories of his break-ins. He knew everything there was to know about buildings and how to get into them. Because of his slight build, great agility and daring exploits, he had come to be known as Squirrel, Billy Squirrel.

He thought of Kershaw and Stammers. 'I'll bleeding show 'em.' He trudged on, stopping from time to time to have a quick gander at a window, or try a foot hold. 'Ay, ay.' What had stopped him in his tracks was a smallish detached house. More to the point, there were no lights on. 'Somebody's away for Christmas.' He stood under the street lamp studying it, looking for clues, trying to work out if the owners had money—there was no point in scarpering with a toffee tin full of farthings. No doubt about it, to have a place like this they had to be worth a bob or two. Billy Squirrel did a quick recce. Fold-over wooden shutters were firmly in position inside the drawing-room window. Around the back it was hard to see anything, but he found two windows, one too small and one out of reach. There was a drainpipe that didn't lead anywhere, and as far as he could work out, no coal holes. Then he saw it. He grinned: 'Blimey, no chimney pots.' He shinned up onto an extension and from there wobbled onto the slates, arms bent upwards, tightrope-walker style. When he reached it, he hugged the chimney stack like a long-lost friend, trying to keep his balance. His head was slowly clearing. Apart from a few loose bricks at the top, it was sound. He'd come across one of these chimney shafts before: it was a piece of cake.

'I'll bleedin' show 'em,' he said as he eased his way down into the chimney stack.

The lights came on again. Robert appeared at the door grinning. 'It was the fuse.'

He held out two fists for Sarah to choose.

'Which hand?' he then revealed the Christmas tree fairy.

'So you found them,' she smiled. 'Your tea's getting cold.'

'Yes Ma'am. Look it's all here: glass balls, glass stars, tinsel and Christmas tree lights in fully working order. And I've got a surprise. Look what I found in the loft.' He nipped out into the hall and staggered back hugging a grimy looking grate.

'Mind the floor—I've just hoovered. What is it, a Roman relic?'

Robert set it down in front of the fireplace and stood back to take a look. It definitely belonged. They had always said that the room was almost perfect, but that there was something missing. Here was the answer. At the heart of a home was the hearth. This was the finishing touch.

The fireplace had been fitted at the turn of the century with all the other 'modern' alterations. The grate itself was a free-standing basket, but it couldn't now be put in position because at some point the fireplace had been blocked up with a sheet of plywood. Robert was on his knees with his tool box, trying to dig the paint out of the screw heads. Sarah was at his side, running a scraper down the edges of the gloss-finished plywood.

'I can't believe it. The screws go into the fire surround. How could they do it? It's such a crime.'

'We'll have to fill them in and repaint'. Robert had put the screws in a neat pile, and was prizing the plywood forward. 'Move out of the way'.

The hearth behind was surrounded with plain green tiles. For a fraction of a second Sarah was disappointed. She had expected something prettier and grander. However, when the basket was in place she loved it immediately and wouldn't have had the fireplace look any different for all the world.

She hugged Robert; it was all so perfect.

The chimney shaft was about twenty-four inches by eighteen. Billy Squirrel manoeuvered his way down by pushing out against the walls and by using the tiniest crevices and cracks as footholds. He moved with the confidence and skill of a circus performer doing a star turn. When he wanted to stop and rest, he pushed his back against one wall and pushed his knees forward against the other, as if sitting comfortably in a high-backed chair.

By his reckoning he must be level with the ridge of the roof

[169]

by now. Just fifteen feet at most, and he'd be in that first floor bedroom.

'First floor,' he chuckled, 'Silverware, ladies watches, family jewels; second floor, bleedin' toy department. I'll show em.'

He continued. He'd thought the Santa's cloak would protect his clothes, but it kept riding up, slowing his progress considerably. He looked blearily up towards the rectangle of lamp-lit sky, wishing it would sit still, trying to work out the distance. He must be there by now. He was trying to focus his mind on the problem of the upstairs fireplace. He felt along the lines of mortar with his fingers, trying to find any irregularities or signs of bricking in. Nothing. The mortar bulged out between the lines of bricks like cream filling in a bun. The shoddy workmanship on the inside of the chimney made his job easier.

Billy Squirrel was deciding what to do next, resigned to moving back up the shaft. Then he thought of Stammers and Kershaw and he thought of his mates back at the stir. 'Go on, Squirrel, you show 'em.'

'Oh well, in for a penny, in for a pound,' and Billy Squirrel continued his downward shuffle.

The grate was now in place. It was a free-standing basket which fitted perfectly with the wide, welcoming look of the open hearth. Sarah put down the phone.

'They say we haven't got a hope of getting a sweep so near to Christmas. Shall we risk it?'

'Oh, come on, Sarah. What could possibly happen?'

'The chimney might catch fire.'

'Well then we'll just have to call the fire brigade.' Robert put his arms around Sarah, reassuringly, pleadingly, but she didn't need persuading. As one, they grabbed their jackets and made for the front door, slamming it as they left the house.

Within minutes they had pulled into the brightly lit forecourt of a petrol station. Outside the pay area, the plant racks were stacked with mounds of mistletoe and holly. Rows of Christmas

[170]

trees were in a line, trussed up in plastic netting ready for easy stowage on roof racks. Their branches were tied like arms, bound and forced upwards.

The couple found what they wanted and bought a bag of coalite, two bundles of split logs and a packet of firelighters.

They stopped off at the Green Man on the way home. The background whirring, clicking and chiming of the pinball and fruit machines made the place seem busy and cheerful.

Robert had his usual pint of Special and Sarah had a dry sherry. They were sharing a bag of crisps.

'That's the nicest Christmas present you could have got me,' Sarah was cooing.

'What, the bag of crisps?'

'No, silly, the grate. It makes the sitting room look so . . .'

'Baronial?'

'No, I was going to say cottagey, actually.'

They moved out into the cold night air. The pub sign was squeaking on its hinges.

Robert and Sarah were in high spirits. 'Come on, let's get back to that baronial cottage of ours.'

Billy Squirrel had descended another four or five yards. He knew he was near the sitting room now because he could feel a slight draught up his trouser leg. The space around him had narrowed considerably, but even so, a moment's inattention sent him slithering down a further eighteen inches. He pushed cautiously with his left foot, but the leather sole would not budge. He was trying to work out what it was that could have caught his shoe in this way. He wasn't concerned, just tired. His mind began to wander. He thought about prison life, how straightforward it was. He was now longing to be banged up again with his mates. It was almost as though he wanted to be caught.

Billy managed to pull himself free, but he lost his shoe in the process.

'Should have worn me bleedin' plimsoles.' His body was

[171]

twisted around now and as he straightened it back, he realized that he could no longer reach his hands down below his shoulders. Billy Squirrel was still cheerful. Any sense of alarm was dulled by the Ramrod and Special warming his insides. He let his head drop back and stared upwards, but there was no longer anything to focus on and no way of judging how far he'd come. The little pool of lit-up sky at the end of the tunnel was gone from sight.

Robert was prodding around with a straightened-out wire coat hanger.

'There's definitely something up there, but I can't quite get at it.'

They had swooped into the house with their smiles and their armfuls of fuel and had immediately set about building the fire. There was some disagreement about how this should be done but Robert, claiming to have the superior knowledge of an ex-scout, won the argument. Harriet had still been muttering about cheats as Robert held a lighted twist of newspaper to the little white firelighter blocks. They had both stood back, arm in arm, and watched the plume of smoke rise up, double back upon itself and then start to fill the room. Robert blamed the excess of smoke on the damp, split logs. They doused the fire with a cupful of water.

It was at this point that Sarah had fetched the coat hanger and she watched with agonizing impatience as Robert gingerly dug the implement up the flue.

'Let me have a go,' Sarah took hold of the coat hanger, trying not to snatch it in her excitement.

A vigorous jabbing and stabbing, combined with a circular movement brought down a shower of soot, and with it, a lace-up shoe.

Robert whistled.

'Well what do you know? Why on earth . . .?', but he was stopped mid-sentence by another shower of objects—a half-crown, a small brown manilla envelope, an open Woodbine packet and a piece of crimson woollen cloth. He picked up the envelope. Most of the writing was smudged, but he could make out the name 'William Squires' and the figure, '55 shillings.'

'Darling, this is pre-decimal currency. Why do you suppose . . .?'

Sarah hadn't heard a word. She was practically climbing up into the chimney to retrieve whatever was up there. She had dispensed with the coat hanger and was now working with her arm plunged shoulder-deep into the hole.

'I've found a trouser leg, she said, 'and there's a walking stick inside it.'

Robert pulled away the fire basket and moved in to take over from Sarah. 'Let me try.'

'Yes, I can feel the trouser leg,' Robert was now reaching in. 'Yes, and there's a sock at the end of it and a . . . Oh my God, it's not a walking stick—it's a leg bone. This is a corpse!'

A uniformed officer was first on the scene. 'I'm afraid you won't be using your sitting room for Christmas,' he apologized, 'I have to seal off the room until we can get someone onto this. It won't be top priority because they're not recent remains.'

Some days later, Scene of Crime officers arrived loaded down with equipment. They dropped lighting down the chimney shaft and took pictures from both above and below the partly mummified corpse. Neither they nor the pathologist seemed to share Sarah and Robert's sense of urgency about the case nor their pity for the victim.

The pathologist caught their worried stares as they hovered by the sitting room door. 'It's alright,' he said reassuringly, 'It wasn't a murder. We'll be finished shortly. You can have your sitting room back today.'

They attended the Coroner's Court at the end of January where they learned a little more about the poor man's fate. William Squires had died with his arms upstretched in the pose of a ballet dancer, mid-pirouette. This elongated body position, together with the fact that neither hands nor feet were bound indicated that the deceased had climbed into the chimney, and had subsequently become stuck. The struggling and reaching movements of the victim, had sent him down further and wedged him more firmly in place.

Photographs of the interior of the chimney showed distinct ridges and troughs some inches above the skeleton-hands, where soot and brickwork had been gouged out in channels. These, together with the scratched and abraded fingertip bones, in particular, the third and fourth phalanges, were consistent with several extremely violent last attempts to claw his way out of the shaft.

A trace on the man named William Squires had turned up nothing. If the brown manilla envelope had indeed belonged to the victim, then his name was William Squires and he had received a pay packet dated 22nd December 1950, from Holdron's, a department store which had long since closed. Nothing more was known about the deceased.

The Coroner recorded a verdict of 'Accidental Death'.

Billy Squirrel knew he was in for a long wait. In his heart of hearts he had known all along he'd end up back in the stir, but he hadn't imagined it would be quite so soon. When the family got back he'd call out, say he was a chimney sweep and how he'd got stuck. They'd never believe him, but he was resigned to going back inside. Inside was home. He wanted to go home. He missed the laughs with his pals.

If he let his right hand drop down it just about reached his top inside pocket. He fumbled for his Woodbines, drawing them carefully out, clasped between his thumb and forefinger. 'Funny bleedin' place to have a smoke,' he chuckled, but as he said this, he realized that his matches were in his trouser pocket. Billy Squirrel was still cocky. 'I'll show em. I'll bleedin' show 'em.'

SWEET CHIMING BELLS

Roger Johnson

A new story by one of Britain's best writers of supernatural fiction. Three of his stories have been included in the prestigious *Year's Best Horror* anthologies ('The Wall Painting', 1983; 'The Scarecrow', 1984; 'The Soldier', 1990), and 'Madeleine' appeared in *Best New Horror* (1992, as 'Love, Death and the Maiden').

'You were singing something!' Philippa Warren looked at me accusingly.

'Was I? Sorry.' No doubt most people find themselves humming or singing to themselves, often without being aware of it. I set down the tray of drinks.

'Something about bells,' she continued. George Cobbett raised his head and peered quizzically at us both from under bushy brows.

'Bells? Oh, right.' I thought for a moment. 'Yes. "Sweet bells, sweet chiming Christmas bells . . ." It's one of the Yorkshire carols.'

Philippa shivered, a reaction I hadn't expected. George and I looked curiously at her. After a second, she smiled, suddenly

[175]

and briefly. 'Sorry,' she said. 'It's just that there's a rather ironic aptness to it. Bells come into the story—oh, yes. And it all happened in Yorkshire . . .

'It isn't my story, I should add. In fact, I'm not going to tell you the full details, names and so forth; they aren't important. It's enough that a distant relative of mine, not long before the war, had moved with her husband to a small town in the West Riding of Yorkshire, where he'd been appointed assistant curate at the parish church.' Philippa sighed. 'They must have been very young, you know. At least, they were only recently married, and very much in love. This was his first appointment, and she had great hopes for him. He wasn't a Yorkshireman by birth, but his father's family had come from Scarborough, and that went some way to overcoming the local wariness of foreigners. The rest he had to achieve on his own, and it seems that he was doing very well, being an intelligent and genuinely good fellow. He'd thrown himself whole-heartedly into the life of the town, supporting the workers at the nearby coal-pit, proving himself very useful on the rugger field, and becoming an invaluable addition to the team of bell-ringers.

'His young wife was very proud of him, and only sorry that her own diffidence and shyness didn't allow her to make the sort of impression in the parish that he deserved. She felt, rightly or not, that the people regarded her with a sort of tolerant contempt. They'd been in the town for some nine months, and were looking forward to their first Christmas there, with rather mixed emotions. When it was nearly over, she wrote down the story as she saw it. I'll read it to you.'

Philippa took from her bag a red-covered exercise book, of the sort that we used at school. She took a drink from her glass of white wine, and then, opening the book to the first page, she began to read.

Christmas is, after all, the time of peace to all mankind, the time when all should see themselves as brothers and sisters. I

hoped that my Edward's popularity would ease the way for me
to be accepted, at this season of all the year, in to the enclosed
little community that was now our home. My intentions, I am
sure, were for the best, but I lacked the social ability to reach
out and touch these people. I was not one of them, though I
hoped desperately that in time I could be. My intentions, I say
again, were good, but I cannot now put from my mind the old
saw about the Road to Hell.

How shall I describe the town? It has that curious quality that
we sometimes find of combining the industrial and the rural,
seemingly without strain. In size, it would scarcely qualify as a
town were it situated in the south and east of the country—say,
in Essex, which is my own home—yet it is, so to speak, complete.
All the usual offices are there, including a small, sedate Town
Hall. The parish church, where Edward and his vicar had the
cure of souls, is a fine building, well kept and well appreciated by
its parishioners. There are also at least two flourishing non-
conformist chapels, belonging to the Methodists and to the Strict
Baptists. The people are fiercely loyal to each other and to the
town itself. I longed to show them that I too was capable of
loyalty, and—for my husband's sake—deserving of it.

As we often find in places where the Methodists are well
established, there is a grand tradition of singing. We had already
attended a number of recitals by the Choral Society, and it was
gratifying to see that men from our own church choir and
members of the Methodist congregation raised their voices
together, making one great and glorious 'joyful noise to God'.
Edward and I were eagerly looking forward to the services at
Christmas.

And then, of course, there were the church bells. Edward had
become an enthusiastic ringer while at the university, and his
superiors at theological college had by no means discouraged
him, though it was understood that his parish duties should
always take preference. The ringing, I remember him saying,
was an expression of praise to God. For some, it was their only

[177]

way of expressing praise; he must respect that, but he as a clergyman had greater means and higher duties. It is no slur upon his integrity to add that he delighted in the bells, and assisted in ringing the changes (as I think they call it) whenever his conscience would allow him.

The holy time approached. It was not a rich town, but the shopkeepers had made brave and festive work of decorating their premises, while the boughs of evergreen in the church were tasteful and somehow comforting in their reminder of my far-away childhood. I made a determined effort to appear less nervous than I felt when meeting the people of the town. It was so frustrating! They had a sort of friendly tolerance towards Mr Barnicott, the vicar, who was an elderly, benign, but rather unworldly old gentleman. Me they still seemed to treat with suspicion. Edward, however, inspired a clear enthusiasm. If only, I thought, I could break through my own reserve, then perhaps I could break through theirs. And so, as I have said, I put myself out to be cheerful and accessible, and it seemed to be having some effect. I refused to mope alone in our little house, but went out into the cold and brightly lit streets, into the shops, greeting the townsfolk by name, forcing myself to appear tranquil, and tranquilly wishing to all the compliments of the season.

It was worth the effort, for the initial suspicious looks mellowed, not perhaps to actual friendliness, but at least to something like the amused patience with which the vicar was treated.

It was particularly pleasing that I should at last attract something more wholesome than silent contempt from Mr Hartley, the captain of the bell ringers. He was a man in his fifties, with that quiet air of authority that the true leader has. A lifetime's work in the colliery had made and nearly broken him: he could have been taken for a man of seventy, bone-thin, but with a wiry strength in him that even Edward could not match. As leader of the ringers, he had achieved a position of honour, admired by all those in the town who were able to appreciate the strength and the delicacy of touch that the bells required. Edward liked and respected him, and I am sure that he in turn liked and respected Edward. There are, after all, few clergymen who truly appreciate the mystery of the belfry. At last, it seemed that he was prepared to like me, and for my husband's sake I was glad of it.

A few days before Christmas, I was permitted to climb the narrow stairs and watch the ringers at work. No doubt I am stupid, or perhaps just unmusical, but I could not even take in the intricacies of their art. I could only look, listen and admire, while my Edward and the others of the team, all under the quiet discipline of their captain, created the wonderful pattern of sound. After the method had been rung, Mr Hartley looked at me, apparently as stern as ever, then turned to Edward and said, 'Maybe the lass would care to see the bells themselves?'

I knew then that a small but significant breach had been made in the barrier. My dear husband looked at me, and there was such a wealth of proud love in that look I felt that Christmas itself could bring no greater joy. And so we mounted the sturdy old ladder and entered the bell chamber.

There are eight bells in the peal, huge creatures of bronze, their weight seeming to strain endlessly at the wooden beams from which they hung. I marvelled that mere human beings could manipulate such mighty things, taming and directing their strength in the praise of God. Ringing was over now, and the great bells were at rest, each hanging below its beam. Mr Hartley reached out a hand and gently stroked one of the bronze giants. 'Aye,' he said, 'near forty years I've rung in this tower, and these bells have been dear friends to me.

'Mind you,' he continued, fixing his intense eyes upon us, 'they demand respect as well as love. Oh, yes—you may smile, young fellow, but you're inexperienced yet, good as you are. I tell you both, you must treat the bells with respect, or they could turn against you. Still and all, they've been good friends to me.'

Very practical advice, no doubt, but it sounded to me like a warning not to meddle in things beyond our capabilities. Very well, I thought; you need have no fear of me. I like and admire the bells, but I do not understand them, and you may be sure that I shall not interfere with them. In an attempt to brighten the sudden gloom of the atmosphere, I asked Edward which of the bells did he ring?

He smiled, and placed his hand on one of them. 'Here she is,' he said. 'This is the other lady in my life. Her name is Honour.'

I was surprised. 'Do the bells have names, then?' I asked.

'Indeed they do, and these are all called after Christian virtues. Let me see if I can remember them all.' He thought for a moment, and then recited the list that I can still clearly recall: 'Faith, Hope and Charity; Patience, Obedience and Honour; Joy and Mercy. Those are the names in order, from the smallest bell, right up to the great tenor. It's a fine peal, Mr Hartley—a wonderful peal.'

The captain nodded approvingly, his thin face momentarily losing its dour expression. 'That it is,' he said, 'and old Mercy, well, she's about the finest tenor I've ever rung.' Abruptly, he took out his watch, glanced at it, and announced that it was time to go.

We descended once more to the ringers' chamber, and thence to the floor of the high tower, where he opened the big door and bustled us out into the churchyard. For a moment, he seemed to hesitate, and then, unexpectedly, he shook me by the hand, saying, 'You take good care of him, lass. He's one of the good ones. Well, I may not see you before the day, so I'll wish you a merry Christmas.'

Before I could recover my composure sufficiently to return the compliment, he had turned his back upon me and was saying earnestly to my husband, 'I hope you've managed to get the vicar's word to join us on Christmas Eve?'

'I think so,' said Edward. 'But you know how vague he can

be. He's still quite likely to demand my services elsewhere.' He smiled, ruefully it seemed, and added, 'After all, I am paid to be a priest and not a ringer.'

'Well, we'll see,' said Mr Hartley. And with that he left us.

It was not until Christmas Eve itself that a visit from Mr Hartley reminded me to ask what special event should call for my husband's presence in the bell tower that day. Edward looked rather sheepish, and said, 'Oh, it is just an old Christmas custom.' But Mr Hartley's bony hand was upon his shoulder, and the fervent eyes were darting sharply, now at Edward, now at me.

'Old custom?' said Mr Hartley, slowly. 'Aye, sir, it's a very old custom. We may believe that it's as old as Jesus Christ himself!'

Ignoring Edward's startled look, he continued. 'Ringing the Old Lad's Passing Bell—that's what it is, ma'am.'

'The Old—?' I looked helplessly at my husband.

'The Devil!' he said. 'It is believed that with the birth of our Lord, the Devil died. Or perhaps it was with the Harrowing of Hell—though in that case, they should toll the bell on Easter Saturday . . .' His voice tailed off, and there was an expression almost of guilty confusion on his face.

I did not understand. This seemed the merest nonsense to me. How could anyone look intelligently at mankind and yet maintain that the Devil was dead?

He made an effort to justify the matter. 'It is, after all, harmless, my dear. The tradition is that, upon Christmas Eve, the great tenor bell should be tolled the same number of strokes as there have been years since Christ was born. Further, the final note should come with the last stroke of twelve, to welcome in the great day.'

Mr Hartley's expression as he listened to my husband did not flicker by so much as a muscle. He had the look of almost feverish determination that we associate with the early Apostles. He spoke quietly and without fuss: 'Welcoming the day—well, that's a nice thought, but it's not the reason.' He turned to me, looking intently into my eyes, as if searching for signs of comprehension in them. 'You see, each stroke is another safe year. It must be the right number of strokes, exactly, and it must end at midnight or the Old Lad won't be held under any more. It doesn't matter whether you understand, ma'am, not really, but please understand that it is important to us.'

I looked at my husband, whose face showed clear signs of embarrassment—and well it might. He cleared his throat and said, 'It is just a custom, my dear, and quite harmless. The same sort of thing used to take place in numerous towns and villages before the Commonwealth, when the Puritan reformers abolished so many charming traditions. Why, even now, you know, there's a similar custom in Dewsbury.' There was a sort of desperate cheerfulness in his voice as he turned to the older man. 'Isn't that right, Mr Hartley?'

'Dewsbury? Aye, right. But in Dewsbury—' (he pronounced the name with some scorn) '—the tradition was revived only a century ago. There's not the same force, you see, because in this town we've never ceased. The Puritans would have got short shrift here if they'd tried to interfere.'

I shook my head in bewilderment. I thought of the great world outside, where the Four Horsemen ran riot, and I wondered again how any sane person could claim that the Devil was dead.

Before I could voice my thoughts, Edward spoke, brightly, as if an idea had just occurred to him: 'It can only be for good, you know. Remember that all the bells are named after the Christian virtues, and that the Devil's knell is sounded upon the tenor—Mercy. It must be good, surely to offer Mercy.'

Mercy to whom? I wondered.

'And to make assurance double sure,' he continued, 'I have just remembered. On one side of the bell's rim is inscribed the word Mercy, but on the other, done it seems rather earlier, is your own middle name—Ruth. And Ruth, as you know, means

[182]

Mercy. I shall think of you, my dear, while Mr Hartley is ringing "The Old Lad's Passing Bell".'

I gave up. The captain was looking meaningly at his watch, and had his hand on my husband's arm. 'Very well,' I said. 'Go and toll for the Old Lad. I shall be in bed and asleep, I am sure, long before you even start, while you are still ringing the changes. Goodnight, Mr Hartley, and a merry Christmas to you.'

The old man's expression relaxed, and he nodded courteously. My husband's face was stamped with relief as the two of them left the house. I closed the door quietly behind them, and made my way to the kitchen, where I intended to tire myself out completing arrangements for the holy day.

But I could not pull my mind away from what seemed to be the most futile and superstitious nonsense. A line from an old song came to me unbidden: 'Some say the Devil's dead . . .' 'Not true!' I said aloud. It was not, and sadly could not be true.

Almost unconsciously, I heard the bells sounding the method—Stedman, or Grandsire, or whatever it was—in its mathematic precision, and I found myself musing upon the names of the bells. It was right, of course, that they should be called after good things; no-one could object to Faith, Hope, Charity and the others. It pleased me to think that my dear husband should have been allocated the bell called Honour, because honour was the keystone of his life and career. But what of the great bell, the tenor, which bore the name of Mercy? God's mercy should indeed flow out over the town, like the sound of the bells, but should mere man presume to offer mercy to the Devil? No, it was too hard a problem for me to unravel. I was even unsure about Edward's idea that some pious benefactor had 'made assurance double sure' by inscribing the tenor bell with both names, Mercy and Ruth. It is true that my second Christian name is Ruth, but even though I am aware of its significance the name has never been one that I cared for. Still, each to his own, as the townsfolk would say.

But the Devil? Perhaps he had been staved away from this quiet, comfortable little town, but he still held sway in the world. The Devil dead? I had only to think of the suffering, the fighting, the disease and the poverty that seemed to over-run our little planet, and from which the holy time of Christmas offered such blessed relief, to know that the Devil was far from dead.

Aloud I said, 'You fools! You claim to keep evil at bay by ringing the church bells, but the Devil is alive—he is not dead, and in your hearts you know it!'

It is difficult to be accurate about what happened then. The very atmosphere seemed to change, to become electrically charged, as during a lightning storm, and I was aware suddenly that the single bell was striking, had been striking continuously, but now, for a moment, had faltered.

So, I thought, they are ringing the Old Lad's Passing Bell. Such foolishness! How could intelligent adults do such things? And one of them a minister of God! It made no sense.

Then I realized: the sound of the great bell, heard but unnoticed, had faltered. It was that very fact that had me aware of the monotonous tolling. Suddenly, I felt light-hearted and, I should say, light-headed. The thought came to me, smug and unbidden, that my own unheard protests had interrupted these men in their silly ritual.

I went to the window and looked out into the night, at the cold, bright stars shining in the infinite darkness, and I felt small and ashamed. After all, as my husband had said, it was a harmless custom, though to my mind dependent upon a blink-ered view of the world. And this was Christmas, the time above all when we can afford to indulge our loved ones. Let him enjoy himself.

In that mellow frame of mind, I made to prepare for bed, but was taken aback by sudden, insistent and frantic knocking upon our front door. Some call, no doubt, for my husband's good offices. Well, Edward would just have to forgo the rest of his time in the bell-tower; being the good-hearted fellow that he was, he would not resent it.

I vaguely recognized the man at the door as one of Mr Hartley's team of ringers, a strong, quiet fellow who earned his keep at a nearby dairy farm. His face, bereft of its usual ruddy and complacent expression, was now white and drawn, the scared eyes not daring to meet mine. The air once again seemed alive with electricity.

'Are you looking for my husband?' I asked, somehow knowing that it could not be so. The only reply was a gulp for breath, and I continued, fearing the truth, 'Isn't he with the ringers, in the church tower?'

My caller began to shake his head, then corrected himself and nodded, the frightened look never leaving him. Fear was upon us both, and I could not raise more words. He found voice at last, seeming to whimper as he spoke: 'You must come, ma'am—to the tower. It's your husband, ma'am. I can't explain—you'll see for yourself!'

What could have happened? I did not know and dared not think. All that came to my numb mind as we hurried across the graveyard to the church was the realization that above us the tenor bell, Mercy, was still tolling inexorably for 'the Old Lad'.

We reached the tower. The young man, in a fever of haste, wrenched open the great door. We hurried up the narrow, winding staircase to the ringing chamber.

Injury, havoc—whatever evils I might have imagined for my poor darling were both unrealized and surpassed. Mr Hartley, with great gentleness, raised the cloth that had been laid over Edward's body, and I saw that in death he looked at peace with himself and with God.

I did not faint, though it would have been a blessed relief to do so. Instead, it seems, I went temporarily mad. I remember nothing of the rest of that night; no, nor of Christmas Day, nor of the two following. On the fourth day, I woke as if from a normal sleep, to find a nurse seated placidly beside my bed. Ah,

I thought, I have been ill. But where is my husband? And then memory rushed back of the devastation of Christmas Eve.

The nurse looked me over, spoke a comforting platitude, and went to call for the doctor. That gentleman arrived quickly, and with him Mr Barnicott, the vicar, who for the moment merely took my hand in his and said nothing. I found his silent presence peculiarly comforting. The doctor's examination, more mental than physical, seemed to satisfy him, though the look of grave concern never left his face. Having assured himself that I was in capable hands, he made out a prescription for some tranquillizing drug, which he handed to the nurse, and then he left.

For the first time, Mr Barnicott spoke: 'How much do you know?' Not waiting for an answer, he turned to the nurse and said, 'Have you told her anything?'

She shook her head, and at last I found my own voice. 'I can speak for myself, and I must know all,' I said.

The old gentleman nodded. 'Yes,' he said. 'It is better that you should. But understand that I cannot tell you as a witness. I was in my own study, polishing my sermon for the Christmas morning service. Mr Hartley, I have no doubt, can give you a first-hand account. For myself, as I say, I was working at the Vicarage, with my ears half-tuned to the tolling of the great bell, wondering idly how the ringers could keep a tally on nearly two thousand strokes. Then the steady progress of the ringing stumbled. It was momentarily interrupted, but only momentarily. Almost immediately, it was taken up again.

'As you will have realized, it was your husband who was sounding the tenor bell. Mr Hartley told me that he had taken a liking to young Edward, and knowing him to be a fine ringer had decided upon this honour for him.'

My feelings may not easily be imagined; certainly, they cannot easily be described. I was at the same time proud for my dear husband of the esteem in which the ringers held him, sad that he could not enjoy the honour done him, and resentful that the same honour had taken him from me. I could not then fully appreciate my loss—indeed, I did not then know the full depth of it.

The vicar continued: 'Suddenly, so the others say, Edward stumbled, pulling clumsily at the rope, falling to the floor in an apparent faint. Mr Hartley's first thought, he admits, was for the bell. Being an expert ringer, he was able to retrieve the rope and continue sounding the old year's passing bell. I doubt that any who had not been listening closely would have noticed that briefest of interruptions.'

And yet I noticed it, I thought, and I had been unaware till then of the bells.

Mr Barnicott had not stopped. 'It was one of the others who knelt beside Edward and tried to rally him. It would have done no good whoever had attended to him, for the poor lad was already dead. Were you aware, my dear, that he had a weak heart?'

I shook my head, dumbly. I was aware of no such thing.

'Even so,' said the vicar, 'the doctor's examination plainly showed that he suffered a sudden and lethal heart attack.

'You were called, I know, to the ringing chamber, though I do think that perhaps the news might have been broken to you more gently. It must have been a most dreadful shock to you.'

A shock indeed, but not really a surprise; I had not realized that before.

He did not seem to expect me to speak, though he paused in his speech for a moment. His lips were pursed, and his fine brow furrowed. He sighed, and continued: 'You did not faint. Instead, and I cannot blame you, you—broke down.' (He was choosing his words, treading very carefully, not looking at me while he spoke.) 'When I arrived, a little before Doctor Lake, two of the ringers were holding you firmly seated upon the bench. You were struggling to reach the bell rope, perhaps seeing it as the instrument of your poor husband's death, and crying out—well—' (for the first time he seemed truly embarrassed. He paused, as if to draw his courage to him, then turned to look me

[187]

earnestly in the face.) 'You were crying out,' he continued, 'upon the Devil for mercy.'

There was no feeling of shame in me; it was as if he spoke of some other person. Instead, I felt a languorous, anaesthetic coldness in my breast. The vicar was a good man, a kind man, but he did not know everything. It was plain that the ringers had not told him the true meaning of that annual tolling of the great bell; not, I thought uncharitably, that he would have understood if they had told him. I do not think that my poor Edward had fully understood, and certainly I had not. How different things might have been otherwise!

'There is little else to tell,' said Mr Barnicott. 'You shortly became submissive, and allowed the doctor and me to lead you home. I arranged for you to have a nurse by you all the time, and we have both looked in upon you twice a day. The nurse was instructed to call us as soon as you recovered—and now you have recovered. Christmas is past, three days past, and a sad time it was.

'My dear, I have not told you how sorry I am at poor Edward's death, but I think you know that already. Besides, I believe—as I am sure you do—that he is in the safest keeping. We must give thought now to your future. You must rest and regain your strength, of course, and for as long as you need you are welcome to stay with Mrs Barnicott and me at the Vicarage. You will not, I suppose, wish to stay alone in this house.

'Well, I have told you all I know, all I can remember. Is there anything you wish to ask me—or anything you think you should tell me?'

No, there was nothing I should tell him. He was a good man, remote from the world. Let him remain so. There was something I should ask, however.

'It was Mr Hartley who showed me my husband's—showed me my husband, and yet you say that it was he who retrieved the bell rope. How could that be?'

He seemed curiously relieved, as if he had expected a different question. 'That is simply answered: having got the ringing back on course, he had delegated one of the others to continue.'

I had been unaware until then of the tension in my body; now I felt able at last to relax. The little town was safe again, and so was I while I remained there.

There was a pause, and I realized that the vicar was considering whether or not to tell me something further. He was a simple, gentle old man, and quite transparent. Eventually he spoke, as I knew he must: 'One curious thing. Hartley seemed particularly perturbed by something quite trivial. "We have lost count," he said—over and again. "We have lost count." As if it mattered!'

The coldness within me became an icy clamp, squeezing my heart. They had lost count! Mr Barnicott did not understand the significance of that simple fact, but at last—and too late, perhaps—I did. What had Mr Hartley said? 'It must be the right number of strokes exactly.' Just so. There was no safety here for me, nor for any other. It would have been good to accept the vicar's invitation, but I knew that danger lay that way. With what grace I could muster, I declined the offer. The decision had been made for me, and for the moment I must stay in the house that was now so empty without my husband's presence. There was no strength in me to weep, though there would be a time for tears. If I had no comfort now, at least there was company in the affectionate little form of Tabitha, our cat.

The vicar left, promising that he or his wife would call upon me each day, and that they would remember me in their prayers. I was glad of that, for if ever a soul stood in need of mercy, it was I. Compassion, mercy, ruth—I thought of the great soulless tenor bell whose pulling had strained my poor Edward's heart. Mercy was a scarce commodity, it seemed.

I dismissed the nurse as well, preferring for the moment to be alone, and in my solitude I wept. How long the fit was upon me I do not know, but at the last I felt emptied of all strength and emotion, with only a great weariness in me. I fed Tabitha, who had been well cared for by the nurse during my illness, and went to my lonely bed, where sleep came directly to me.

I was half woken at some early hour by Tabitha's mewling and the movement of the bedclothes as she tried to pull them off me. Too tired for movement; aware vaguely of the coldness outside the bed, I called sleepily to her to stop, which she did, and I drifted again into sleep, to a world of dreams that I could never afterward recall.

Only upon waking fully in grey daylight did I remember that before going to bed I had put the cat outside and closed the door behind her.

There was a sickness upon me, not of the body or the mind but of the soul. They had lost count. Mr Hartley's words came back to me; it would be a sad jest to say that they haunted me. The ringers had lost count! The town was no longer protected, and I above all was in danger, for I above all had been arrogant and foolish. I should leave, as soon as I could, for only then might both be safe.

I had neither family nor close friends upon whom I could impose. Besides, the proprieties demanded that I should stay at least until my husband's funeral was over. These things take time, and I must resign myself to that. In God alone could I confide, and it seemed that He had abandoned me to the Old Lad.

The days that followed were like a living dream. I try to recall detail, but all evades me; nothing is substantial. My nights were not my own, and I grew drawn and hollow-eyed for lack of rest. Again and again there came that tug at the bedclothes, and the pleading animal sound, until at last—whether consciously or not I do not know—I murmured an invitation. After that, something warm and momentarily comforting shared the nights with me, going some way toward assuaging my grievous loss.

The old couple at the Vicarage may have noticed some change or deterioration in me; except on one specific occasion, I cannot now remember if they said or did anything to indicate it. That was upon the day when I found just outside the kitchen door the sad little heap of fur and bones that had been my beloved Tabitha. Someone, it seemed, would brook no rivals, and that would be hard to forgive.

The captain of the ringers tended to avoid me, and perhaps that is to be expected, for he at least had the knowledge and the native shrewdness to realize what I had done and what I had become.

The day of the funeral came. Many compliments were paid to Edward's sweetness of character, his honesty and strength, his courage and intelligence. Many pitying looks were directed at me, but no help was offered. The day went as it had come, bringing nothing and leaving nothing. My husband was dead, and nothing remained of him. There would be no children now. It was as if he had never been.

At last, with what money I could raise, I was able to arrange to move away from the town and from the area. The chance came none too soon, for the new curate had already been appointed and was due to take over the house that I could no longer call mine.

I went first to Cheshire, where I took a post as secretary to a lady, but after some weeks we parted, 'by mutual agreement' as she said. After that, I tried my hand once more at teaching, near Northampton; there was something in the faces of the children, however—a calculating knowingness that no child should be capable of—that I was glad shortly to leave. So I have made my way by stages, as perhaps I had known that I would, back to my home county. It has been a curious experience on my progress to observe the demeanour of those I meet, and to gauge whether they realize that I do not travel alone.

Each morning I find myself almost surprised to wake, for sleep and I seem to be strangers these days. My nights bring little repose, but there are other things, and I usually find that there is an impress in the pillow beside my head.

Those strange events in Yorkshire—how pin-sharp some

aspects are in my memory, while others are all uncertain. Nearly a full year has passed, and soon Christmas will be upon us again. Will Mr Hartley again sound the Old Lad's Passing Bell, I wonder? I hope he does, that the town may still have protection. He need have no fear that the barriers are useless now, for whatever came through last year left the town with me and has been my companion ever since.

It is a tale of irony above all, and the greatest irony is the name of that bell, the great tenor. Mercy it is called—but mercy for whom, I ask? Mercy for whom?

Soon it will be Christmas, and my baby will be born.

Philippa closed the book, quietly but decisively, and put it down on the table in front of her. 'The poor creature was found dead a day or so before that next Christmas,' she said. 'The verdict was death by natural causes. The family found her book and tried to dispose of it, thinking it reflected on their sanity. Somehow—I don't know how—it survived, and my brother found it some months ago. There was no baby, and she wasn't pregnant.'

Philippa drank what was left of her wine, and looked pointedly at me.

'Uh-uh,' I said. 'This is George's round.'

The old man glared at me as if I had betrayed him, but eventually he took out his wallet and handed me a note, saying, 'I'll pay for 'em, but you can fetch 'em—and don't worry! We'll say nothing more about Philippa's story till you get back.'

He was as good as his word, though I could see when I returned with the drinks that there was a question demanding to be asked. Typically of George, though, he put it off until we were settled and he had his pipe going satisfactorily. At last, he took a swig from his glass of bitter and said bluntly, 'Look here, young woman! Just how true is this story? You'll forgive my asking, but you've refused to give us names, or even a date. So I repeat: is it true?'

Philippa waved a slim hand. 'The book at least is genuine,' she said, 'and you're welcome to look at it. As to the story, I have no doubt that the poor woman believed it. But no, I won't tell you her name.'

'Hm!' He was clearly dubious. 'Well, I suppose I could look this Barnicott up in Crockford. That should give a lead to the identity of the town . . .'

'You can if you want,' I said, 'but as it happens I know that town. It's grown a bit since the thirties, of course, but it hasn't changed that much. I was there a few years ago with a friend who's a bell-ringer; he showed me the church and the bells.

'The tradition is officially known as "tolling for the old year", much as Mr Barnicott knew it—or rather, it was called that. The Puritans didn't manage to silence the bells, but Adolf Hitler did: the custom wasn't continued after the war, though I understand that there's talk of reviving it now. No mention of the Devil, however. That bit seems to have been what you might call secret knowledge.'

I picked up my glass and drank, finding when I put it down that Philippa and George were both gazing expectantly at me. I looked as innocent as I could, but said nothing, though the question in their minds was obvious. Perhaps I was being rather hard on Philippa, but it's a rare situation when I know something that George doesn't.

At length, the old man lowered his bushy eyebrows, har-rumphed, and turned to Philippa. 'Will you ask him, my dear?' he said, in a tone that suggested that his patience was wearing thin.

'Very well,' she said. 'Roger, you told us that your friend had shown you the church bells. Was there anything strange about the tenor bell—could anyone tell you why it should have two names, Mercy and Ruth?'

'It's not usual, is it?' I said. 'George has probably guessed the answer, though: despite what your unfortunate relation was told, the bell has only one name. It's called Mercy. But also inscribed

[193]

on the flange is an appropriate reference to the Bible . . .'
George nodded grimly, and I saw understanding in Philippa's
eyes. I continued: 'Yes, to the book of Ruth. Rather worn, but
still legible, it says, if memory serves me rightly, "Ruth I, XVI".
You'd recognize it as the loyal words of Ruth to Naomi.'

'Very appropriate,' said Philippa.

'Appropriate and ironic,' I said. 'Almost the last entry the
young woman made in that book, you'll recall, was a comment
on the irony of the name Mercy. The real irony is in the biblical
text, because it contains the words of Ruth—go on, George.
You can quote more accurately than I can.'

He closed his eyes and appeared to be searching his memory,
but the words came fluently and precisely: '"Intreat me not to
leave thee, or to return from following after thee: for *whither
thou goest, I will go; and where thou lodgest, I will lodge.*"'

FANCY THAT!

Stephen Gallagher

A new story by the bestselling novelist Stephen Gallagher. In the past ten years he has produced an impressive number of acclaimed psychological horror novels: *Chimera* (recently dramatized as a four-part television series), *Follower*, *Valley of Lights*, *Oktober*, *Down River*, *Rain*, *The Boat House*, *Nightmare*, *With Angel* and *Red, Red Robin*.

I t was around five o'clock on Christmas Eve when the battered white van slowed at the sign. It slowed, but it didn't stop. Not until it was about a hundred yards further on down the road, which was about the distance that it seemed to take for inspiration to root itself with finality in the driver's mind. There he finally braked and seemed to hesitate for a moment. Then a single dirty-white reversing light came on at the rear of the vehicle, and it started to weave its way backwards.

'Fancy Rats for Sale', the sign had read. Handpainted on hardboard, and the board wired to the post at the end of a gateless driveway. The van overshot, the gears crashed, and then the van turned nose-in and bumped its way onto the drive.

The daylight was going now, all but gone. That's how it always was, at this time of the day and at this time of the year. People hurrying home in darkness, with a sense of the day's business not quite done. Wet ground, electric light. That vague excitement, attached to nothing specific.

And Christmas Eve, to sharpen it even more.

The house at the bottom of the downward-sloping driveway was a dull box of a bungalow, modern but by no means new. Behind it the land dropped away, down to a wood and a small reservoir whose surface caught and reflected the last hint of pearl in the sky. It was countryside, but it wasn't *good* country-side. This was high industrial country with pylons and silos, and a view of the nearby city laid out beyond it all like a big, sparkling map.

The driver got out. It hadn't snowed this end of the year, but it was damp and it was cold. He walked down to the house and rang the doorbell.

And waited.

The door opened with a faint, outward belch of warm air. Unpleasantly warm, and full of the wafted scent of stewing vegetables. There stood the householder, a middle-aged man in a dingy cardigan and carpet slippers. He cocked his head to one side, like a small dog looking for some hint of a biscuit.

'I saw your sign,' the visitor said. 'I've been working up on one of the farms and I never had the chance to get to the shops. I still need a Christmas present for my Lucy.'

'Oh, yes?' The man in the cardigan waited.

'So when I saw the sign on my way home, I thought . . . bingo.'

'You want to buy her a fancy rat?'

'I want to give her something different.'

'It's not like a bag of sweets, you know. These are living creatures.'

'She loves animals. She's had mice before. And a hamster, once. She loved the hamster. She'll love this when she sees it.'

[196]

The rat breeder stood there for a moment. As if studying the driver.

Then he said, 'Wait just a minute,' and disappeared back inside.

There was a piece of yellow curtain tacked against the glass on the inside of the door, probably for insulation as much as privacy. The driver could see nothing until the man re-emerged a couple of minutes later with a car coat drawn on over his house clothes. He hadn't changed out of his slippers. He'd a keyring with about half a dozen keys in his hand; padlock or deadlock keys, at a guess.

'We'll just have to go round the back,' he said, pulling the house door shut. He tested it with a shove before leading the way around to the side of the bungalow. The driver followed him. Their breath feathered in the cold air.

'Your Lucy,' the man said. 'How old is she?'

'Nine,' the driver said.

'Nine ought to be old enough,' the breeder said. And then, as they turned the corner, 'I've always reckoned that looking after a pet helps to develop a sense of responsibility.'

Around the back of the house, not visible from the road, stood a long, narrow garden. Filling most of the garden were two long, narrow sheds. They stood side by side, raised above the ground on brick pilings over concrete bases. They had the look of old chicken sheds, restored and re-roofed for habitation. The roofs had been covered with tarpaulin. The windows, of obscured glass, were protected by wire.

'There's an alarm on,' the breeder said. 'Just give me two seconds.'

Moments later, they were inside. There was light already, from a bathroom-style reflector. The driver had been expecting a smell. There *was* a smell, but it wasn't a particularly unpleasant one. It was like warm sawdust and musk. He closed the shed door behind him and looked around.

He'd been expecting lots of small cages in the style of a pet

[197]

shop but these were bigger, glass-sided tanks on two levels. There were pet rats in all of them. Some were rearing eagerly at the glass, others slept together in the corners in breathing, heaving masses. There were minks, cinnamons, silver fawns, hooded rats, and no more than two or three albinos. They'd been separated according to sex, about half a dozen to each of the pens.

'What line of work are you in?' said the breeder, moving down to the far end where a greenhouse heat-and-humidity unit stood. He bent to make an adjustment. In the nearest cage, a digging rat sprayed sawdust up onto the glass.

'I'm a plumber.'

'A plumber? You'll have seen a few wild rats in your time, then.'

'Not really. I don't do drains.'

'What, then?'

'Milking machines. I used to service the pumps in all the pubs up here when I was apprenticed to my uncle. But that's going back a bit.'

'Are you local?'

'I live in town.'

The visitor took a closer look into the nearest run, where the digging stopped and the digger turned to look at him with curiosity.

'Those are Agoutis,' the breeder said, turning from the humidifier after a tweak of the thermostat. 'They're almost the same colour as the wild brown, and that can put some people off. And those are all mature adults, as well. I could only fairly sell them as breeding stock. You want to be looking at a kitten if it's for a present.'

The visitor moved on to the next run.

'You know,' said the breeder, 'rats get a terrible press and it's completely undeserved. I've had women walk in here and take one look and scream.'

'Oh yeah?' the visitor said, looking at him with interest, but the breeder didn't follow it up. Not by talking about the women, anyway.

'Rats are very social animals,' he went on. 'The tame ones love to be handled and they keep themselves clean. They don't attack people, that's a myth. I mean, if you just lie there and look dead they'll have a go at you—just the nose and fingertips to start with, that kind of thing—but to be honest, if you're just going to lie there then you'd be fair game for any predator. Rats, or anything else. All you have to do is blow on rats and they'll run.'

The visitor was eyeing what appeared to be the bones of a Sunday roast, stripped almost clean in the corner of one cage.

'But they will eat anything and everything, including each other. All that gets left is the tips of their tails. Now, *that's* what you can call population control. Breed fast, eat anything, and die young. That's rats for you.'

As he was saying this, the breeder was lifting a gate in the top of one of the lower cages. He put his arm inside. A vari-coloured black and white quickly clambered into the palm of his hand and then up to his shoulder, where it disappeared under the collar of his coat and down into his shirt. It signalled its presence only moments later as a moving lump across his waistband as it tunnelled under his clothing.

'You don't mind when they do that?' the driver said.

'They'll all do it, given the chance. This one's my oldest. He's two and a half.' He undid a shirt button and fished the animal out. The rat sat hunkered on the palm of his hand, haunches overhanging the sides. Eyes bright, ears alert, the strong, down-covered question mark of a tail curled loosely over the breeder's wrist. The pale whiskers quivered, vibrant with the electricity of life.

The visitor searched for something complimentary that he could say.

'Huge pair of bollocks,' he offered.

'I know,' said the breeder. 'Personally, I wouldn't care to have

[199]

to drag 'em around. And they can be a bit of a spectacle. I'd suggest a doe for your particular purpose.'

'Can we pick one?' the visitor said. 'I'll have to be getting home.'

They quickly settled on a mink Irish kitten. 'Not too big,' the visitor said. 'She won't be able to handle anything too big.' The young rat was lithe and sleek and reckoned by both to be ideal for the purpose. She was eleven weeks old.

'Fine for anything except showing,' the breeder said. 'If you show her, those belly markings are going to let you down. That's taken into account in the price.'

The visitor looked, but hadn't got a clue what the breeder was talking about so said nothing.

'What about a cage?'

'I've got a cage.'

'A mouse cage won't do.'

'It's bigger than any of these.'

'Food? Bedding?'

'I don't think we'll need it.'

'I'll give you some to get you started, anyway. Just hold her for a minute.'

The visitor stood awkwardly with the warmth and weight of the rat in his hands as the breeder reached under one of the benches. Its fur was fine, like air-dried silk. From under the bench came a flat-folded box which, under slight pressure at the corners, sprang up into a fully-formed cardboard transport case with punched-out airholes. A couple of tugs and tucks, and it was rigid.

'Now, listen,' the breeder said, taking the animal from the visitor. 'If there's any problem, you come back with her. I don't look over anybody's shoulder, but I do take an interest. These are more than just pets to me. They're family. Do you understand that?'

'I understand,' the visitor said.

The breeder kissed the mink kitten rat on its head, between

the two shell ears, before letting her slide from his hand into the box. She went like an otter into water, and he closed the lid.

Money changed hands. The breeder said he'd throw in a little book, just a brochure really but with a few useful tips, but then he couldn't find one. The visitor said it didn't matter. He said he'd draw up some breed papers. Again, the visitor said it didn't matter.

As he was locking the door up behind them, the breeder said, 'I'm assuming that you'll clear all this with the mother. I wouldn't like to think there was going to be any awkwardness. Rats bring on strange emotions in people who don't know better.'

The visitor said, 'I haven't seen her mother in years. I wouldn't know where she is, these days.'

'So there's just the two of you?'

'That's why I need to be getting back.'

'Well,' said the breeder, sticking out his hand as if suddenly gripped by a surge of seasonal humanity, 'you have a really good Christmas.'

'You too,' said the visitor, shaking hands awkwardly around the livestock box. 'Sorry if I kept you from your dinner.'

Back at the van, he moved some of the crap out of the footwell on the passenger side to make room for the box. He wedged it securely so that it couldn't slide or tip over. He could hear the small animal shift around inside a couple of times, but mostly it stayed quiet.

It was properly dark, now. As he drove down from the hills and into town, the roads were more or less clear. McDonald's was the brightest light on the main street, outshining the nativity scene in the church foyer across the way by an order of magnitude. The church put out the same set of little plaster figures every year with some fresh straw and Christmas carols playing from a speaker around the back. One of the Three Kings must have been dropped and broken at some time, and had

[201]

been replaced by an Action Man in a velvet cloak and a crown shaped from a KitKat wrapper. He wasn't quite to the same scale, but nobody worried because neither were the animals. Townspeople would bring their children to gaze in wonder, and this would probably be the nearest they'd ever get to a church door until the day when they were carried through one. There was an alms box, and every morning the verger would open it up and clean out the cold fries that had been posted in throughout the previous evening.

The white van turned from the main street, out under the shadow of the viaduct and into that part of town where the houses were old and crammed together and only left standing, it seemed, because everyone had forgotten that these streets existed at all. The van stopped before a house at the end of a brick terrace. A few of the other houses in the row had strings of crossed lights or small Christmas trees showing in their windows, but many of them were Muslim households now and celebrated some other festival.

He entered, carrying the box.

'Lucy!' he called out, pushing the door shut behind him with his heel. 'I'm home.'

He set the box down in the hallway as he paused to hang up his coat. 'And guess what Daddy's brought you.'

Lifting the box again, he went through into the main room where the light was. He could feel the fancy rat scrabbling around nervously as the world shifted under her claws.

Lucy was waiting there. She looked as if she'd just woken up.

He set the box in front of her, and opened it. 'Look, Lucy,' he said. 'A fancy rat. A *fancy* rat. Nothing but the best for you.' And then he picked up the rodent by her tail in the way that the breeder had warned him not to, and held her where Lucy could see.

Lucy stared, and her face betrayed nothing.

Then he moved the stone off the lid which covered the aquarium tank, lifted the lid aside, and dropped the rat in beside where the big snake lay coiled. The rat dived over into the corner, and the snake didn't move.

But later, when the man was popping a few Mister Kipling's mince pies into the microwave, there was a slithering and a scuttling from the direction of the tank.

'Happy Christmas, Lucy,' he called from the kitchen, and he smiled indulgently.

More than just pets, but family.

There was a feeling that he could understand perfectly well.

TWENTY PENCE
WITH ENVELOPE
AND SEASONAL
GREETING

Terry Pratchett

Terry Pratchett (b. 1948) sold his first short story
'The Hades Business' to *Science Fantasy* magazine
at the age of 13, and his first children's book *The
Carpet People* was published in 1971. His fantastic
'Discworld' series of novels are a modern
publishing phenomenon, and several of his earlier
titles (notably *The Dark of the Sun, Strata, The
Colour of Magic*, in addition to *The Carpet People*)
are among the most sought-after and highly-prized
first editions of recent times.
This tale originally appeared in the Christmas
edition of *Time Out*, 16–30 December 1987.

From the *Bath and Wiltshire Herald*, December 24, 1843:

'CALNE—A Singular Mystery surrounds the disappearance to
the London Mail Coach on Tues last in a snowstorm of
considerable magnitude, the like of which has not been seen in
the memory of the oldest now living. It is thought that the
coachman, missing his way in the driving blizzard at Silbury,
took the horses off the road, perhaps to seek the shelter of a

Hedge or Rick, and became overwhelmed in the drifting. Search parties have been sent out and the coachman, who was found wandering in a state of severe anxiety in the snow, has been brought back to Bath . . .'

From the journal of Thos. Lunn, Doctor, of Chippenham, Wilts:

The world is but a tissue spread over the depths of Chaos. That which we call sanity is but a circle of firelight, and when I spoke to that poor mazed man downstairs he was several logs of a full blaze.

Even now, with my own more Natural fire drawn up and the study curtains shut again the Christmas chill, I shudder at the visions he imparted. Were it not for the solid evidence, which I have before me as I write, and which catches the firelight and sparkles so prettily, I could dismiss it as the mere ravings of a deranged mind. We have made him as comfortable as the ropes allow in my front room, but his cries punctuate this Christmas Eve like skulls in a flowerbed.

> *Is Father Christmas Coming/Or Is He Just Breathing Heavily?*
> *Lots of Stuffing This Christmas!!! Snugglebottom Ex Ex Ex!'*

There is a sound outside. Carol singers! Do they not realize the terrible, terrible risk? Yet if I were to throw open the window and warn them to quit the streets, how could I answer their most obvious question? For if I attempted to, I too would be thought mad also . . . But I must set down what he told me, in his moments of clear thought, before insanity claimed him for its own.

Let my readers make of them what they may.

His were the eyes of a man who had looked into Hell and had left behind something of himself. At times he was perfectly lucid, and complained about the ropes the searcher had put him in for fear that in his ravings he would hurt himself. At other times he tried to beat his head on the wall and ranted the slogans that had sent him mad.

[205]

'Twenty Pence, Plus Envelope and Seasonal Greeting!'

In between he told me . . .

Gateway to Hell

It had been a wild day, with the snow blowing off the Plain and turning the hills west of Silbury into one great white waste. At such times it is possible to miss the road, and he had got down off the box to lead the horses. Yet, despite what one may read in the papers, the snow was not impossibly deep on the hills, and had abated so that the sunset could be seen. Spirits were generally high, for the lights of Calne were visible and one and all looked forward to being off the freezing roads by darkness.

And then, as he tells it, there was a creaking noise and a flicker of shadow and the world changed or, he believes, they stepped from this world into another. And, ahead of them, there was a great square hole in the landscape.

He avers now that it was the gateway to Hell, and while it was not the Hell that Dante visited there is to my mind some internal evidence to suggest that his ignorant guess might be the truth. There was something a-glitter at the edge of the world and, when he examined the drifted snow, he found the same curious substance strewn haphazardly on the crest of each hummock. It appeared to be thin plates of silver, scattered so as to reflect the light in what would have been, in better circumstances, a pleasing manner.

The coachmen and several of the male passengers considered the situation. The sun was sinking fast into a western sky that was now a mess of livid red and purple tones, and to the east more snow threatened. Besides, it appeared to those who ventured a little back along the coach tracks, which were already being erased by the blowing snow, that the road had been well lost and a white wildness stretched all around.

At length, there appearing to be no alternative, several of

the party resolved to venture closer to the rectangle that obliterated the sky a score of yards away.

It was then that they saw for the first time the monster that appeared to be the guardian of the gateway, perched on a snow-covered log.

It was a giant Robin, several times larger than a Turkey. It watched them with malevolence in its beady eyes, and they feared greatly that it would attack, but it remained unmoving as they reached the rim, and peered out on a blur of colour. Warm air, tinted with tobacco smoke, was blowing into the world, and according to the coachman they could hear strange sounds, distorted and distant . . .

One of the party was a scholar from Oxford who, having in the coachman's opinion refreshed himself mightily during the journey, suggested that some of the party climb through the opening, beyond which lay, at a depth of perhaps three feet, a wide expanse of brown plain, because, uncertain though this course might be, it appeared to offer a more certain chance of survival than a night in hills which seemed increasingly alien.

'Season's Greetings! From all at the office!'

Bold Spirits

Several bold spirits in the party, with whom the scholar had been sharing his brandy, resolved to do this. The coachman was not among them, he told me, yet eventually decided to accompany them out of a sense of duty. They were still his passengers, he said, and he felt it incumbent upon him to bring them safely to Bath.

It was the view of the scholar that Bath may be found across the plain, for, he held, if this was a window out of the world then it followed that there may be a window back into it . . .

Strange though it may seem, this appeared to be the case. They had not gone above a hundred yards before they saw,

[207]

looming out of the mists in front of them, another rectangle very similar in appearance to the one they had vacated.

Imagine their joy to see that it opened on to a friendly street lined with yellow-lit windows. One of the party declared that it was in fact a street very close to his own home in London, and while many of the travellers had left London some time before, the prospect of a return now caused them to greatest joy; the traveller promised to open up his house for them, and one of the men volunteered to go back alone to the coach to fetch the rest of the party. For it seemed to all, in those last few moments of hope, that Almighty Providence had foreseen their fate upon the bitter road and had opened a gateway into the warm heart of the greatest city in the world . . .

It was then that they noticed a party of anxious people clustered near the rectangle, and the coachman saw with a falling heart that it too was rim'd with the glittering plates. This party, composed both of men and women, were bearing lanterns and, after some hesitation, approached the coachman.

The man who had a house nearby gave a cry of recognition and embraced the stranger, claiming to know him as a neighbour, and then recoiled at the dreadful expression on his face. It was clear that here was another victim of a similar fate.

After some refreshment from the Oxford scholar the newcomer explained that he had, with a party of friends, gone out carol singing. All had been well until, an hour before, there had been an eerie creaking and a shifting of shadows, and now they were somehow in a world that was not of the world.

'But—there is a street, and lighted windows,' said the London man. 'Is that not the Old Curiosity Shop, so ably run by Mrs Nugent?'

'Then it is more than decently curious, because the doors do not open, and there is nothing beyond the windows but dull yellow light,' said the carol singer. 'What were houses, my friend, are now nothing but a flat lifelessness.'

'But there are other streets—my home, not a hundred yards away . . .'

The carol singer's face was pale. 'At the end of the street,' he said, 'is nothing but white cardboard.'

Their companion gave a terrified scream, climbed into the frame, and was soon lost to view. After a few seconds they heard his scream, which the coachman screamed to me, also:

> *'May This Day Bring You, Every Year,/*
> *Joy And Warmth And All Good Cheer!'*

Menacing Banality

Several of the ladies in the carol singers' party were quite hysterical at this point and insisted on joining the company. Thus, after much heated debate it was resolved to return to the mail coach and, with considerable difficulty, snow and luggage and the glitter were piled against the frame sufficient to allow it to be manhandled down on to the plain.

At this point the coachman's tale becomes quite incoherent. It would seem that they set out to seek yet another entrance to the real world, and found for the first time that the strange windows had an obverse side. If I can understand his ravings, they seemed to be vast white squares in the sky on which some agency had written lengthy slogans of incredible yet menacing banality, whose discovery had so unhinged the London gentleman.

I can hear the coachman's mad giggling even now: *'I have come a long, long way,/To bring you Joy this Christmas Day!'* and he would bang his head on the wall again, in time to what I may, in the loosest sense, call the rhythm of the phrase.

Then he would drum his heels on the floor.

'Merry Xmas to All at No 27!' he would scream, *'From Tony, Pat and the kids. Remember Majorca?'*

And *'Get lots of crackling this Christmas!'* This last one seemed particularly to affect his brain, and I cannot but wonder what the poor man must have seen. '*Merry X-mas from Your Little Willy!!!*' and it was at this point that I had to get the gardener to come in to help me restrain him, in the apprehension that he would otherwise manage to do himself an injury.

How long were they on that fateful plain? For it appears that they were in a world outside Time as we know it, and sought for days an entrance into a world that was more than a flatness.

And they were not alone.

There were other people on the same dreadful journey. And Monsters also.

I fear that his mind is quite gone. No sane man could have seen such things. There was a window, if such I may call it, into a world of desert sands under a night sky, wherein three men of African or Asian appearance had made their camp. One of them spoke passable Latin, which the Oxford scholar was still just able to understand, despite his state of near inebriation. They too had found their world running out into a cardboard waste, and after considerable study had put it down to some event, possibly astronomical, which had severely distorted Space and, who knows, perhaps even Time itself.

They made common cause with the party, much to the chagrin of the ladies present, but it would seem that they were well-educated by heathen standards and indeed kept up the spirits of the company with their tales and outlandish songs. They were also men of considerable wealth, a fact of some importance when the swollen caravan of benighted travellers met a party of Shepherds, orphans of their world, and were able to purchase several Sheep which the coachman, who had been raised on a farm, was able to slaughter and dress.

The Shepherds, being nomads by persuasion, had been wandering for some time from their Window, and told of many fearful wonders.

> '"*Happy Christmas!/It's Your First One!/Wishing You Joy/ And a Lifetime of Fun!*" Sweet Jesus! The dreadful Beagle!'

Giant Kittens

What more dare I write? He babbled of four giant kittens with blue bows around their necks, and a rectangle within which was a vast Pie of mincemeat, which they carried for their continued provisions. There were also several glasses, taller than a house, which were found to contain—after considerable effort with ropes and the utilization of a giant sprig of Holly—a sweet Sherry, in which the Oxford scholar unfortunately drowned.

And there was the bellowing red giant, bearded and mad, sitting on a rooftop. And other things, too dreadful to recount— men who were merely coloured shapes, and the enormous black and white Caricature of a Dog watching them balefully from the top of its Kennel, and things which even as a man of Science I would blush to record.

It seems that at last he resolved to quit the company, and came back alone across the plain, believing that to die in the bitter hills of Wiltshire in mid-winter was a better fate for a Christian man than life in that abominable world.

No sooner had he reached it, and was crawling *in extremis* across the strange glittering snow, than behind him he heard once again the eldritch creaking and, upon looking around, saw the dreadful oblong slot disappear. Cold winds and snow immediately forced themselves upon it, but he felt it to be a benediction after that dreadful warm world of the brown plain. And thus, staggering in the fresh blizzard, he was found . . .

It is now fully dark. The carol singers have gone, and I trust it is to their homes.

And now my housekeeper departs, having brought me the strange news of the day. A blackamoor on a Camel has been arrested near Avebury. In Swindon a man has been savagely pecked to death in his own garden, and all there is to be seen in the snow are the footprints of an enormous Bird. Here in Chippenham itself a traveller has reported seeing, before it leapt a tall hedge and ran across the fields, a cat larger than an

Elephant. It had a blue bow about its neck. What monsters have been let into the world?

And on my desk I see my reflection in the shining, tinselly shard that the coachman had clutched in his hands. Who would cover the snow with this to make it glitter, and what fearful reason could there be?

I open the curtains, and look out upon the busy street. The local coach has come up from Bath and is outside the inn, and all is bustle and Christmas cheer, a world away from the sad ravings and pleadings of the man downstairs. It is a picture of hope, a reminder of reality, and perhaps he is, after all, no more than a man mazed by exposure, and the tales of giant Beagles and flying sledges are no more than strange jests. Except for the shard of tinsel . . .

'The tinsel on the straw! Amen! "Wishing you all the best, Mum and Dad!"'

And I see the falling snow, how it glitters . . .
And I hear the creaking.
God help us, every one.

THE BOMMIE
AND THE
DROP-OFF

Richard Adams

A new story by the author of *Watership Down*
(1972), now generally recognized as the best
novel about wild animals since *The Wind in the
Willows*. Among his other books are *Shardik*
(a remarkable fantasy of war, adventure and
horror), *The Plague Dogs*, and *The Girl in
the Swing*.

Again and again I have resolved to tell someone—a
former scuba-diving companion, or some professional
diver, like Monica Ferring, whom I used to know
personally, or simply a friend—any friend at all—of the experience which I underwent more than two years ago; the experience whose recollection obsesses me to the preclusion of all
normal, day-to-day thoughts, and of books and music; the
recollection which makes solitude unendurable; only to realize
yet again that I cannot speak of it. But I may be able—at
whatever personal cost to my mind—to write an account. Well,
I have had no peace of mind for the past two years; no proper

[213]

sleep, no proper appetites. So perhaps I need not worry about any worsening of my state of mind. It couldn't be much worse.

I think I'll start cautiously, with a bit of skating round the subject, so that I can stop—in other words run away—if things get too bad. If I were an ancient Greek, I might call on Poseidon to possess me; or better still, perhaps, a deified Monica, that most level-headed and undauntable of scuba divers.

Some years ago—ever since I discovered it, in fact—scuba diving was for me a consuming passion. It wouldn't really be exaggerating to say that there were only two things in life; diving, and making enough money to go diving again. Was I happy? you may ask. Oh reader, I was happy beyond my wildest dreams. I had found the only thing in life worth doing; the greatest source of joy, the revelation of God's truth. (But God has more than one aspect, so the Hindus believe, and one of them is Kali.)

I was teaching at a university in Florida when I took it into my head, almost idly, to sign up for a qualifying course in scuba. I thought it might be a bit of fun. I certainly caused a raised eyebrow or two, for at fifty-five I was easily the oldest member of the course. The others were mostly young men and their girls (or in two cases, I rather think, young men and their young men) plus a few oddballs like me; and like Trevor Fishlock, the only other Englishman among us.

Trevor was also teaching in Florida, on a sabbatical. We took to each other at once, although he was a good twenty years younger than I. We found we had the same difficulty in comprehending—or at any rate, in applying, which comes to much the same thing—Boyle's Law, atmospheres, nitrogen in the blood-stream and all the rest of the physics, for graduates though we might be, our subject was history.

This affinity happily answered for us the question of 'Buddies'. It is one of the absolute fundamentals of scuba that when you dive, you must have what the Americans, with characteristic banality, call a 'buddy'—a mate or comrade. You must never, in any circumstances, dive without a buddy. Underwater, your first concern is the welfare and safety of your buddy. The two of you must never become separated. The worst scuba crime you can commit is to leave your buddy, for whatever reason. This admirable rule, the 'buddy system', has saved any number of lives, and failure to practise it must have lost a good many, I would think. Naturally, to have a permanent buddy of long standing, who knows you well, is far better than going down with just anybody who happens to be available. During the course, Trevor and I became well used to each other's strengths and weaknesses. (Where is Trevor? What does he think now, since—no, I won't anticipate. It will be quite bad enough when I get to it.)

The course exemplified very well the American commercial outlook. In England a qualifying course lasts six months and if you don't know your stuff at the end, you fail. This course in Florida lasted six weeks, and our instructor—a nice fellow— told us that while nobody who'd paid up ever failed the course, you could pass it with conditions expressed by the staff. The syllabus was certainly demanding, since, while as far as I know nothing essential was omitted, it was all very compressed and I fear that as far as I was concerned, a good deal of the theory (which matters very much in scuba) went in at one ear and out at the other.

Anyway, we were duly presented with our cards, certifying our proficiency, and away we went. (Without producing your proficiency card, you are not supposed to be able to get air for your tank before a dive. In practice, sometimes you can and sometimes you can't.) What left me dissatisfied—and Trevor also—was that all our diving on the course had taken place in fresh water and inland; that is, in pools and lakes. Florida rather resembles Connemara in consisting of a lot of lakes, rivers and pools joined together by bits of land. I'm told Finland is similar. Some of these pools have caves, and every dissuasion is advanced to deter divers from going into them. People have

[215]

died in them, as the warning notices proclaim. (We never entered them.) It seemed to Trevor and myself that we had not really done any true scuba-diving until we had experienced the sea. We took the first opportunity to visit the West Indies.

It was here that the true fascination of scuba took full possession of me. Of what does it consist? First, I think, in the amazing brilliance and intensity of underwater colour, which cannot be described but only experienced. Fishes, plants—even stones—seem actually to glow, to be alive with colour as nothing is on land. Tannhauser must have felt like this about the Venusberg. There is another world, infinitely more beautiful than this. Most of it is unspoilt and much of it is accessible. It existed for millennia before ever human eyes beheld it, and most of it remains still unseen.

It has the innocence of Paradise, for its creatures are unafraid of Man. None or few of them have experienced death or cruelty at the hands of Man, and therefore have never developed any instinct to avoid him. The smaller fish, in their vivid shoals, seem heedless of a human approach, and continue their idle movement and quick dartings to and fro within inches of a diver's mask—before his very eyes, in fact. Larger fish will certainly avoid a diver's approach, but their motion resembles not so much flight as a kind of sensible getting out of the way, for which they feel there is quite time enough. A diver who keeps perfectly still can soon be sure that he is observing the natural world of the water round him.

That world is silent; and since the sea covers the greater surface of the planet, this means that that blessed silence is earth's natural condition. It is possible, certainly, to utter sound—perhaps to attract your buddy's attention—by shouting or crying out inside your mask, but the noise is muted, carries only a few feet and seems not to alarm the fish. On dry land, we have all come to be subjected to so much intrusive noise that we take it for granted and seldom try to do anything to stop it.

We are like ignorant, untaught partners of an unconsummated marriage; unaware that there is anything better. Imagine that underwater silence that extends round the world like the enfolding arms of the Great Mother. That is such a peace as cannot be known outside the sea; cannot be known except by its creatures, for whom it is part of their natural condition.

In the past, men have assumed unthinkingly that the world and its creatures were made for them to rule over and exploit as they would. And a sorry, arrogant, irresponsible mess they have made of it. But in the sea lie vast realms inhabited only by fish and the like, and inhospitable to air-breathing men. It is no more than the truth that most of the world has never been seen by human beings, but is no less beautiful and marvellous as anywhere that has.

It was this component of the excitement of diving—seeing what had never been seen before—which particularly appealed to Trevor and myself. We delighted in feeling that we were diving into the as-yet-unseen, and we used always to press for this when engaging the divemasters with whom we went down (for we never dived without a divemaster—some experienced professional). In the course of a few years we visited most of the recognized diving areas of the northern hemisphere. We went all over the West Indies and the Mediterranean, and to the Gulf of Aqaba and other parts of the Red Sea. We went, too, to the Seychelles and the Maldives, sometimes diving with people who spoke virtually no English. We became as experienced as amateurs could well be.

I remember clearly the time and place when I first propounded to Trevor what we later came to call the Grand Design. One evening in June we were sitting on the verandah of a modest hotel in Alexandria, looking out over the countless ships in port and the calm, blue sea beyond.

'Do you know what we ought to do?' I asked Trevor, signalling to the waiter for a couple more gin-and-tonics.

'What?' he answered. 'Turn professional? I've sometimes

considered it. It would really make things simpler for us in some ways, wouldn't it? But I've no idea how you go about it.'

'No, I don't mean that,' I answered. 'I meant our next destination.'

'Well? Murmansk? Alaska?'

'No, seriously,' I said. 'I think we're ready for it. We've never yet been to the southern hemisphere. We must go to Australia and dive on the Great Barrier Reef and the Coral Sea.'

'Strewth!' said Trevor. 'It certainly *is* an idea. But shall we ever be able to afford it?'

'It won't be easy financially, I agree,' I replied. 'I shall have to sell the spoons, or mortgage something. But I'm determined to do it, before I get too old. Cairns would be the place, wouldn't it? I've often heard of Cairns as *the* place for scuba, haven't you?'

Well, I needn't go into details. Somehow we raised the money, and in December of the following year we found ourselves in Cairns, on the Queensland coast; Cairns, whose entire waterfront is devoted to every possible aspect of scuba-diving; in whose bars scuba is the general topic of conversation.

We were more than lucky, for we found what we had certainly not known beforehand; that Bill and Monica Ferring were accepting experienced people for a trip, and had a few vacancies left. Less than a week later we embarked on one of two launches outward bound for the Reef and the Coral Sea.

We found we liked Bill and Monica very much, and soon thought of them as personal friends. They were two of the most genuine, unassuming people I have ever met. In spite of their world-wide fame and reputation, they were quite unselfcon-scious, and not at all given to talking about (what we all wanted to hear at first hand) their incredible and spine-chilling work with sharks. Monica had frequently dived among all kinds of sharks and had often excited them to feeding frenzies, remaining calmly among them while Bill filmed her. 'But haven't you *ever* been bitten?' I asked her. 'Only once,' she replied, 'in the thigh.' 'And what on earth did you do?' 'I hit the shark to make it let go, which it did.'

'I'm just an ignorant peasant,' she said once, when Trevor happened to say something about Kipling as a poet. 'But none of you Poms know anything about Banjo Paterson or 'The Man from Snowy River'. Now there's a poet.' She undertook to lend me Banjo Paterson when we got back.

Diving in those waters largely revolves round what are called the 'bommie' and the 'drop-off'. Here and there are to be found great columns of rock, which rise from the sea-bed to about twenty or thirty feet below the surface. The tops are more-or-less flat, covered with well-established plants and inhabited by anemones, small crustaceans, shoals of small fish and the like. These easily accessible tops are the 'bommies'; some relatively small in area, others as big as a meadow or even bigger.

You can have a very enjoyable dive without leaving a bommie. Usually the dive-boat is anchored above, and the pairs of divers go all over the bommie and see all it has to offer. A tank of air, at this relatively slight depth, can last you a good hour or more, and you don't have to bother about nitrogen intake and the bends, since you aren't lower than one 'atmosphere' ($33\frac{1}{3}$ feet).

At the edge of the bommie is sheer cliff, often plunging hundreds of feet to the ocean floor. This is the 'drop-off'; where the fun begins. The weightless diver is like a fly on a wall, and can go effortlessly wherever he likes. The face of a drop-off is splendid beyond belief, being inhabited by anything from anemones and shell-fish to giant conger eels (not dangerous unless molested) and swarming with shoals of small fish which never venture far beyond it. This prolific life doesn't extend to much depth, and you can have as exciting a time at forty feet as at eighty.

Our party had been moving about, outside the Barrier Reef, to various places known to Bill and Monica, for about a week, when on Christmas Eve Bill announced that conditions were perfect for a dive onto a particularly splendid drop-off no more than half an hour away. When we reached the place in our Zodiacs, I felt full of a Christmas spirit of adventure, ready for anything—even a few sharks as long as Monica was about. The sea was dead calm and there was none of the tossing about among waves, which I always dislike, while waiting for everyone to assemble.

The drop-off was amazing, and Trevor and I spent plenty of time in going all over it, up and down as the spirit moved us. I suppose we had been down a little over half an hour when I found myself possessed by the notion of going really deep. Trevor and I had never been deeper than about eighty feet—had never particularly wanted to—but here, where you could see the drop-off going on down until it was lost to sight, I thought it would be exciting and perfectly safe (you couldn't lose your way) to follow it and establish for ourselves a personal depth record. Of course we wouldn't be able to stay there long—the deeper you go the more air you use up—but it would be another opportunity to see a place which had never been seen before. I signalled my idea to Trevor by pointing downwards most emphatically; he responded with a nod and the thumbs-up, and down we went.

I wasn't thinking of anything much, simply watching the drop-off becoming barer and barer of life, observing my depth-gauge gradually falling to a satisfying 200 feet, when I saw, in the dim light, that we wouldn't be able to go deeper. A little below, the drop-off ended in a right-angled turn outwards, curving to form a kind of smooth, underwater beach, quite featureless, which stretched away into the ocean, without gaining any noticeable depth, as far as the eye could see.

I went down the remaining few feet, stood on the floor of the beach and turned to signal to my buddy. You can hardly imagine how dreadful it was to me to see that whoever was near my side, it was not Trevor. And as I stared through my mask, I passed from dread to sheer terror, for it was not a human being.

The figure facing me was upright, and I suppose a little over five feet in height. It wore no mask and carried no air-tank. It had two extremities like legs, on which it was standing, and two arms which were stretched out towards me. Each ended not in a hand but in a sort of webbed paw, with great claws instead of fingers. In colour it was uniformly grey, and scaly from head to foot. Its neck was very short and thick, and had gills on either side. It was looking at me from two large, unlidded eyes, set above a short, almost flat excrescence which had no nostrils. Below this was a wide mouth, open to show long, pointed canines—the teeth of a carnivore. As I stared at it, transfixed with horror, it took a step forward and raised one clawed arm above its head.

I fled upwards. My utmost speed was too slow for my panic. If I had thought of it I would have ditched my weight-belt. As I gave one glance below, I saw that, although the creature was pursuing me, I was too fast for it; but this did little to diminish my mindless anguish. In so far as I thought at all, I wanted to be out of the water.

Looking up, I saw three stationary human figures above me on the drop-off, and I made for them, still at the same speed. They turned out to be Bill, Monica and Trevor, who had evidently and most sensibly sought out the divemasters on losing touch with his buddy. Bill took my arm, but I tore myself free and went on, up to the bommie and thence into the dive-boat, where I lay moaning and trembling.

As soon as everyone had come up, Bill, who was plainly troubled, tried to get me to say what was the matter. I could only shake my head and say 'Later, later', as I sat on the rim of the Zodiac and held Trevor's arm. Back at the launch I got into my bunk and slept, I suppose. I don't remember eating, or talking to anyone. Bill and Monica were waiting for the bends— the excess nitrogen sickness—to begin. I certainly deserved to get the bends, but for some reason I didn't.

Next morning—Christmas Day—I felt a little better, and Monica gave me the dressing-down of my life, in front of everyone, for coming up as I had. I stood facing her, silent as a schoolboy, while she scolded me for a good ten minutes. 'And in Cairns I can show you a row of graves of people who've *died* of the bends,' she ended. 'You deserve to be there.' Then, more gently, she asked, 'What upset you? Did you think you were out of air, or what?' I only shook my head. 'And why did you leave your buddy?' Here Trevor, like the good egg he was, tried to intervene and take some of the blame, but it made little difference to Monica's anger.

I didn't dive that day or the next, and the day after that we returned to Cairns, and Trevor and I went home. Trevor was much concerned for me. All I could say was that I had had a very bad experience and would tell him about it later, when I felt equal to it. I never have felt equal to it, and I haven't dived again. Nor shall I.

I suppose someone might say 'What's all the fuss about? You only *saw* it: it didn't hurt you.' Do you remember the old story about the man who agreed to spend the night in a haunted house? He was found the next morning uninjured but stark mad, and couldn't speak of what had happened. Neither can I speak of what I saw. I suppose it may wear off in time, but at present I still remain most horribly preoccupied and—well, haunted.

And suppose I *did* say 'There are anthropoids—an anthropoid species—dwelling under water in the Coral Sea, and I have encountered one,' what would follow?

Our descent from the apes goes back millions of years. Is it not possible that an amphibious group became separated and adapted itself over the millennia to develop into—into what I saw? It would be carnivorous, of course, for no creature that is not can live in the sea.

We still know almost nothing about the sea and its inhabitants. Not only are many unclassified, but it is safe to say that many are still unseen and unknown.

That is all I have to tell. Some day, no doubt, more will be discovered.

THE FERRY

Joan Aiken

A hitherto unpublished story by one of Britain's
most popular writers, equally well known for her
ghost stories, children's books, historical novels
and crime fiction.

J udith stuck up a sprig of holly, and then looked round for
another site; she still had an enormous bundle to use up.
No, really, there wasn't a single space left, and she gathered
up the scratchy, rustling armful and took it into the porch
to form a sort of berried nest which would, she hoped, look cosy
and encouraging to callers.

She went outside for a moment to gloat over the house. They
had only been in it for a fortnight and it still seemed hardly
credible—to be here, beside the sheet of glimmering water with
gulls crying plaintively above, instead of in the dusty warren of
a suburb and Ken catching the eight-thirty every morning. How
a not-very-large legacy can alter your life, she mused; a month
ago we thought of Cornwall only as an Ultima Thule, a horizon
to be attained some time after the age of sixty; and now here we
are, already equipped with a boat and some hens, and Ken off
getting in the Christmas drinks.

The house was small and white; Judith thought it looked

rather like a shell left lying by the water, with firelight throwing a pink light on the walls inside and the curved steps leading down to the landing-stage. It had been a boatman's house when the ferry was running, and was still called Ferry House. The hill rose up steep and bare behind it; there were only three other cottages on this side of the river and they were much further out towards the point. The village proper was all over on the other shore and she could see lights beginning to shine out from windows down by the water and the coloured gleams from the pub Christmas tree on the quay.

It was cold. Judith shivered and told herself that she had better go indoors and begin changing to go to the Martins' cocktail party. But for some reason she felt a strong reluctance to go indoors, and an even stronger impulse to stay here idling on the landing stage. She would have liked to sit down and dangle her legs over the side as if it were an August afternoon instead of dusk on Christmas Eve. She knew now that decorating the porch had only been an excuse to get outside the house.

'But why?' she demanded in protest, of that other Judith who was so dumbly, insistently urging her to stay out on the landing stage. 'You've simply got to get used to being by yourself, you city-dweller. There are bound to be lots of times when Ken is out, and you can't get into a state of jitters whenever you're alone in the house. It's a nice little house, a dear little house, there's nothing whatever the matter with it.'

She stood staring at the black square shape of the open door with the wide water and the lights behind her, and felt as if she were at the entrance to a rat hole. With a strong effort of will she stepped inside. After all, Ken would be back any minute now with the drinks—she strained her ears for the chug of the motorboat—and soon they would be starting off for the Martins' party. Everything was all right, everything was fine—why was she standing in a corner of the scullery like this, wringing her hands and biting her lips in an agony of nerves?

Angrily she shook her head and ran up the stairs, took out

her favourite dress, tomato-coloured wool, and dragged it on over her head. Then once again she found herself, hairbrush in hand, by the window, gazing fixedly at the landing stage steps. Was that Ken coming up them? No, it was not—nothing but imagination. The telephone bell interrupted her as she recrossed the room.

'Darling?' said Ken's voice. 'Look, a tiresome thing's happened. The engine conked out on me as I was starting back. Old Weaver thinks he can fix it in an hour or so, in time for us to come home from the Martins, but it means I can't get over to fetch you. Can you come over with the Joneses? They're going to the party too, aren't they?'

'Yes, but I've an idea they went over early to do some shopping. I'm not sure—I'll go and see.'

'Well, call me back if they can't and I'll try and find someone this side. I'm at the pub.'

'Right. I'll only be five minutes.'

With a feeling of relief and purpose she hung up and started along the waterside path to the Jones's house.

'Like it in Ferry House?' asked Mr Hocking the landlord, hanging red and green paper balls over the bar in preparation for opening time. 'Settling in all right?'

'Yes, we love it,' Ken answered. 'We're very happy there. Has the house any history, do you know? Wasn't there a lot of smuggling round here?'

'No, there's only one story I've heard about Ferry House,' said Mr Hocking slowly, 'and smuggling doesn't come into it. It happened a long time ago—in the witch-burning days, before the smuggling started. There was an old woman running the ferry called Mother Poysey, and it was generally believed in the village that she was a witch. Well, nobody cared much—live and let live is our motto in these parts, and always has been— but the squire got to hear the story and he said she ought to be ducked if she was a witch.

'There's a custom round here, used to be, that is, when the ferry was running that the ferryman took everyone over for nothing on Christmas Eve. In memory of some local saint, it was. Of course people used to give a present instead, so it came to the same thing.

'Well, one Christmas Eve the squire, with four or five other men, came down to the ferry and asked to be taken across. They'd all been drinking, and they carried bundles under their arms, saying they were presents for Mother Poysey. She untied the boat and started pulling them across, but halfway over they undid their bundles and took out ropes hung with lead weights, tied her up and dropped her overboard. Her body was never found. Oddly enough, on the following Christmas Eve the squire himself was missing, and his body was found later, washed up on the White Rocks out by the headland. So people began to say that she appeared in her boat on Christmas Eve offering to take people over on the ferry for nothing, but if they accept they're never seen again alive. Of course it's a lot of nonsense really—I've never heard of anyone who honestly claimed to have seen her. A chap *was* drowned last Christmas though, and washed up on the White Rocks. He was a stranger; people said afterwards he'd been seen trying to find someone to row him across.'

'Jolly,' Ken commented.

The telephone rang.

'It's for you,' Mr Hocking said.

'Oh, hello darling, is that you?' came Judith's voice. 'Listen, a lucky thing's happened—Mrs Jones *had* gone already, but just as I was walking back I met a funny old crone who's going across to the village, so she's going to take me. I offered to pay her but she said she'd do it for nothing, as it's Christmas. So I'll be there in ten minutes. OK?'

'Hey, wait—Judith!' he said frantically, but she had rung off. 'Exchange, get me Polhale 320 again, please.'

'I'm sorry, there is no reply,' said the girl after a moment.

[226]

Ken ran out on to the quay and stood by the lighted Christmas tree staring across the water. It was really dark now and the tide was coming in fast, bringing a fog on its back. He could not see the lights on the far shore. There was cold behind the fog too— he shivered, straining his eyes and ears, wondering if he could hear the creak and splash of a boat or voices in mid-river. But there was no sound.

When Judith rang off she hurried outside again.

'I won't keep you a moment—I must just powder my nose,' she said to the old woman. 'Goodness, you do look cold. Won't you come in and have a cup of tea while you wait? I've just made some.'

The queer old thing seemed to be shivering uncontrollably. Judith caught at her hand—heavens, it *was* cold and drew her in.

'Do sit by the kitchen fire, it's lovely and warm. I was just wishing I had somebody to share it with. Do you take sugar?'

'I thank you Ma'am.' The crone sat stiff and upright in her rusty black clothes. 'I used to live in this house once.' But she hardly glanced round; her eyes were fixed on Judith.

'*Did* you?' said Judith, powdering her nose at the sink mirror. 'It's a lovely house. You must have been sorry to leave.'

'Yes, I was sorry to leave.'

'Do have one of my mince pies, they're quite good this year. Oh, you haven't begun your tea yet. Drink it while it's hot, it'll warm you up. What a curious bracelet,' said Judith, noticing the lead weights hanging from her wrist. 'Is it a charm?' She was chattering in her relief at having company at last, and hurried off to get her coat, hardly waiting for an answer.

Ten minutes later when Ken jumped out of a borrowed dinghy he saw his front door wide open casting a square of light down the steps. The house was quite silent.

'Judith!' he called.

The holly in the porch caught at his sleeve as he raced through. Judith lay in one of the armchairs by the kitchen fire. At his entrance she sat up dazedly and rubbed her eyes.

'Ken! Goodness, how extraordinary—I must have gone to sleep. Where's Mrs Poysey?'

'*Who?*'

'The old woman who was going to take me across. I suppose she got fed up and went on. She was rather odd, a bit mental I think. She said: "You've a bold heart, my dear. There's few cares to take sup with Mother Poysey," and something about her house being in good hands at last. I suppose she moved farther up the river when she left here. What are you looking at, Ken?'

He was staring at the other chair. Draped over it, and tangled round the untouched cup of tea and mince pie, was a mass of sodden rope, to which were attached a number of little lead weights.

'Those were what they weighed her down with,' he said. 'Let's hope she's free of them now.'

They never saw the old woman again.

THE MAID

Jane Beeson

Jane Beeson has written for radio, television and
theatre. She has also produced three novels and
her latest, *Scarhill*, will be published in 1995.

It was in 1959 that we came to live here. By here I mean
Dartmoor—a thousand feet above sea level and in those
days prone to long snowbound winters with temperatures
remaining below freezing for up to eight weeks at a time. With
no snow-plough to open up the lanes the moor was a bleak and
desolate place—a landscape of white, black, brown and ochre.
The motorway had not been built and the area not yet become
a weekender belt for London. The predominant population was
local—tradesmen, craftsmen and farmers. Richard farmed,
while I looked after our children and helped when necessary out
of doors, but that was not often as labour was cheap and farm
help abundant.

Arch worked for us. Arch was ageless and bent like a dwarf.
He wore a sack cast over the shoulders of his baggy tweed jacket,
his bandy legs were bandaged in more strips of sacking to the
knees, a pipe dangled from the corner of his mouth. He spoke a
fast disappearing Devonian dialect that I gradually came to

understand. Arch had come with the farm, had worked for our predecessors who were Devonian themselves; he knew all that was worth knowing about hill farming and was excellent with stock although he never appeared to look at them, what could be seen of his face beneath his cap looked at the ground. It was from Arch I first heard about Jay, which I must admit came as a shock as I am not partial to ghosts and had carefully asked before we came if the house was haunted. Absolutely not, had come the reply, the former occupants had been there twenty-five years and never seen one yet. Of course, it was a silly question!

At the time we, Arch and I, were over in Canna yard, used for cattle sorting. Canna had once been a neighbouring farm but now stood deserted and was included as a part of our property. It was a curious place with a central yard, on one side of which was a deserted cottage and shippon and opposite this a massive barn. The other two sides were enclosed by stock buildings. All was built of the usual moorstone. The cottage was perfectly distinguishable by its fireplace over which lodged a massive granite lintel supporting the chimney breast; a beam remained slung from wall to wall, and small blocked-up openings set at odd heights suggested there must once have been an upstairs. To the left and sharing the same roof was a shippon with a loft above; beneath this a central passage led through to what must have once been the front door, humans and animals in those times sharing the same humble dwelling. Certainly Canna had not been lived in by humans in living memory which had already puzzled me, and the only reason I had been able to supply in my mind was the cold. Canna was a cold place ill sheltered from the north by three sycamores which, even on the warmest days of summer, were swayed by a chill wind. I describe all this in some detail so that it will be possible to follow my movements later.

Arch stood in his usual bent pose, hazel stick in one hand, craning his head back awkwardly to look up at the beam above.

[230]

'Aye,' he said. 'Hanged 'erself on that one, poor maid.' 'Maid,'
I came to learn, was Devonian for young girl.

'Why?' I asked.

Arch shook his head. He was filling his pipe, an occupation
that had to be repeated frequently and took all his concen-
tration. In the dark desolate cottage I studied the beam above
us, looked up to the roof timbers.

'She must have been small,' I said. 'If it was this beam.'

'It were higher then. The dung has built up, see.' Arch spat,
poked the ground with his stick. 'Her's buried up top at t' Cross,'
he said, waving his stick at the moor that rose in black silhouette
under an ominous looking cloud across the valley. I hoped he
would elucidate further but he seemed disinclined.

That evening I passed on the information to Richard who showed
little interest, he was not one for folk-lore. But it prompted me
to take the children on a fine and sunny afternoon for a walk up
to 'the Cross'. We viewed in silence the grass-covered mound
with a jam jar of drooping flowers set in front of an uprighted
lump of granite. It was set in the centre of a lane that widened
out to join the present road; a track and bank indicated where
once the lane must have continued on over the moor.

'Is there bones in it?' my eldest asked.

'Yes, I think so,' I said.

After which they ran off in the heather opposite and I was
left alone by the isolated grave. Wind snatched at the wizened
thorns on the bank beside it, and even on such a day it seemed
to me a strange choice of place to bury someone.

After that I forgot 'the maid' until the builders arrived in late
September, three of them in all, as handsome a looking gang of
young rogues as ever was seen with their dark hair and blue
eyes. They set to work.

Two days later in the custom of local builders they had gone,
leaving the work unfinished and a variety of their tools behind.
We assumed that when the more lucrative job they had gone to
was accomplished, they would return to the paltry task of putting

on ridging tiles and replacing gutters. But when after two weeks there was still no sign of them, I rang their number. Mrs Elder senior, clearly the mainstay behind the business, answered me.

She sounded cagey the moment I said who I was and gave the name of our farm. The men were out, she told me. I asked when they would come to finish our roof?

'I don't think as how 'em will, my dear,' she said. 'They had a bit of a scare from what I heard. Jack says he aint goin' out there again for money nor nothin'.'

I absorbed this depressing bit of news. 'Did he fall?' I asked.

'Oh no, dear, gracious me no. It was the maid.'

'Oh,' I said, my brain ticking back to my conversation with Arch, 'What exactly happened?'

Mrs Elder became even more guarded in her information. 'He didn't tell me exact, like. But it gived him a scare. He don't like to talk about it, see. He wants to forget it, like.'

'Oh I see,' I said feebly, my curiosity both aroused and frustrated, 'Doesn't he even want to collect his tools?'

'I wouldn't like to say, dear. Maybe he'll get Nicky to pick 'em up when he's passing.'

And there the conversation ended. I reported it to Richard who swore. In due course the tools did disappear so presumably Nicky must have made a furtive visit. We got some other builders to complete the job and no further mention was made of 'the maid'. Meanwhile I came across a short paragraph in one of the only guides to Dartmoor then written. I quote: *The road we now follow skirts Swine Down, the enclosures of Hedge Barton being on the left. A path runs off left and here we shall notice a small mound with a headstone. It is the burial place of a suicide and is known as Jay's Grave. She is said to have been a young unmarried woman who many years ago hung herself in an outbuilding belonging to Canna Farm, and in accordance with the barbarous custom of the time, was interred at the crossway.*

At least I now knew her name.

*

It was shortly before Christmas that I was over in Canna yard bottle-feeding an orphaned calf. I had left it rather late and darkness had fallen suddenly. I had with me a small pocket torch with a fading battery, but I was not worried for outside I could still see, and the wide doorway of the cottage where the calf was housed let in what remained of the light.

The calf sucked vigorously, I had quite a job to keep a grasp of the bottle. I did glance over my shoulder once at the dark recess of the cottage behind me which was inky black, but then owing to the blocked up openings it is dark in the day as well as at night. The weather was wild and worsening, it was attempting to snow.

The calf had finished and was butting me for more, when it seemed to me I heard a sound other than the calf's rustle in its straw bed. At the same time the air stirred inside the cottage with one of those unexpected gusts of wind. I stared into the impenetrable blackness behind me but saw nothing; it was then the noise started in the loft to the left of the chimney breast and over the shippon. It was as if a chair was being dragged across the floor, then a sudden loud thump as if something had fallen; at the same time I quite distinctly heard a young baby's cries.

There was no denying I was afraid. I reached for the calf's warm body for reassurance, but it had moved away into the darkness. The air round me seemed to have dropped in temperature and was deathly chill. I summoned my courage, left the cottage and walked along a few paces to the door beneath the adjoining loft from where the sounds had come. I pushed it open and listened. Not a sound. I took a deep breath and climbed the few rungs of the wooden ladder, pushed my head up through the trap, and flashed the weak beam of my torch round. Nothing. Absolute silence. I climbed down and hastened home across the single field and road dividing Canna from our farm. I told Richard.

Together we went back with our powerful calving torch, climbed into the loft. Nothing. Most remarkable of all, the floor was completely covered with the old straw of our predecessor so nothing falling would have made anything like the thud I had heard, nor could an object dragged across the floor have made the noise. Richard put the thuds down to cats, the baby's cry to a marauding tom. I knew better. The calf, as though to take Richard's side, lay curled asleep in its nest of straw. Before I fell asleep that night I said to Richard, 'It was a baby crying, I'd know that cry anywhere. You know perfectly well what they sound like.'

'Yes,' he said. 'I agree it is very odd.' Then promptly fell asleep. I lay awake. It wasn't my imagination, I knew I had heard it all exactly as I have described. I felt an involuntary prickle of fear even as I lay in bed beside Richard.

For the next few days I took care to feed the calf well before dark. The happening began to recede in my mind as dreams do, due in part to the proximity of Christmas, and the thought of getting in enough food should we be snowed in, and the need to fill Christmas stockings. The weather forecast was not good.

Exactly one week before Christmas the next disturbing incident occurred. I was again feeding the calf and musing on whether to buy a turkey in the market or a frozen one from a supermarket, when I felt the same cold draught of air behind me. Instantly I felt my throat go dry, I was sure there was someone—some thing—there, but I was too afraid to immediately look round. When I did the shadowy space of the cottage, the dark recess beside the chimney, was empty. Yet the cold struck right through me. Involuntarily I shivered in spite of the comparative mildness of the evening. Relieved at the empty space and chiding myself for silly imaginings, I shut the gate on the calf and was about to leave when I again heard a baby's cry—even more distinct and unmistakable than the last time. I had no doubt it was alive and had been left on the far side of the shippon, in front in fact of what must have once been the building's front door. I crossed the yard and without fear because I was so sure the baby was alive, I fumbled my way through the dark building determined to find it, prove to Richard it was not my imagination. As I reached the door the crying cut off as sharply as it had begun. I wrenched it open towards me, looked down on the weathered flagstone. Nothing. I ran out into the small field in front that had almost certainly once served as a vegetable garden, looked all round me. No one. Equally no one could have gone that quickly holding a baby, there would simply not have been time. Besides, instinctively if irrationally I felt it was a woman. I could not face going back into the building, so I hurried round the outside and went home across the field.

When the children were in bed and we were alone, I said, 'I heard it again—the baby crying.'

'Did you?' said Richard, looking mildly interested. But I could see he didn't believe me and thought there was a perfectly good explanation.

'Yes,' I said. 'You feed the calf tomorrow, see if you hear anything.'

'All right,' he said. 'I will.'

The next day I went shopping, took the children, did all the usual things prior to Christmas. Father Christmases abounded in every store, lured my children with bulging sacks, it all took time. We got home late to find Richard in his usual chair beside the stove.

'Did you remember the calf?' I asked.

'Yes.'

He said no more and I put the children to bed, came down eventually to join him. He had lighted a fire and was crouched over it; the weather had gone colder again as predicted. When he looked up I noticed something rather strange about his expression, not quite focussed. He did look like that sometimes when his mind was on other things. I sat down, took up the Radio Times. When he didn't speak my curiosity got the better of me. I asked if he had heard anything, sure that he would say No.

[235]

'As a matter of fact—yes.'

'What?' I felt an odd mixture of triumph and fear.

'What you described—a baby crying.'

'I told you,' I said. 'But you didn't believe me.'

'I admit it is very odd, but there must be a rational explanation.'

I made him tell me exactly what happened. He stayed crouched over the fire, not looking at me, and I could tell how hard it was for him to admit to something his rational mind did not believe. It had the quality of a confession. He had gone over to the cottage late, not bothered with a torch (he sees well in the dark), fed the calf, felt the sudden 'down draught' as he described it, felt the icy chill. Then the noises had started—a chair had been dragged across the floor, the footsteps of someone moving around, a pause, then a thud as though something quite heavy had fallen, followed by a baby's cries . . . It seemed he had heard even more than I had.

'Was the baby outside what must have been the front door?' I asked.

'I'm not sure I know where you mean.'

I explained.

'I couldn't tell,' he said, but then he doesn't have directional hearing.

We sat in silence watching the smoke curl up the chimney above the flickering flames. Our wood was not seasoned and didn't burn well. The room felt damp, I even thought I detected a sweet, faintly mouldy smell similar to that of the cottage at Canna. I prayed it wasn't dry rot.

'So what do you think it was?' I asked finally.

'God knows,' he said.

In the morning snow was on the ground, a sense of excitement was in the air at the thought of a traditional white Christmas. From my window I spied Arch in the yard bent over a wheelbarrow of dung. I went out and waylaid him. After discussing the weather at Christmas over the last two decades I got round to the point. 'Arch,' I said, 'the maid haunts, doesn't she?'

'They says her do,' he said scratching the back of his neck.

I waited.

'They says 'er bones was buried down the lane on t'other side to Canna afore they was dug up with the plough. Ploughed 'em up where the lane opens up in to that there rushy field.'

I waited.

'They took 'em up to the cross and put 'em in the grave where the parish boundaries meet, see. Then neither one nor t'other has to own to 'er. But some of 'em youngsters back along opened up the grave, took out the bones.'

'Would that make her restless?' I asked.

'Restless?' Arch laughed a grave-like throaty gurgle. 'It'd make me restless. Aye, it would that.' And still gurgling he picked up the barrow and walked on.

On Christmas Eve our electricity generator packed up; we heard the doomed noise of it revolving and revolving without picking up. There was nothing for it but for Richard to go out and switch it off completely, it looked like a candlelight Christmas. As a result the calf got forgotten until long after dark.

'Shall we both go?' I asked.

'What about the children? It's not very safe to leave them here with candles.'

'No,' I agreed and at that moment the door opened and Harry, our youngest, arrived in tears. He had had a bad dream. He sat on my lap and clung to my neck for comfort. I tried to get him to tell me his dream but he wouldn't, or couldn't, and any further persuading seemed to increase his distress.

Richard took up the torch. 'I'll go and get it over with,' he said. He put on his boots and left. The back door shut behind him. I felt a little shiver of apprehension. I took Harry up to his bed, sat with him a few moments until he settled if not slept, and went down to the sitting room to make up the fire. The room looked rather fine lit by candles, it seemed to increase the thickness of the walls, the depths of the recesses. But it was less friendly than electricity and owing to the need to economize in candle power so as not to run out until the shops opened, I had to space them at infrequent intervals. It was while I was blowing up the fire with the bellows that I heard the crying. I stopped blowing and listened. It came again. I ran upstairs to see if it was the children but knew perfectly well it was not. They were all asleep including Harry, nightlights on the dressing table, stockings laid out at the foot of their beds. I steadied myself, tiptoed out, shut the door as quietly as I could, stood with a prickling feeling at the back of my neck, straining to hear what I most dreaded. After a few minutes of absolute silence I began slowly going down the stairs, stopping with every step to listen. I reached the bottom, was about to go into the lighted sitting room when quiet distinctly from outside our front door I heard a baby crying. It was in the porch. I slid silently through into our shadowy hall, picked up the lighted candle off the table and made my way down the cobbled passage towards the front door. I was aware the temperature round me had grown icy, a cold breeze dragged at my legs. I was not more than halfway down it when the candle suddenly guttered. I automatically reached for the light switch, fumbled, found it, switched it on. No light. In my panic I had forgotten the generator wasn't working. The cries continued, I could feel cold sweat under my armpits trickling down the inside of my sleeves. Then I saw the front door opening towards me, and in the same instant the candle flared up and went out in the draft. In the complete darkness I heard the door scrape over the floor, stick, then be forced wider. No wind could have shifted that hefty door open over the upward-sloping cobbles—the bolt rattled. I heard the sounds of someone, something, moving up the passage towards me. It stopped just in front of me. I was too afraid to move or make a sound of any kind; I knew what-ever-it-was was trying to get me, say something. For a terrifying moment I thought it must touch me, then the air stirred and I heard it moving away from me down the passage, the heavy door closed, and the baby's cries started so loudly that I was sure it was inside the door with me. The sound echoed off the walls on either side, I put my hands over my ears and screamed and screamed.

Richard was beside me. 'What are you doing out here?' He was holding the torch on me.

'The baby,' I said. 'The baby. Can't you hear it? She was here, that woman, beside me. Didn't you hear me screaming?'

'No,' said Richard. 'I didn't hear anything. I came to look for you because I wondered where you'd got to.' He led me through into the lighted kitchen, gave me a glass of brandy.

'I don't believe you didn't hear me scream,' I said. 'You must have.'

'I didn't,' he said. 'And nor apparently did the children or they'd all be downstairs by now.' He paused. 'Bad news, I'm afraid,' he said. 'The calf is dead.'

'No!' I exclaimed in horror. 'No! How did it die?'

'Heart attack, I suppose. It was stretched out in the straw when I got there, still warm. I've been all this time trying to revive it.'

'Richard,' I said. 'I don't think I want to stay here, I don't think we're going to be happy.'

'Don't be silly. If you're worried about the noises we'll get them exorcized.'

'You don't understand,' I said. 'It was here. Right here in this house.' And I described exactly what I had been through. 'It's the bones,' I finished. 'I'm sure it's because they've dug them up, taken them away. Or perhaps it's because they are separated from the baby's.'

But in Richard's mind the tragedy of the dead calf far superseded any ghost. I could tell that he wasn't fully listening to me and he didn't connect the two happenings as I did. With a shudder I wondered if the poor calf was my scapegoat.

*

[239]

We did get our local rector to come and perform an exorcism ceremony. It was hard to believe it would work but it did. No more was heard of Jay until the Flower People came for their 'Loving' on the moor. They must have disturbed the loveless maid, for on the same night a contractor and his girlfriend were on the way home from a party in their car followed by two other male friends in a separate car when, as they neared the grave, they saw what they at first took to be a moor pony up against the hedge, but as they got nearer, discovered it was a faceless figure in a long cloak hovering over the mound of grassy turf. It sounded far fetched even to me.

By then my family were grown and I was at University reading Psychology. I decided to search out the haunted couples, ask them for first hand information rather than the distorted story of the local Press. The couple in the second car I eventually learned had gone 'up country', no one knew where or had their address; the contractor and his girlfriend, now his wife, I located only with difficulty in a small brick terraced house on the side of a hill in Newton Abbot. He was in his garage, she was in the house when I arrived at their back gate. I asked if he could spare me a few moments and he willingly agreed, wiping his oily hands off on a rag. But when I mentioned what I had come about, his face changed. No, he didn't want to talk about it, he'd forgotten it. Would his wife consider seeing me, I asked. He looked angry but went to ask her. He was gone some time and I began to think he was never coming back, but at last he reappeared looking even more hostile. No, she wouldn't talk, wouldn't even see me. I told him I was not from the Press, anything said would be strictly in confidence, explained my own interest and involvement. His anger if anything increased. I apologized for my intrusion, turned to go. I had all but reached the gate when he caught up with me, said it had scared them both so much they were frightened if they talked about it, 'it' might come after them, follow them. The shock had so affected his wife that she had been ill and in bed for some time afterwards. If I didn't believe him ask the other two in the car behind, they'd seen it just the same. He was a brawny great chap of about six feet four inches, I calculated, but his eyes were scared and his hands trembled as he nervously lit a cigarette, offered me one. They had moved down here, he said, to get away from it all. What was more, people mocked them, didn't believe them, but his wife was a healthy woman and didn't get ill for nothing.

I told him not to worry, I believed them. I left rather shaken, closing the gate carefully behind me. As I walked down the narrow back street away from the house an icy little wind whipped round my legs. As soon as I was round the corner, I ran, pelted down the street so passers-by looked at me curiously. As I waited at the traffic lights I became aware of a baby crying, but then in the centre of a town, I reassured myself, that was not only possible but probable.

'IT WILL ALL BE OVER BY CHRISTMAS'

Alan McMurray

Alan McMurray (b. 1930) retired from a 35-year career in Education in 1988, and now spends his time as a public relations consultant, a School Inspector, a writer and photographer, a choral singer and a railway modeller. His articles appear regularly in a wide range of trade journals, and he has just completed his first novel.

'Don't worry, love,' said Dad, giving my Mum one last hug. 'They say it will all be over by Christmas.' Poor Mum. Her voice choked with her sobs.

'Oh, Harry,' she gasped. 'I love you so much.'

'And me you, Isabella. I'll be back. You'll see.' Gravely he took my hand. His proudly waxed moustache seemed to complement his new uniform. 'Look after yourself, Tommy. And take care of Mum. You're big enough now to take my place. Christmas, then.'

A whistle shrilled. There was a surge of khaki towards the carriage doors, and men vanished like ghosts into the steam rising from below.

*

[242]

The regimental band standing beneath the flickering gaslights struck up. Very quietly and slowly, the pipes, mournful in the cold night air, played the haunting bars of 'Will ye no come back again?'. Women buried their faces in handkerchiefs, the few men stood stiffly, while the children seemed as much overcome by the pageantry of the occasion as by its sadness.

The locomotive wheels skidded on the icy rails, and clouds of smoke erupted in staccato bursts from its chimney. Momentarily the dirty carriages seemed to pause, as if deliberately prolonging the agony of farewell, before gathering pace and gliding smoothly into the tunnel of darkness at the end of the platform.

The Second Battalion of the London Scottish Regiment had left for France.

I felt a sudden chill and pulled my coat collar tighter. I slipped my hand into Mum's, giving her a quick squeeze. She turned, her brown eyes still filled with tears. There was a dignity about her sadness which reminded me yet again how different had been her upbringing from my father's. She put her hands on my shoulders, turning me to face her. Small weeping groups of people drifted slowly past us.

'We'll look after each other, won't we, Tom,' she said, trying to smile. I was always happier when she called me Tom: it made me feel more grown up. 'You'll be able to leave school at Christmas. Then you'll really be the man of the house, won't you?'

I had forgotten that. I would be twelve in November, but it would make sense to stay on at school until the end of the term. Then I could get the job at the dairy that Mr James, Dad's foreman, had always promised me. Talk about 'Like father, like son.' I knew it would be some time before I could hope to join my Dad on his milkround, but at least he would be able to teach me a lot. I could hardly wait to start.

We made our way across the cobbled yard into Waterloo Road.

'Come on!' said Mum. 'Let's walk over the bridge to the Strand, and get a bus there. It will help to blow some of our cobwebs away.'

Arm in arm we set off briskly across Waterloo Bridge. Even at that late hour the road was bustling with people, cabs and omnibuses, with an occasional car blowing its horn to make people scuttle for the safety of the kerb. Everything looked so normal. What difference was the war making? How many of the scurrying people had husbands, fathers and sons in France? They said that France was only twenty-one miles away across the English Channel. But it might as well have been another world.

That feeling of normality gradually faded as October lengthened into November. We read of the retreat through Belgium of the British Expeditionary Force, and of the terrible loss of life at a place called Wipers. The need for more men to enlist became urgent, and the East India Dock Road seemed to be covered with recruiting posters with a finger that appeared to be pointing at you all the time.

Every night my Mum and I knelt together and prayed for the safe return of my father. She hid her fears from me very well, but every morning I could see her eyes were hollow with the lack of sustained sleep. No-one who saw them together could ever doubt my parents' love for each other. And a real love-match it was; she the youngest daughter of a Sussex squire, he the head groom at the manor house where she had lived. She had known from the moment she had announced her intention of marrying my father that her family would have nothing more to do with her; and consequently she had become totally dependent upon the two men in her life—my Dad and me. We were a very close-knit family.

Any hope of seeing my Dad again at Christmas seemed to become less and less certain, although we both looked eagerly each Tuesday morning for his weekly letter, which was as regular as clockwork. It was difficult to guess how he was, for so much of what he had written had been scored through with blue pencil by his platoon commander. So we supplemented what he wrote with the stories in the 'Daily Sketch', which painted a depressing picture of life in the mud of Flanders.

Those letters were a life-line.

The first occasion on which I was awoken by the sound of hooves on the cobbles in the street was a cold, sharp morning in early December. It was still dark, probably about half-past five. I assumed that that was the time because that was when I had so often been awoken by my father stopping outside the house to fill our milk can which had been placed on the corner of the doorstep. Often, particularly in the summer when the dawn was breaking behind the cranes peering over the tops of the houses opposite, I had rushed to the window to wave to him. This morning I did the same, as much out of habit as curiosity. But even in the darkness I could tell the street below was deserted, and thinking it was a dream I returned to bed to snuggle back beneath the blankets.

A week later, the same thing happened. Half asleep, I went to the window and raised the corner of the curtain. Again the street was deserted.

The third time it happened, about ten days before Christmas, the hooves sounded as though they were pawing the ground impatiently, just as Jenny, the mare that had pulled my Dad's milkfloat, had been in the habit of doing. Even before I reached the curtain I knew she was going to be there, and that I would see her breath forming two jets of steam in the cold morning air.

She was. There was no doubt about it. As if to confirm the truth of what I had seen a voice suddenly cried 'Giddyap!' and she was away, down the road and round the corner. But there was no sign of a horseman.

I turned away from the window, and lit the candle beside my bed. It was low in its holder, and the pale flame guttered and flickered eerily in the darkness. I took my dressing gown from behind the door and clambered back into bed.

Although I could divine no reason for what I was quite sure I had seen, I felt no fear. I tried to re-call every detail of those few brief moments in my mind's eye, turning them over and over and scrutinizing them closely. Of one thing I was certain: it was no dream.

Eventually I fell into a half-sleep. The next thing I heard was my mother's voice.

'Tom? Tom?' she cried. She was shaking my shoulder, firmly but not roughly. 'It's ten past eight. If you don't hurry up you'll be late for school. Whatever happened? Have you had a bad night? Why didn't you come and tell me?'

'No, Mum,' I replied, struggling up on one elbow. 'I've seen—' Something inside me made me stop abruptly.

'Seen? Seen what?'

'Oh, nothing, Mum. I must have been dreaming.'

She looked at me, obviously expecting me to describe my dream. But I could see apprehension in her eyes. Then it dawned on me. She, too, had heard the hooves, seen the milkfloat. She made as if to say something, but instead waved her hand as if to dismiss her thoughts from her mind. 'Hurry up, then,' she said, and went downstairs.

The next few nights passed without disturbance. But I felt certain that the milkfloat would return.

It did. Two nights before Christmas I was again awoken as before. I leapt out of bed, threw open the bedroom door and ran to my mother's room. She was standing by the window, looking intently into the street below. The moon was low in the sky but full and bright enough to create sharp shadows which threw everything into high relief. The milkfloat was again in the road, with the horse pawing at the cobbles. Standing on the rear of the float, the reins in his hand in readiness for setting off, was my father.

I say my father, because I am in no doubt that that is who it was. The characteristic stoop of the shoulders from years of balancing on the float, the striped apron under the thick jacket, even the waxed moustache, were all quite visible in the moonlight.

He looked up, and waved. Almost involuntarily, my mother waved back. We turned to each other. There was a clatter of hooves on the cobbles, and when we looked back into the street it was deserted again.

Neither of us spoke. I went slowly back to my room, my mind racing. Was it really Dad? Why had he not come into the house? How long had he been back in England? Why had he not said in his letters that he was coming home? And why on earth was he driving his milkfloat when he was still in the army?

At breakfast, my mother said nothing, although I noticed that her eyes seemed to have taken on a look of even deeper sadness.

That afternoon, which was Christmas Eve, we walked down the road to buy some treats for Christmas. The shops seemed as well stocked as they had been the previous Christmas, when thoughts of wars and partings had never entered the minds of people like my Mum and Dad and me. The butchers' shops seemed to be filled from floor to ceiling with enormous hams, plump turkeys and chickens, huge joints of beef and apparently endless strings of sausages. Along the kerb were barrows laden with fruit and nuts, the colours made brighter and cleaner by the naphtha flares stuck on the handles of the barrows.

My mother bought busily, almost as though she suspected, as many other people did, that next Christmas would be very different. I sensed that this would be our last opportunity for some time to celebrate Christmas in the way that we had done for as long as I could remember in my short life.

As I struggled home beside her, two heavily laden bags

in each hand, I said to her, 'This is rather a lot, isn't it Mum?'

'No,' she replied, with her gentle smile. 'You know what your father said, that he'd be back for Christmas.'

That evening I helped her in the kitchen, as best I could, mainly picking off stalks, washing currants, and other odd jobs. I could not help thinking about my father's return.

'When do you think he'll be here, Mum?' I asked several times, with the impatience of a child.

'He'll be here as soon as he can, Tom. You know what he said. And in all the years I've known him, Harry MacDonald has never broken his word.'

But by the time my bedtime had come, he had still not arrived.

'Off you go, Tom,' said my mother. 'He'll be here by and by.'

My exertions round the shops and in the kitchen helped me to fall asleep fairly quickly. But it was not the sound of hooves which awoke me on this occasion. It was the click of the latch of my bedroom door.

I sat bolt upright in bed. I could feel my heart pounding. The door swung slowly open, creaking on its hinges as it always did. I was aware of a lighted candle on the landing. Framed in the doorway was my father's stooping figure, in his soldier's uniform.

'Dad!' I cried. 'Dad! It's you! You're back!'

'Yes, Tommy,' he replied, in a voice that sounded unnaturally hoarse. 'I said I'd be back for Christmas.' I flew past him to my mother's door. She was sitting sobbing on the edge of the bed.

'Mum! Mum! It's Dad! He's come home!' I shouted.

She looked at me and smiled. The tears were coursing down her cheeks.

'I know, Tom,' she whispered. 'He said he would.'

I rushed back out on to the landing. It was deserted. On the floor outside my bedroom, where moments before my father had stood, was a small red stain.

*

The telegram arrived at eleven o'clock on Christmas morning. My mother took the buff envelope from the boy and placed it behind the clock on the mantelpiece in the kitchen.

There was no need to open it.

ACKNOWLEDGMENTS

The publisher has made every effort to contact the Copyright holders, but wishes to apologize to those he has been unable to trace. Grateful acknowledgment is made for permission to reprint the following:

'Jeremiah' by Jessica Amanda Salmonson. Copyright © Jessica Amanda Salmonson by kind permission.

'Two Returns' by Terry Lamsley. Copyright © Terry Lamsley by kind permission.

'Billy Drops In' by Jill Drower. Copyright © Jill Drower by kind permission.

'Sweet Chiming Bells' by Roger Johnson. Copyright © Roger Johnson by kind permission.

'Fancy That!' by Stephen Gallagher. Copyright © Stephen Gallagher by kind permission.

'Twenty Pence with Envelope and Seasonal Greeting' by Terry Pratchett. Copyright © Terry Pratchett by kind permission.

'The Bommie and the Drop-Off' by Richard Adams. Copyright © 1995 Richard Adams by kind permission.

'The Ferry' by Joan Aiken. Copyright © Joan Aiken by kind permission.

'The Maid' by Jane Beeson. Copyright © Jane Beeson by kind permission.

'It Will All Be Over By Christmas' by Alan McMurray. Copyright © Alan McMurray by kind permission.